T0155325

IMPEACHMENT

IMPEACHMENT

A Novel

MARK SPIVAK

A City of Light Imprint

Published by Blacklight Press,
A City of Light Imprint

City of Light Publishing
266 Elmwood Ave, #407
Buffalo, New York 14222

info@CityofLightPublishing.com
www.CityofLightPublishing.com

Book design by Ana Cristina Ochoa

ISBN 978-1-942483-96-0

Printed in South Korea
10 9 8 7 6 5 4 3 2 1

Prologue

Ten Months Earlier

President Khaleem Atalas leaned back in his chair, closed his eyes and rubbed his forehead. He allowed himself this gesture of fatigue because he was alone in the Oval Office with Joel Gottbaum, his closest political advisor. The chair had been a birthday gift from his wife many years before, and it had travelled with him from his home outside Philadelphia to his Senate office and down Pennsylvania Avenue to the White House—a journey almost as remarkable as that of Atalas himself. At the time he received it, he had been an unknown community organizer and the chair seemed like an extravagance. Now, the leather was worn and fraying in spots, and the contraption resembled something from a garage sale. His insistence on using it had less to do with humoring Korinne than reclining in one of the few places he felt truly comfortable.

"You'll have to make a statement about the troop levels," Gottbaum said when the President opened his eyes. "And I'm afraid you'll have to do it soon. Both Fox and CNN are pressing me on it."

"They can wait a couple of weeks."

"That gives them a couple of weeks to continue comparing you to Cane. We can't afford it—the election is eight months away."

"I'm waiting for the CIA to cough up some information on Al-Akbar. They thought they had a lead on his whereabouts. If we can catch the son of a bitch, people will forget about the troop levels."

"They don't much care about them now, to be honest. We're talking about containing the network noise. Remember, you've reduced the force in Sumeristan by 30 percent since you took office."

"Yes, and we've put 100,000 troops into Kabulistan. With nothing to show for it."

"Here's the narrative," said Gottbaum. "You inherited this mess from George Cane—people understand that. It doesn't hurt to keep reminding them of it, regardless of what *Saturday Night Live* says. Sooner or later someone will give up Salman Al-Akbar, and voters will forget how many troops we have in Kabulistan."

"Maybe so, but that's not going to stop the insurgency in Sumeristan."

"So you do a George Cane, and propose another troop surge. It worked for him."

"Look Joel, as a political operative, you're the best in the business. I wouldn't be sitting here if it weren't for you. But this goes beyond politics. People are sick and tired of being at war, and I don't blame them. It's sucking our economy down the tubes. We're making no progress. It's one thing to tell them that we're engaged in an ongoing battle against the forces of terror, but this has been going on for nearly a decade."

"And it's been a decade with no domestic terror attacks inside the U.S. You need to keep reminding them of that as well."

"Is that what I tell working mothers in the ghettos? That we can't expand social programs for their kids because we're funding 100,000 troops in Kabulistan?"

"You could tell them that because of your efforts, no suicide bombers have committed mass murder in their neighborhood."

"Every single one of those attacks that we've foiled was scripted to take place in rich, white areas—gated communities, luxury condos. These guys know they won't get any mileage out of bombing the 'hood." He drummed his fingers on the desk. "Cane and Hornsby had it easy. All they had to worry about was the Dua Khamail and Husam al Din. I'd like to see them take on the New Caliphate for a week."

It was difficult for anyone to believe that less than two years had passed since Husam al Din had spawned their latest mutation, the New Caliphate. Dismissed at first by the CIA as a radical but harmless fringe group, the organization had swelled to nearly 50,000 members dedicated to establishing an Islamic state in Sumeristan. The first beheading had occurred six months earlier when the group executed a captive from Doctors Without Borders; since then, the brutal videos of the decapitations had become a staple of the nightly news. The New Caliphate troops were organized into military brigades and wielded weapons supplied to them by Russia and China filtered through allies in Persepostan. Even worse, they fought with a fearlessness totally absent in the Sumeri army units who opposed them, and they were starting to accumulate territorial gains in the provinces.

"If we play our cards right," said Gottbaum, "maybe we can get them to start beheading the Republican primary field. One every few weeks ought to do it."

"Sure." The President grinned. "At least you can still cheer me up."

"Just trying to earn my princely salary."

"You want to earn it, you can worry about what happens if these people start capturing provincial capitals before the election. If they're marching on Baghdad by the middle of the campaign, the Republican nominee can stroll in here with his head in his hands and a higher approval rating than I have right now."

"With all due respect, you're starting to get tunnel vision. You're at 48 percent, within the margin of error, and trending upward. We've locked down all the key Democratic constituencies, even the ones that were wobbly last time— particularly gays and Hispanics. The economy has moved out of recession, and real estate prices have rebounded. You need to tell people of all this."

"I do."

"I mean, on a regular basis. Like weekly."

"You're right." Atlas rubbed his forehead again. "Who's worried about a few dozen beheadings when the stock market is doing better?"

"People vote their pocketbooks. Never forget that. The video of yesterday's beheading is ultimately not as scary as the increase in food prices, or the decline in the value of retirement accounts."

"Shit." Atlas grinned again. "You're pretty slick for a white guy."

"That's because I play basketball. I can also dance, by the way."

Atlas rose, walked to the window, and stared at the manicured grounds.

"The one thing I don't want to do, Joel, is kick the can down the road. If we don't figure out a way to contain and defeat the New Caliphate, we're no better than the Cane crew. I don't want somebody else sitting here ten years from now, bitching about my mistakes."

"First, let's focus on having you sit here next year. Then you can do the rest. But we need every possible edge we can get. The word on the street is that the Haft brothers are prepared to spend hundreds of millions to defeat you."

"All right. What do you suggest?"

"Stay on message. Repeat the catechism: We're in this mess because of George Cane's invasion of Sumeristan. You're doing everything you can. You've reduced the troop levels by 30 percent, and you've strengthened our forces in Kabulistan. Your dual motivations for this were ousting the Dua Khamail and restoring the legitimate government, which you've done, and catching Salman Al-Akbar, which you're going to do at any moment. You're on the verge of a breakthrough. In the meantime, those troops are holding the New Caliphate at bay."

"Sounds encouraging."

"It's all true."

"And how long before we start bringing those troops home?"

"With any luck, you'll catch a break and find Al-Akbar before the election. In the meantime, we'll issue a projected timetable for withdrawal." Gottbaum smiled. "The public loves timetables."

Chapter 1

Paul Gilliam, the Chief Justice of the U.S. Supreme Court, unlocked the back door of his Northwest Washington home. He reached into the plastic bag and placed the bottle of Doxepin on the kitchen table. Gilliam then pulled up a chair and stared at the bottle.

The pills had been prescribed for him several years earlier, when he was having trouble sleeping after the death of his wife. He insisted on picking up the refill himself, despite repeated offers from his personal assistant. Gilliam always retrieved the prescription at night. His routine was inflexible. He returned home, put the bottle on the table, and contemplated the possibility of taking all sixty pills at once.

He imagined it would take several minutes to swallow them, preferably with a glass of milk. He would then walk into his bedroom and lay down. He envisioned he would have to take a wastepaper basket with him, since significant vomiting might set in. The side effects would be unpleasant, but it would be over within ten minutes.

He wouldn't do it, of course—or probably wouldn't. He didn't think of himself as a coward. He didn't regard himself as a person who wallowed in his own depression, either, but once every two months he allowed himself this luxury. At least he was clear about the source of that depression. In the course of his scrupulous self-examination while contemplating the Doxepin bottle, he realized that his problem went way beyond loneliness caused by the absence of his wife. Paul Gilliam considered himself a failure.

Five years earlier, things had been very different. During his confirmation hearings before the Senate Judiciary Committee, Gilliam had droned on pompously about the majestic impartiality of the law. The law transcended individual opinion, he remembered saying. Onlookers could debate its spirit and intent, but judges were charged with enforcing it to the letter. His pronouncements made such an impression on the committee that he was approved unanimously, then confirmed by the full Senate by an overwhelming margin.

His first inklings about the devious complexity of the law occurred when he voted with the majority to deny a stay of execution to a convicted murderer. The eyewitness testimony against the man was ironclad, even though DNA testing had been inconclusive. After the man was put to death, further DNA tests exonerated him. Gilliam was initially haunted by this, but his guilt was assuaged by informal conversations with his colleagues. Many on the Court had played a role in executing an innocent person before learning from their mistake.

Then came *Democracy Unchained.*

The real name of the case was *Cole vs. Federal Election Commission* when it came before the Court. Herbert Cole was the sponsor of a right-wing interest group that produced a documentary on Bethany Hampton titled *Bethany: The True Story*. Hampton was the wife of former President William

Hampton and was serving as junior Senator from New York. She was also running for President against Khaleem Atalas. The film was negative and inflammatory, and the goal of Cole's company was to air it on HBO before the end of the year, in order to inflict the maximum damage on Hampton during the Democratic primaries. The U.S. District Court for the District of Columbia had ruled that it could not be shown. Cole appealed, and the case reached the Supremes in May.

The initial consensus was 5-4 in favor of showing the documentary, with the majority falling back solidly on the First Amendment. But then the Court's senior conservative began to argue that the majority's interpretation was too narrow. He urged his colleagues to view free speech in the broadest possible sense. Why was it possible for a film company to express its opinion on political matters, when other corporations or labor unions were prohibited from doing so?

Right-wing think tanks and interest groups began to pile on in favor of unlimited free speech—which meant, of course, unlimited campaign contributions. Organizations funded by the Haft brothers were calling the case *Democracy Unchained*, and the name went viral in the media. Gilliam watched helplessly as the process spiraled out of control. The final majority opinion stipulated that political contributions were a form of speech. Although the opinion placed no restrictions on the amount of contributions, it did specify that the source of donations had to be disclosed (rules that were later skirted or ignored). Paul Gilliam was torn, but he recognized that according to the letter of the law the opinion was correct. He joined the 5-4 majority.

Khaleem Atalas eventually defeated Bethany Hampton to win the Democratic nomination, and the impact of the Cole documentary was insignificant. Of far greater importance were the effects that *Democracy Unchained* had on the electoral process. By the next election cycle, the cost of a Presidential campaign had escalated to a billion dollars, and half of that money on either side came from a handful of donors.

Paul Gilliam was horrified. He watched as election contests morphed into shouting matches between billionaires. The content of campaigns was no longer about the issues. They had turned into a series of vicious and continual attack ads, which when taken together gave the impression that both sides were desperate. Even worse, the polarization turned Congressional terms into long stretches of gridlock between campaigns. Everybody seemed to hate everybody, and nothing was getting done. His worst moment came during a State of the Union address, when he and his fellow Justices had to sit through a blistering attack on *Democracy Unchained* by Khaleem Atalas in the House chamber.

He had spent his life trying to be fair, to interpret the law impartially according to the text on the page. He also placed high value on the importance of admitting his mistakes. When Gilliam looked honestly at *Democracy Unchained*, he couldn't deny one simple fact: He had single-handedly fucked up the American political system, and he had done so out of his own rigidity and inflexibility.

He mused on this as he spread the Doxepin tabs out on the table before him. This was also part of his ritual. He separated the pills into piles of five, then methodically scooped up each group and put them back in the bottle. There were sixty, but he would not take them tonight. He would attempt to live long enough to make things right.

Gilliam rose from the table, poured himself a glass of milk, and swallowed one Doxepin tablet. *Goddamn Democracy Unchained*, he thought as he staggered off to bed.

Chapter 2

One morning in early December, as the executives of Haft Industries were contemplating what they might buy their families for Christmas if the brothers ever gave them a day off to go shopping, Richard Haft sat in his office watching the year's first snowfall. As usual, the atmosphere at corporate headquarters outside St. Louis was quiet and peaceful; the turbulence of politics never influenced the company's drive to make money. He picked up the phone and hit the button on his console that connected him directly to his brother.

"Morning, Dickey."

"Do you have some time for me this morning?"

"Let me check the calendar." There was a ten-second pause. "Come by at 11:30. We'll make it work."

Roughly three weeks after President Khaleem Atalas was reelected, *Rolling Stone* published a lengthy profile of the Haft brothers titled *Trouble in River City*. The massive contributions made by the two brothers during the campaign had opened them up to scrutiny, and *Democracy Unchained* had suddenly revealed their existence to large numbers of

Americans. What was remarkable about the piece was the line of thought pursued by the magazine.

Unlike the previous year's story in *Mother Jones*, *Rolling Stone* did not take the Hafts to task for being two of the largest polluters on the planet. They refused to focus, as *The New Yorker* had, on the ongoing war between the brothers and the President, a conflict that had been raging since before Atlas took office. Nor did they follow the path of *Forbes* and recount the bitter family conflicts that began when the Hafts were children, forming the basis for decades of litigation.

The author of the *Rolling Stone* piece didn't even fall back on the familiar story line that the brothers were attempting to reshape the government in their own conservative image. Instead, he put a startling theory on the table: The Hafts were committed to fomenting a revolution that would bring down the U.S. government. Only after that revolution was successful, and the society lay in tatters, could they begin to transform the culture.

At 11:30, Richard walked into his brother's office and tossed a copy of *Rolling Stone* on Sheldon's desk.

"Ah." His brother chuckled. "The art of fiction."

"Amazing stuff, yes."

"Look at it this way: Did you ever think we'd see the day when a pair of rich conservatives were referred to as revolutionaries by *Rolling Stone?*"

In fact, the brothers were beyond rich. They were estimated to be worth more than $40 billion apiece, which placed them in the top tier of Forbes' Wealthiest Americans list, on a par with Bill Gates and Warren Buffet. The true extent of their assets was unknown. Haft Industries was a privately held company, but most experts put their revenues in the range of $120 billion annually.

"I've got a scenario for you," said Richard. "Let's have some fun with this."

"Okay." His brother leaned back, half interested and half amused. "I take it this is a 'what if?'"

"Very much so, but just hear me out."

"Shoot."

Looking at the two men, hardly anyone would assume they had control of one of the largest corporations on the planet. Sheldon's graying hair and wire-rimmed spectacles made him seem professorial and distant. On the surface, Richard was the more assertive of the two, although he consistently deferred to his soft-spoken brother.

"Ultimately this story doesn't matter," said Richard. "Forget that *Rolling Stone*'s circulation is around 1.3 million. It's only really important in terms of the possibilities it raises."

"And I assume you'll tell me what those are."

"Of course, we don't want to create a revolution and bring down the government. We want to reshape it for the future. But assume for a moment that *Rolling Stone* is right, and that our effectiveness has hit the wall."

"Well, we don't know. That's the thing. Obviously, we're both disappointed about the outcome of the election, but we can't tell if it's a temporary setback or a watershed."

"True."

"And there's another possibility, which is that this whole thing has to run its course. Four years from now, people may be just as disgusted with Atalas as we are. They may be ready to accept real change."

"We're not getting any younger, Shelley."

"No, but we're not dead yet, either. Sixty-nine and seventy-three isn't old by today's standards. Dad lived to be ninety. Hell, Germans live forever."

"Well, let me spin this out for you."

"Go ahead." Sheldon smiled indulgently at his younger brother. "I can see your mind is in hyperspace."

"Okay, look." He leaned forward earnestly. "We've been putting money into these campaigns for years—since the 1980s. We've had considerable success on the local level, but we've never snagged the big prize. The best we ever seem to get is some guy who claims to be a conservative and turns out to be a moderate. But we back these people anyway. Sometimes they get in, but we're never happy with the results."

Sheldon laughed. "I gather you're talking about the Cane family."

"Perfect examples, both of them. Even Reagan wasn't much better, and he was the best we've had."

"No argument there."

"So how much would you say we plowed into this race to beat Atalas? Two hundred million?"

"Well, that was just the amount that came from us. It was more than double that, if you count the anonymous donors and the PACs."

"And I know that's not the point. The money doesn't matter—it's all generated from foundations and people who agree with us. It's not principal."

"Yep." Sheldon grinned again. "Dad would be proud."

"Absolutely. But at the end of the day, what are we doing? We're making the TV guys and the consultants rich."

"So what do you suggest—that we live up to the *Rolling Stone* description of us?"

"We don't invest in groups that would actually bring down the government, no. But say we took the money and focused it in areas that would throw Atalas into crisis?"

"Such as?"

"Here's an example." He pushed a sheaf of papers across the desk to his brother. "This is a bunch of guys who basically function as Good Samaritans. They're organized along the lines of the police, but they're harmless. They help keep order at public events, escort old ladies cross the street, whatever."

"Hmm." Sheldon's brow compressed as he read through the report. "The Angels of Democracy. Sounds like a passion play. What's this about being descended from the Knights Templars?"

"Who knows? It's their mythology, as far as I can tell—it gives them a sense of noble purpose and allows them to run around in funny uniforms."

"How many are there?"

"A few thousand, believe it or not. Most of them are concentrated in California."

"Surprise, surprise."

"But there are branches in a number of major cities as well. Basically, it's a fraternal organization."

"Do these guys claim to have police powers? Because if they do, we don't want to get within a hundred yards of them."

"No, no. As I told you, they're do-gooders. But their Supreme Commander, Jasper Marshall, is a piece of work. This guy has charisma—six-four, jovial as the day is long, great speaker. He can make a crowd sit up and whistle."

"So where are you going with this?"

"Okay, this is a hypothetical. Say we fund these guys, really fund them. They get to the point where they've got maybe ten thousand people around the country, organized into squads. Then we give them missions to enhance our agenda."

"Such as?"

"I don't know. We station them on the Mexican border to enforce our immigration policy. We have them guard the construction of the Trans-Canada pipeline. That kind of thing."

"And how does that throw the government into crisis?"

"I'm thinking off the top of my head. Say we pick a situation that will put Atalas into turmoil, demonstrate how weak and inept his regime is. I have no idea what, but we'll find something. Then we get him impeached. It's not hard to do. The Republicans control the House, remember. If Bill Hampton could get impeached for fooling around with an intern, we can get this guy and make it stick."

"And then we've got his bozo Vice President. He's just as bad."

"As I told you, Shelley, it's a hypothetical. We'd have to work out the details. Obviously, we'd have to find some way to get rid of him as well."

"I don't know." His older brother shook his head. "This is awfully risky, Dickie. For starters, we'd have to make damn sure the money couldn't be traced back to us."

"Whoever's trying to trace it now isn't too sharp. Nobody has the slightest idea how much money we spent this year. You read the *Rolling Stone* story. They don't have a clue."

"Even so." Sheldon removed his spectacles and wiped them with a cloth, a reflexive action when he was analyzing a situation. "We could afford another two hundred million, but it's still a lot of money."

"Particularly when you lose."

"Yes. So you have to wonder exactly what *Democracy Unchained* did for us, other than blow our cover to the outside world."

"I've been thinking the same thing."

"Anyway." Sheldon felt himself smiling and trying not to. "You've raised a possibility. And an intriguing one, I have to admit. It goes against our traditional way of operating in the political arena. We've always set up the think tanks and foundations first to formulate the policy, then looked for politicians to carry the message."

"That's exactly my point. Maybe someone else can carry that message more effectively."

"Let's look into it. You say this guy is a good speaker. Get some video of him, and we'll review it together. Let's see what he's all about."

"Actually," said Richard, "I'm already working on that."

Chapter 3

C hester Wallko looked up from his desk in the Senate Office Building and stared at a picture of a pig.

The picture graced an overhang that covered the sitting area of his spacious office and was visible only to him. It had been drawn years ago by a political cartoonist in his native Indiana and was given to him as a gift when he became President Pro Tempore of the Senate and Chairman of the powerful Foreign Relations Committee. The animal was depicted in hot pink. It had sprouted a set of wings and was flying over the landscape of Washington, D.C. The cartoonist was inspired to create the drawing after the frustrated Senator had declared, years before, that "a moderate Democrat will hold another position in this government only when pigs fly." It was Wallko's habit to glance at the picture several dozen times each day.

"So give me your thoughts, Chet. Can we count on you for this?'"

Across the desk from Wallko sat Joel Gottbaum, chief political strategist for President Atlas. The public perceived Gottbaum to be the person who got Atlas elected, while many in Washington viewed him as the power behind the throne.

"I honestly don't know, Joel. I'll have to review the options, do some research. You know how I operate."

"That's not what I was hoping to hear."

"Well, I'll buy you a donut and a cup of coffee if it'll make you feel better. But I can't give you a snap answer on whether I'd support a more open relationship with Cuba."

"Why not?"

"For starters, they were Communists the last time I looked."

"Give me a break, Chet—this isn't the 1950s. I think they're about as Communist as Google at this point."

"On the highest levels, maybe. But the majority of the population is living below the poverty line, as you're well aware. They don't have freedom of speech, or freedom of much else. The regime's human rights record is terrible. I thought that was supposed to be important to you guys."

"It is, absolutely." Gottbaum's tone was patient and measured. "That's exactly why the President believes we should open a relationship with them. It will lead to trade and tourism, and ultimately lift up conditions for the Cuban people."

"Forget the donut and coffee. I'll buy you a fucking violin."

Wallko was almost as well-known on the Hill for his characteristic bluntness as he was for his moderate ideology. The son of a steelworker, he might have turned out to be a Republican had it not been for the strong union genes in his DNA. By the time Khaleem Atalas vaulted into the Oval Office, some of Wallko's positions made him seem stranger than a flying pig within his own party: he was pro-life, hawkish on defense, and cautious in fiscal matters. All those beliefs played well back home in Indiana, but in Washington he was regarded as a quaint anachronism. The ranks of moderate Democrats and liberal Republicans had been shrinking for decades. The two groups of endangered species held many convictions in common, and increasingly found themselves forming coalitions on important issues.

While Wallko's brutal honesty sometimes created problems with the public, it endeared him to his Senate colleagues, most of whom secretly harbored the desire to speak their mind. Their affection for him was the primary reason he had been elected President Pro Tempore—an honor that by tradition should have gone to Marcus Kaplan, who became the majority's longest-serving Senator after Curt Bassen was elected Vice President. Wallko's contrary nature galvanized him to conduct a vigorous and successful campaign for the position, which he didn't even want: His primary motivation was to send a message to the newly-elected Khaleem Atalas that the Democrats' slim Senate majority was no guarantee of a rubber stamp.

"We've had tough sanctions on them for 50 years, Chet. They haven't worked. How long should we keep this going?"

"Until the regime is toppled, I guess. Isn't that why the sanctions are there in the first place?" He glanced up at the pig. "Okay, here's track two: last I heard, they were committed to undermining the United States by any means possible. Am I wrong, or have they said that repeatedly?"

"They say things, we say things. Let's not confuse rhetoric with policy."

"You're a political operative, Joel. How do you think this will play in the heartland? How do you think it will play in Miami?"

"We're not worried about Miami at this point."

"Maybe not, but the next Democrat to run for President might want to carry Florida."

"Cuban immigrants in Miami were never going to vote Democratic. Not in a million years."

"You're probably right." Wallko looked at his watch. "We'll have to wrap this up in a few minutes, fascinating though it is."

"I appreciate the time."

"You want to give me the closing pitch?"

"Sure." Gottbaum grinned. "Cuba's small potatoes—you and I both know that. It's an island nation with a population of 11 million, and one of the last three or four Communist states left in the world. But the opening to Cuba is symbolic, and it's the first step toward a dramatically different U.S. foreign policy. The step after that is the big one: a treaty with Persepostan that will lift sanctions, normalize relations, and limit their nuclear program."

Persepostan had been a close ally of the U.S. until 1979, when a spontaneous revolution had dethroned the American-backed dictator and installed a strict Muslim state ruled by clerics. As relations with the West deteriorated, the new government had actively pursued a policy of acquiring and refining nuclear technology. The regime insisted that the goal was to provide alternative sources of energy. Since Persepostan was one of the most oil-rich nations on the planet, most observers felt their real goal was a weaponized nuclear arsenal.

"It's inevitable, Chet. We can't have a radical Islamic state in the Middle East that hates our guts and has atomic weapons. Somebody has to do it, and we want it to be us. And don't tell me it can't be done. Nixon reached out to China, remember."

"Very eloquent." Wallko rose to his feet. "The way things are going, I'd be more concerned about the New Caliphate. If they keep beheading a few dozen people each week, the body count will eventually be worse than a nuclear attack. And you won't be able to make a treaty with them, either."

"That's another conversation."

"So it is." The two men shook hands. "Send the President my regards."

Chapter 4

J asper Marshall stood erect, his bulk towering over the podium. His bald head gleamed in the bright lights of the hall, and his baritone ricocheted against the concrete walls.

"Back where I come from, we have a saying." He gave the audience a radiant smile. "We say you have to stand on the tops of the redwoods if you want to see the horizon. And that's good advice, after all—I'm sure most of you folks here tonight would like nothing better than to climb to the summit of the universe and behold all the marvels below.

"But you know what? Things aren't that simple anymore. The wisdom I grew up with in the Northwest just isn't enough to meet the challenges of today. And why not? Because the government is cutting down those redwood trees, folks, and they're making it illegal to climb the ones they still allow us to have."

"That's damn right," yelled a man wearing a John Deere cap at the back of the room. The crowd murmured appreciatively.

"Now I think everyone here knows that it doesn't matter how many times you write your Congressman—things aren't going to change. A lot of folks are sitting around waiting for the government to empower them, but people in Washington just aren't listening to us anymore. We're talking to them, but nobody's home."

"You tell 'em, Jasper," said a woman with a beehive hairdo.

"And that's exactly why I founded the Angels of Democracy twelve years ago. Some of our country's leaders may have experience and wisdom, but many of them lack the courage and vision to bring the great promise of this country to life. They need our help. They need the help of every man, woman and child in this room. They need our help to ensure domestic tranquility, to make sure every citizen achieves greatness, and—most importantly, folks—to see that the spirit of the law is applied along with the letter of the law."

Jasper took a dramatic pause.

"Are you ready to help them?"

A hundred voices shouted in unison, and fists pumped in the air. He had them now. The room was filled to overflowing, and several dozen people stood at the rear. This had been carefully engineered: Marshall always told his staff to book a room smaller than the crowd he expected. And even though this rally was being held in an auxiliary building at a high school just south of San Diego, about 15 miles from the Mexican border, the densely packed crowd gave the impression that Jasper Marshall was commanding an exciting and exploding movement. In fact, he had traveled to San Diego to address the hundred or so local members of the Angels of Democracy and hoped to pick up a few recruits in the bargain. The rally was open to the ranks of the curious, and there was little doubt that curiosity was on the rise.

"Now some people ask me why we need an organization like the Angels of Democracy. Some of these folks are just cynics and nay-sayers, but many of them truly don't understand. We have the police to protect us, they say, we have the fire department to put out our blazes, and we have some very good people donating their time and resources to charity. So why do we need the Angels of Democracy?

"I'll tell you why. Because the police, God bless 'em, are too busy enforcing the law to try to prevent crime in their communities. By the time they get involved, a crime has already been committed. They've got too much on their plate to be proactive, and we certainly can't blame them for that.

"But long before we had an organized police force, we had watchmen. These were men who patrolled their neighborhoods, usually as volunteers, and made sure that everything was under control. They knew their communities inside out, and they could spot trouble before it developed. They performed an important and essential function, although they largely ceased to exist after police departments were organized.

"And some of you folks here tonight probably remember when the cops on the beat did the same thing. It wasn't unusual at all, even up until thirty or forty years ago. But the sad fact is that our society has changed. Today our families are fragmented, our young people lack direction, and our neighborhoods are filled with transients. I'm sure you don't need me to tell you that, as we sit here just a few miles from the Mexican border."

The room erupted in spontaneous applause.

"And long before we had watchmen, we had valiant organizations like the Knights Templar. They were the bravest of the brave—warriors who fought for the good of mankind simply because it was important to do so. They were also the purest of the pure. They took vows of poverty and chastity, and they stuck to them. I'm proud to say that the Angels of Democracy follow in the footsteps of the Knights Templar. We're not too strong on the chastity business, but we've got the poverty part down pretty good.

"And that's why," he said over the laughter of the crowd, "I'm proud to wear this jersey with the red cross on it, the insignia of those brave knights. That red cross was a symbol of martyrdom for the Knights Templars, a reminder that they never needed to be afraid of dying in battle, because there was a place reserved for them in heaven. The Angels of Democracy don't fight real-life battles, but we are engaged in a constant struggle to restore the values of our society. That cross reminds us every day that we have a mission bigger than ourselves, a mission that needs to be fulfilled."

He took another dramatic pause, scanning the crowd to eye contact with as many adult males as possible.

"I want you to join me in that mission. If you have a pure heart and an open mind, we have a place for you in the Angels of Democracy. You won't get rich. You won't become famous. But you'll have the satisfaction of knowing that you helped restore this country to its roots. And I can tell you that there is no more noble cause on earth.

"Will you join me?"

The crowd rose to its feet and applauded, and men made their way to the podium to shake Marshall's hand. At the rear of the room, the representative from Haft Industries stopped recording on his iPhone.

Chapter 5

I
t all started when Gunther Haft was splattered with mud.
Gunther came to the United States with his parents in 1892 at the age of twelve. The family headed for Missouri, a collection point for German immigrants. The Hafts settled in Gasconade County, where the population consisted almost entirely of transplants from their native region of Saxony.

Young Gunther was a bright and headstrong child, but his intelligence was easily eclipsed by his physical strength. By the time he finished school at 17, the boy stood well over six feet and tipped the scales at a muscular 220. No wonder he was attracted to the Missouri Bootheel. The southern tip of the state comprised parts of seven counties, and word had reached Gasconade that the Bootheel was a logger's paradise: densely wooded and virtually uninhabited. By 1897 access to the area was opened by railroads, and Gunter headed south to pursue his fortune.

His physique made him a standout in the logging camps of the Bootheel. He was calm and quiet, never seeking confrontation but never shying away from it. He had the stamina to work harder and longer than anyone else in his crew, and he was so thrifty that he quickly accumulated far more money than his workmates. In 1903 he founded Haft Lumber, and soon he was supervising dozens of men.

During his filial trips back to Gasconade County he met and courted his future wife, Julia. He sired two daughters and a son, Jacob, born in 1899. Gunther continued to prosper during the first decade of the 20th century, and as World War I came over the horizon he was one of the wealthiest men in the Bootheel.

Then came the moment that changed the direction of his business completely, affecting him more profoundly than the tales of endless forests that had enticed him to move south.

One day in 1913, Gunther was out in the field with a logging crew when he heard the noise of a machine in the distance. The sound grew louder as the apparition came into view, and he realized it was a Model T. Ford's production had begun to explode the previous year. Gunther had heard of these cars but had never seen one—common as they might have been in St. Louis, they were a rare sight in the isolated Bootheel. His crew stopped working and gaped at the vehicle as it approached. The car bounced along the rutted field toward them at its top speed of 45 mph. As it passed the men it lurched through a ditch filled with the remnants of that morning's rain and splattered mud all over Gunther Haft.

Fastidious though he was, Gunther was more astonished at the significance of the event than with the mud that fouled his neatly pressed clothes. Like many in rural America, he had dismissed the automobile as a fad of the moment. The fact that the Model T had penetrated into the Bootheel meant that the world was changing more radically than he realized. Over the next few months he read everything he could about Henry Ford's business. He learned about the assembly line method that had produced nearly 70,000 cars the previous year, and which was projected to turn out 200,000 in 1913. Within five years, Ford claimed he could be making 500,000 cars annually.

The future, Gunther realized, was oil. He temporarily placed the management of Haft Lumber in the hands of foremen and embarked on a tour of the nation's burgeoning oil industry. As he visited oil fields from the Gulf Coast to Oklahoma, he had another revelation. Drilling for oil was not only messy and dangerous—it was also expensive. Gunther decided that he had no interest in the costly, time-consuming roulette game of extracting oil from the ground. The real future lay in the process of transforming oil into gasoline, then transporting the fuel to the millions of people who would soon own cars.

He focused his efforts in Louisiana, where Standard Oil had never been able to establish a significant foothold. He opened his first refinery in Shreveport in 1916. By the mid-1920s, when his son Jacob joined the company, it had annual revenues of $6 million. When Gunther died in 1935 and Jacob took over, it was known as Haft Petroleum.

Jacob may have lacked Gunther's physical strength, but he was even shrewder than his father. In the 1930s he realized the war was coming, that America would eventually get involved, and that oil would become more important than ever. Between 1936 and 1941 he doubled the refinery output of Haft Petroleum and kept the company debt-free.

World War II turned out to be the winning lottery ticket for Jacob Haft. Even though he detested what he perceived to be the Socialist policies of Franklin Roosevelt, he used the New Deal to accumulate a formidable fortune. His own sons—Sheldon and Richard, born three years apart—grew up on a steady diet of dinner table lectures about the dangers of government intervention in business and the blessings of the free market system. It was a catechism: Government meddling was bad, individual entrepreneurship was good; pure capitalism meant that the strong survived and the weak perished; fiddling with the Darwinian order of things would wreak untold havoc on the universe. By the time the boys were teenagers, they could repeat it in their sleep.

They were also indoctrinated into their father's political opinions, positions that grew more extreme as the years passed. Jacob Haft had been a staunch Republican throughout the Roosevelt years. When the war ended and the country's economy boomed during the Truman era, he realized that Socialism had become permanently embedded in the American system: as individual entrepreneurs accumulated more wealth, they were steadily subjected to a flood of regulations that hampered their activities. He came to believe that it was no longer merely a case of the government wanting their cut of the pie. The authorities wanted to tell him how to bake it, a situation he found galling.

When the young Barry Goldwater was elected senator from Arizona in 1952, Haft followed him closely and liked what he heard. Goldwater had bucked the system and snagged a Senate seat as a Republican in a heavily Democratic state. He was both a friend of Herbert Hoover and a bitter opponent of the legacy of the New Deal. He fought against labor unions, Communism and the pervasive interference of the federal government into states' affairs. When Goldwater's book *The Conscience of A Conservative* came out in 1960, Haft called it "the most important literary work since the Bible." He purchased several thousand copies and distributed them to friends, family and business associates.

One morning in December 1958, before Sheldon and Richard had been trained as engineers at M.I.T. and had completed their education at Wharton Business School,

Jacob Haft walked into a large Tudor home in the suburbs of Indianapolis. He took a seat in the living room surrounded by a dozen of the country's leading right-wing academics and industrialists. For the next two days he listened as Robert Welch, a retired business executive and rabid anti-Communist, outlined his perception of the worldwide Soviet menace. According to Welch, the U.S.S.R. had conceived a plan for global domination and was executing it flawlessly, both in America and abroad. On the evening of the second day, Welch finally outlined his vision of how to combat this menace. It would be a coordinated effort involving public education, support for conservative media, organization of interest groups, and political action. It would be called the John Birch Society.

John Birch was an American military officer and Baptist missionary who had been executed by Chinese Communists in 1945. Welch referred to him as "the first American casualty of the Cold War." The group that took his name attacked the Communist conspiracy on many fronts. They wrote and distributed pamphlets and magazines, produced informational movies, lobbied for U.S. withdrawal from the UN, organized field offices and sponsored letter-writing campaigns. Jacob Haft supported them financially from the beginning. He traveled widely giving speeches about the unseen dangers of Communism and wrote his own pamphlet, *One American's View of the Communist Threat*, distributing several million copies around the country.

Jacob Haft continued to be involved with politics until his death in 1990. He was a major contributor to conservative candidates on both a local and national level, constantly searching for people who displayed enthusiasm for the free market system, disdain for government regulation and a hatred for all forms of Socialism. He became fascinated with the Libertarian Party when it surfaced in the 1970s and passed his passion on to his sons. Sheldon, the eldest, inherited many of his father's hard-core beliefs, even opening a John Birch Society bookstore in St. Louis in 1978. Richard was more balanced, although he ran for office unsuccessfully on the Libertarian Party ticket. Above all else, the brothers learned from their father the importance of using their wealth to influence the direction of the country.

Many years later, had he lived, Jacob Haft would have been amazed and delighted to see how far the boys took it.

Chapter 6

C het Wallko was maneuvering his way out of the Senate chamber when he saw the vice president coming toward him. Curtis Bassen flashed his usual grin, wide and brilliant, as he extended his hand.

"Surprise, surprise," said Wallko. "I never expected to see you on the Hill today."

"Chet." The vice president placed his hand on the senator's shoulder. "How the hell are you?"

"Not too shabby, for a middle-aged moderate."

"We're hoping you'll be able to help us out on this committee vote."

"I'm sure you realize the answer to that question is no."

"Can we talk privately for a minute?"

"Sure. The committee can wait."

The two men ducked into the Democratic cloakroom, which was deserted except for a cluster of aides in the corner. Startled, they looked at the two men and headed for the door.

"The President would appreciate your help on this, Chet."

"Can't do it, sorry. I believe you know the reasons."

"Run down them for me quickly."

"This is a worthless deal. Cuba gets everything out of it, and we get nothing."

"I disagree, and so do a lot of other people. I think it will greatly improve the quality of life for the Cuban people."

"It will greatly improve Atalas' image as the savior of the downtrodden. That's about it, really."

"Still the sarcastic son of a bitch I know and love." Before running on Khaleem Atalas' ticket, Bassen had spent five terms in the Senate, the last three of which had overlapped with Wallko. "Cuba hasn't been a threat to our security for decades, Chet. It's time we tiptoed into the 21st century."

"I agree with you there," said Wallko. "But here's what concerns me. Say we make this worthless deal. What's next? Persepostan, according to Gottbaum, and you'd be hard pressed to find a greater threat to our security than them. They're bankrolling the New Caliphate, for God's sake. If we give Atalas Cuba, the next four years will be a parade of concessions to our enemies. We might as well put our nuclear secrets on the Internet and call it a day."

"I think you're overreacting."

"Everybody's entitled to their opinion, Curt. That's the beauty of America."

"Look, I won't lie to you. We'd love to have you on our side on this."

"And it'll look bad if you don't."

"Maybe so. But the President would really like to have a closer working relationship with you."

"Gosh, let's see. Maybe he could give me some subsidies for sausage-making factories back in Indiana."

"Go ahead, have some fun. But you do realize that if the treaty doesn't pass—or if it isn't even reported out of committee for a floor vote—he's going to go ahead and open a diplomatic relationship with Cuba anyway."

"As I say, it's a free country. There are people around here who question how long we should be funding 100,000 troops in Kabulistan. I'm too busy holding them off to worry about Cuba."

"We appreciate that, we really do. But that's another conversation."

"Better believe it."

"Apparently there's nothing I can say to change your mind. But I can tell you that the President will be very disappointed with this."

"Tell him one thing for me."

"What's that?"

"Remind him that he's the president—not the emperor or king."

● ● ● ● ● ● ● ● ● ● ● ● ● ● ● ● ● ● ●

Wallko stared at the gavel, turning it over in his hand. Unlike the famous ivory gavel of the Senate chamber, this one was made of wood—snakewood, one of the hardest and most expensive varieties of wood on earth. It was plain, although at first glance its intricate natural markings made it look engraved. His fascination with the gavel dated to the day he first assumed chairmanship of the Senate Foreign Relations Committee. It was a rare day in the committee room when he failed to study it carefully before using it. A staffer had once asked him what he found so intriguing about it.

"This time around," he told the aide, "banging that gavel's about as close as I'm going to come to being in the movies."

Slowly and forcefully, he thumped the gavel three times against the wooden sound block in front of him.

"The committee will come to order. The clerk will note that all nineteen members are present, and I want to thank all of you for coming here today.

"Today's session should be a short one. We've already had extensive debate on the administration's proposed treaty with Cuba, and I'm sure that further discussion won't change any minds. Therefore, I'll ask each member to deliver a concise, two-minute summary of their position, and then we can vote. And speaking of concise, two-minute summaries, we'll start with the distinguished gentleman from Mississippi, Mr. Caldwell."

"Thank you, Mr. Chairman." The slow drawl of James "Bull" Caldwell (R-Miss.) rang out over the laughter in the room. "I'm sure the distinguished gentleman from Indiana would agree that loquaciousness in the pursuit of liberty is no vice." It drew another laugh from the press corps. "That being said, my statement today will be a short one, and one that I suspect even our illustrious chairman wouldn't argue with. The gist of my position, as you know, is that this treaty will not just weaken the stature of the America in the world. It will pave the way for a series of foreign policy deals that will deliver us into the hands of our enemies. For the first four years of his presidency, Khaleem Atalas was intent on redistributing the balance of wealth and power within the United States. Now he seems intent on taking our global influence and handing it over to those who bitterly oppose us. And as they say where I come from, that dog won't hunt.

"There are people in this great land who would tell us that the Communist menace is a thing of the past. Those folks would insist that Cuba is harmless, and they characterize the fight against Communism as a long-gone by product of the Cold War. To those people, I say this: Who do they think is supplying all the money and weapons to Persepostan—resources that are being channeled to the New Caliphate in their crusade to transform neighboring Sumeristan into an Islamic state? I'll tell you who: it's China, by God! The

Chinese Communists aren't content with weakening our country by owning all our foreign debt. No, they want to take the most important achievement of the past decade—namely, the liberation of Sumeristan and the removal of its brutal dictator, Hussein Ghazi—and subvert it by funding a group of radical Muslims hell-bent on our destruction."

In 1945, a weak and dying Franklin Roosevelt had flown to the Pacific for his last summit with Churchill and Stalin. Against his better judgment, and perhaps because he was too tired to fight it, FDR gave in to Churchill's half-assed plan to carve the bulk of the Middle East into three massive superstates: Kabulistan, Sumeristan, and Persepostan. There had been nothing but trouble since, and, up until recently, the worst-case scenario was Persepostan. In 1979, fundamentalist Muslims overthrew the American-backed dictator and established an Islamic state. They seized control of the U.S. embassy and took more than fifty hostages who were held in captivity for more than a year. While the hostages were eventually freed, the people of Persepostan were not: Islamic law was rigidly enforced, violators were routinely stoned to death, and personal expression outside the boundaries of religious life was non-existent. Now they were expanding their sphere of influence by backing the New Caliphate in Sumeristan.

"Therefore, Mr. Chairman, I urge all members of this Committee to vote against the ill-advised Cuba treaty. It will be nothing less than the first step toward the Communists attempting to reassert their global reach, and it does not deserve the attention of the Senate." He looked at his watch. "One minute and fifty-six seconds, dammit."

"Thank you, Mr. Caldwell," said Wallko. "Next we'll hear from the ranking Democratic member, Mr. Kaplan of New York."

"Thank you, Mr. Chairman." Getting Marcus Kaplan on board had been a coup for the administration. The Senator had been critical in the past of Khaleem Atalas' deteriorating relationship with the Israeli Prime Minister, and Capitol insiders assumed that his support for the Cuba treaty was linked to promises of enhanced foreign aid and defense assistance to the state of Israel.

"You know, when my children were little, I used to read them a story every night. And before I left the room, they would always ask me to check underneath the bed for the bogeyman. Because, you know, they were convinced that he was lurking under there and would pop up the minute I said goodnight.

"I've known Senator Caldwell a long time and have a lot of respect for him, but he and I are simply looking under different beds. When I look, I don't see a bogeyman. When Mr. Caldwell looks, he sees the specter of the New Caliphate and their 50,000 followers. But here's the thing: last time I checked, we had about a million and a half troops in the U.S. armed forces, plus nearly another million in the National Guard. And those troops are the bravest, best trained, and best equipped in the world. Currently we have 100,000 of them stationed in Kabulistan mopping things up in the wake of restoring that country's legitimate government.

"So I'm not worried about the bogeyman of the New Caliphate, because I realize that those troops could be repositioned back into Sumeristan and defeat the terrorists without breaking a sweat. Whether or not we have the political will to do that is another debate, but we all know it could be accomplished easily.

"This treaty will be a Godsend to the Cuban people. It will help alleviate the hardships they face, and it will also welcome Cuba back into the community of nations. It is the morally right thing to do. I support it, and I urge all my colleagues to do so."

When the speeches were finished, Wallko called the roll. As expected, the treaty failed by a vote of 11-8, and would not be forwarded to the full Senate for approval or disapproval. All nine Republicans voted against it; Wallko and Senator Insfield of South Carolina were the two Democratic defections.

In the Oval Office, Khaleem Atalas and Joel Gottbaum watched the proceedings on C-SPAN.

"Shit," said the President when the results were in.

"No worries, no surprises. We were expecting this."

"I guess I was hoping Curt could charm them at the last minute."

"What are you going to do?" asked Gottbaum.

"Exactly what I said I'd do. I'm going to issue an executive order lifting the trade embargo. I don't need Congress for that—JFK levelled the embargo by executive order in the first place. Then I'm going to reopen the U.S. embassy and normalize relations. And after the U.S. flag is flying over Havana again, I'm going to send an autographed picture of it to Insfield and Wallko."

Chapter 7

Despite growing up in the affluent Town and Country suburb of St. Louis, Sheldon and Richard Haft had no idea their family was wealthy.

"I actually thought we were poor," said Richard. "We were always working. We had jobs after school and on the weekends. Every minute we weren't studying or playing sports, we were earning money. It was my father's way of not spoiling us. During the summers, we'd go out to Montana and work on the ranch."

In 1939, Jacob Haft purchased a 350-acre tract in rural Montana. It was a working farm with hundreds of head of cattle, thousands of chickens, and well over a hundred acres of wheat. The boys toiled from sunrise to sunset assisting the ranch hands, who were given explicit instructions not to go easy on them.

"I remember being really depressed at one point," recalled Sheldon. "We had spent the summer cleaning chicken shit out of the coops while our classmates were swimming in the country club pool. When school started again, I told a friend of mine that I looked forward to the day when we could afford to join the country club. My classmate looked at me in disbelief. 'Are you kidding?' he said finally. 'Your father could buy and sell my family five times over. Hell, he could buy the country club.'"

Jacob himself was the product of a severe German upbringing, and he was determined never to coddle his children emotionally. He left the hugging and kissing to his wife and steered clear of any display of affection with his sons. "We knew he loved us," said Sheldon, "but he never showed it. I think it was all part of his strategy to make us better businessmen."

Haft's absolute insistence that his sons not grow up to be playboys succeeded better than he had hoped. By the time they were in high school the boys had both an old-fashioned set of values and a sense of caution about money. To make sure they didn't become overly cautious, Jacob was constantly educating them about the risks and rewards of entrepreneurship. Sheldon remembers one July day when he and his brother were home on summer break from their engineering studies at M.I.T. They spent the day with their father, touring a series of local copper mines. Almost without exception, the mines were dilapidated and on the verge of bankruptcy. Copper had been in high demand during the Korean War, but since the Armistice that demand had become insignificant.

"So," asked their father that night at dinner, "what did we learn today? What did all those mines have in common?"

"They were depressing," said Richard. "Output was down drastically, and the equipment was deteriorating."

"They all looked like they'd be out of business in a year," said Sheldon.

"You're partly right." Jacob smiled. "They were depressing, of course. But here's what they had in common: I'm going to buy all of them."

"What?" Simultaneously, the boys exploded with incredulity.

"What on earth for?" asked Sheldon.

"You've heard of air conditioning?" asked his father patiently.

His sons nodded.

"Well, copper is an essential material in the construction of air conditioning units."

"But there are hardly any of them," said Richard.

"At the moment, you are correct. But twenty years from now, almost every home in America will be air conditioned, along with most cars—there are already models that offer it. And when that happens, we'll have the market cornered on copper."

He turned out to be right, and the boys never forgot the lesson: Think and plan decades ahead, bide your time, and make your killing down the road. It became one of the central precepts of their business careers. Eventually, they were to apply the same axiom to their political activities. Of the two, Richard was always more willing to risk a public profile, while Sheldon preferred to quietly manipulate things behind the scenes.

By the 1970s both brothers had completed their MBA degrees and were back home working for Haft Petroleum. They had fallen easily into the pattern that was to continue throughout their careers: Sheldon was Jacob's anointed successor and heir apparent, while Richard was the idea man, the creative spark plug that made the business work. As Jacob grew older, he gradually decreased his role in the company and placed more responsibility on his sons. Sheldon became President and CEO, while Richard was Chief Operating Officer.

They took control of Haft Petroleum at the worst possible time. Nixon had just resigned, the Vietnam War was over, and the country had sunk into one of the worst recessions in the past century. As the decade of the 1970s limped toward a conclusion, things got even worse. America's problems with Persepostan led to an oil crisis of unimaginable proportions. Gasoline was being rationed, and lines at many service stations coiled around the block. Consumers were on waiting lists to purchase fuel-efficient cars. Oil companies were about as popular as sexually transmitted diseases.

The Haft brothers were unperturbed. They embarked on an ingenious expansion plan that effectively took the country's energy crisis and converted it into a corporate asset. While their competitors drilled feverishly for oil around the world, Haft bought businesses that manufactured parts for drills and rigs. They expanded into coal mining, trading of petroleum coke and delivery of propane gas. They purchased the largest wastewater treatment plant in the United States. When the brothers took over, Haft Petroleum had $100 million in revenues; five years later, it hit the $1 billion mark.

The brothers responded to this milestone by holding a press conference and announcing that they were changing the name of the company to Haft Industries, in honor of their father. In the years to come they expanded into real estate, building shopping centers and apartment complexes around the country. They became one of the world's largest producers of nitrogen fertilizers. They were the major player in cattle, with more than 500,000 acres of ranch land under their control, and also built more than 4,000 miles of pipeline to transport oil, natural gas, and chemicals. Over time, the $100 million company they inherited from their father grew into the largest privately held business in the United States, with annual revenues totaling $125 billion and a profit margin of nearly 10 percent.

As their business grew, so did their involvement in politics. In 1977 they created the Freedom Institute, the country's first conservative think tank. It was followed by the Democracy Foundation, the Sheldon and Richard Haft

Foundation, Americans for a Free Society, and several dozen other organizations that reflected their views. The brothers micro-managed these groups as thoroughly as they did Haft Industries, making sure they never swerved off the ideological track. Over the years, their think tanks and foundations churned out position papers that formed the basis of the conservative revolution in America. Most importantly, the groups allowed the Hafts to remain in the background and exert their influence on the system anonymously.

When Khaleem Atalas received the Democratic nomination , the brothers were panic-stricken. They perceived Atalas as a dangerous Socialist, a man who would tax them to death, nationalize health care, and pile so many government regulations on them that they would barely be able to operate. Aided by the *Democracy Unchained* Supreme Court decision, they drastically increased their personal contributions and used their extensive network of contacts to raise a fortune for the Republican candidate. It didn't work. The electorate was fed up after eight years of George Cane, and resented his pointless invasion of Sumeristan. Atalas was elected easily, but what was even more annoying to the Hafts was the realization that they had been outwitted.

"The electoral map for national politics had changed," said Richard Haft. "The country was so polarized that there were only about 12 to 15 percent of people in the middle who could be swayed one way or the other. The Atalas folks targeted that group with surgical precision. They had less money than we did, but they used it far more effectively. We probably spent a hundred million dollars running ads that were aimed at voters who agreed with us in the first place."

Four years later, they also realized that they had over-estimated their ability to defeat a sitting president. And so it happened that Sheldon and Richard sat in their St. Louis offices reviewing the purloined iPhone recording of Jasper

Marshall addressing the faithful near the Mexican border south of San Diego.

"Well," Richard asked his brother after they had watched it twice, "what do you think?"

"Damn." Sheldon shook his head. "I'm not sure. He's got passion, obviously. He's got guts, brains, and balls. He's certainly a good speaker, as you said. Is he a Savonarola without an audience? We won't know for sure until we get him out here and talk to him."

"That won't be easy."

His brother yawned. "It won't be as difficult as you think. This guy obviously needs funding as much as he needs direction. If you get the right people to approach him, he'll jump at the chance to talk to us."

"You could be right."

"You handle it, Dickie. Let's get him out here."

"Will do." Richard paused. "And speaking of guts, brains, and balls, what did you think of that Foreign Relations Committee vote on Cuba?"

"Brilliant." His brother laughed. "I'm sure a lot of people thought the entire spectacle was engineered by us."

"Wallko's a good man. Hell, he's a gem. It's hard to believe he's a Democrat."

"Well, he's an old-fashioned Democrat—a Harry Truman kind of guy. Somebody you can reason with."

"That's why I think he might fit into the grand scheme here."

"I have to admit, your plan is intriguing. And God knows that *Democracy Unchained* didn't do us much good, despite all the effort we put into getting the case made into law. The only thing it accomplished was convincing a large chunk of the population that we were the Devil incarnate."

"Agreed. That's why I also have an idea of what to do about it."

Sheldon leaned back in his leather chair, removed his glasses and grinned. "I thought you might."

"I say we get the decision repealed."

"How do you propose we do that?"

"There are a couple of different possibilities. I've commissioned some studies on them."

"Well, even if we're seen to engineer the reversal, it won't do much for us in the eyes of the public."

"The hell with the public," said Richard. "I say we make the arrangements behind the scenes, then issue a statement in favor of it. At the very least, we get to have some fun with the state-controlled media. And as you say, the decision isn't doing us any good."

"I like it." Sheldon nodded. "Full speed ahead."

Chapter 8

Two months after the second inauguration of Khaleem Atalas, the Haft brothers' plans to disrupt the president's agenda suffered what would be referred to in the political world as a "hiccup."

In a dramatic nighttime raid, several teams of Navy Seals killed Salman Al-Akbar. The operation was the culmination of nearly a year of surveillance. The leader of the worldwide terrorist network called Husam al Din had been hiding in a compound outside the capital of Kabulistan, within walking distance of the Police Academy—in fact, the Superintendent had been a frequent guest of Al-Akbar's for tea. The Seals took off in helicopters from nearby Sumeristan, flew to the compound without the approval of the Kabulistan government, and assassinated the terrorist along with several members of his immediate family.

Salman Al-Akbar had first become known to the public during the administration of William Hampton. Despite a number of bombing raids designed to eliminate him, Al-Akbar had consistently eluded his predators, and Hampton was ultimately blamed for using the raids to distract attention from his own domestic scandals. To most Americans, the tall, gaunt, and bearded leader of Husam al Din was best known as the mastermind of the Mayday attacks.

On May 1, 2001, a hijacked 757 had crashed into the Mall of America. Members of Husam al Din had seized control of the airliner shortly after takeoff in Minneapolis. The plane was packed with fuel and headed for Los Angeles. They forced their way into the cockpit and slit the throats of the pilot and co-pilot with box cutters. The men then turned the plane around, headed south toward Bloomington, and smashed into the side of the Mall. The Mall of America, presumably chosen as a target for its symbolic significance, erupted into a fireball that could be seen for nearly twenty miles in all directions. The scene was chaotic. Fire trucks were dispatched from all over the state, but they were slow to respond due to the distance of rural communities from the Mall. Before the day was over, nearly 2,000 innocent shoppers had perished; many had been trampled to death.

Things got worse. Later that day, suicide bombers walked into carefully chosen targets around the country and blew themselves up. The venues included an elementary school in Virginia, a synagogue in New Jersey, a U.S. Post Office in New Mexico, and a high school football practice in Texas. By midnight, the death toll had reached 3,000.

The terrorists also hijacked a second airliner, which proved to be the only redeeming moment of the day. The second plane, United flight 546, took off from Boston's Logan airport headed for Chicago. The Husam al Din agents who commandeered the second 757 placed it on a direct course for Washington. In an act of spontaneous heroism, the passengers of United 546 overcame the terrorists and took control of the aircraft, which crashed in a field south of Wilmington, killing all 103 people on board.

During the years that followed, Salman Al-Akbar became the public face of terrorism for the American public.

He eluded capture for the rest of President George Cane's administration—through the invasion of Sumeristan, the removal of its dictator Hussein Ghazi, and the painfully slow withdrawal of American troops—despite an ongoing effort by the CIA to track his whereabouts. Al-Akbar took special delight in the production of taunting videos, which were released to the media at holiday time or on the anniversary of the attacks. Even worse, Husam al Din eventually spawned the New Caliphate, a paramilitary group with 50,000 troops and the sworn goal of turning Sumeristan into a strict Islamic state.

Al-Akbar's assassination was greeted with jubilation throughout the country. Crowds spilled out spontaneously into the street, waving American flags and chanting *"USA!USA!!USA!!!"* Their enthusiasm seemed unaffected by the fact that the New Caliphate had beheaded 22 Westerners within the previous month, including two journalists, three missionaries, and five members of the Antiquities Department at the University of Baghdad.

"Last night," declared President Atalas in an address to the nation from the East Room of the White House, "the brave men of our Navy Seals struck a blow for democracy and against terrorism. They successfully eliminated one of this country's most bitter enemies, and they did so without collateral damage to local citizens. This was an extremely dangerous mission. It was undertaken without permission from the Kabulistan government to use their airspace, which meant their helicopters could have been shot down at any time. I want to express my gratitude to them for their heroism, and I congratulate the CIA for a sustained and successful struggle to isolate the whereabouts of this brutal terrorist. I think we can all sleep more soundly tonight knowing that he has been removed as a threat to our society.

"However, we need to be mindful that the struggle against terrorism goes on. Over the past month, I'm sure most of us have seen the atrocities committed by the New Caliphate, that group of murderers who have inherited the mantle of Husam al Din. We must remain vigilant in our fight against this menace. As President, you have my promise that we will continue to do so."

Despite the fact that Salman Al-Akbar no longer posed much of a threat to anyone, the administration indulged in some celebrations of their own.

"This man has a spine of steel," said Vice President Curt Bassen, in a TV interview recorded the following day, as he shamelessly heaped praise on his boss. "Obviously we succeeded, but the raid was a considerable risk. We had no idea if the Kabulistan military would track the helicopters or not. If they did, they would certainly have interpreted them as the vanguard of a hostile attack, and they would have launched retaliatory action. Being present in the Situation Room while the raid was taking place was one of the high points of my forty years in public life. We had a very tense couple of hours, but the President never betrayed any signs of stress—he was as calm and collected during the operation as he would have been on the golf course."

However, not everyone was celebrating. Two days after the raid, as Chet Wallko headed for the Senate chamber, he was waylaid by a reporter and camera crew from Fox News.

"Senator," said the reporter as he held the microphone up to Wallko's mouth, "the country is overjoyed at the killing of Salman Al-Akbar recently by a team of Navy Seals. Any plans to sponsor a Congressional resolution honoring them as heroes?"

"I won't be sponsoring one, no. I'm proud of the Seals and admire their bravery, as always, but this is very far from a triumph for the United States."

"What do you mean, sir?"

"Salman Al-Akbar hid out in Kabulistan for many years. He practically sunned himself in the backyard of the Police Academy and played backgammon with the Superintendent, while we had no clue as to his whereabouts. The Kabulistan government obviously knew where he was. So if I sponsor any resolutions, it'll be for the removal of the CIA Director."

"Senator—"

"This guy could have been ordering from Domino's, if they had Domino's in Kabulistan. He could have joined the rewards program and gotten himself a slew of free pizzas during those twelve years."

"Sir, don't you think you're being a bit harsh?"

"Not at all," said Wallko flatly. "I certainly can't criticize the president for taking action when Al-Akbar's whereabouts were finally confirmed, but this whole situation points to a systemic failure in our intelligence community. And it's far from new—Robert Hornsby was a former CIA director, and we were still blindsided by the Mayday attacks. It never seems to get any better. So before we start popping the Champagne, let's get to the bottom of why our intelligence guys are sleeping."

Out in St. Louis that afternoon, Richard Haft sat watching the bank of TVs in his office. He systematically went from Fox to CNN to MSNBC as Wallko's remarks went viral.

Chapter 9

Jasper Marshall's rented Hyundai glided across the flat plains west of St. Louis. At the wheel was Joe Guthrie, his friend and confidant. The two men had met fifteen years earlier, when Marshall managed a Home Depot store and Guthrie worked as the foreman of an oil rig. From the beginning, they had complemented each other perfectly. Marshall was outgoing and charismatic, the type of person other people followed; Guthrie was taciturn, blunt, and shy, but scrupulously honest and loyal.

"Thanks for coming out here with me, Joey."

"Hell, thanks for havin' me. I still don't know what you need me for."

"Moral support, I guess."

"Hope you can get it by remote control." He grinned. "I'll be waitin' for you in the parking lot."

"That's good enough."

"You got any idea what these boys want with you?"

"Not a clue. I was hoping you could give me some background on them, since you were in the oil business."

"Hell, I wasn't in the oil business—I was in the business of squeezin' the shit out of the ground. But I did meet some folks that worked for the Hafts."

"And?"

"The way I hear it, they're a trip. Total control freaks, the kind of guys that look at everything. And their people in the field were as twisted as they come. They were always usin' some underhanded trick to suck more profit out of a deal."

"Well, look on the bright side. Maybe they want to make a donation."

"To us? Better hope not, unless you're ready to sign over your first-born." He chuckled. "Of course, you never liked that kid much anyway, did you?"

When Marshall founded the Angels of Democracy twelve years before, Guthrie had come along as his Operations Commander. Shortly afterward, the two men took early retirement to focus on the group. Guthrie made out better on his retirement plan than Marshall, largely due to stock options, but the financial side of the organization had been a struggle from the beginning.

"Whatever it is," said Jasper, "it was important enough for them to pay our way out here."

"That's about the equivalent of buyin' a candy bar for those guys. Tell you one thing, though: when you talk to the Haft brothers, you'd better hold on to the fillings in your teeth. Way I hear it, they can take 'em out without you even knowin'.'"

The unassuming main entrance to Haft Industries was set into a twelve-foot high chain link fence that surrounded the complex in all directions. An armed security guard checked their credentials, then printed out a map to the building that housed the offices of Sheldon and Richard Haft. The Hyundai passed several miles of production facilities, squat buildings that resembled airplane hangars.

"Look at this," marveled Guthrie. "These boys own some acreage, don't they?"

"So it appears."

"Guess they can afford it." He pulled up alongside a sleek, modern office building and checked the map. "Here we go, buddy. I'll be out here if you need me."

"Joey, thank you. I really appreciate it."

"Nothin' to it," he grinned. "If you're not out in a couple of hours, I'll call the police. You hold on to those teeth, hear?"

On the top floor of the building, the elevator opened to a sprawling suite of offices. Another armed security guard checked Jasper's appointment slip and wordlessly motioned him to the right. He opened the door marked Sheldon Haft, President and Chief Executive Officer.

"Good morning, Mr. Marshall! Thank you so much for coming."

The woman shook his hand firmly. She was perhaps sixty, with perfectly coifed gray hair; she wore a tweed suit accented with a single string of pearls.

"Well, thank you very much for having me. Would you be Mrs. Haft, by any chance?"

"Oh, dear." The woman laughed. "No, I'm Mr. Haft's executive secretary, but thank you for the compliment. Please come this way—Sheldon and Richard are expecting you."

She led him into an elegant, wood-paneled room that contained more square footage than Jasper's house in Pasadena. The brothers rose and greeted him with enthusiasm. They were tall and physically imposing, but their finely chiseled features somehow made them seem smaller. Their silver hair was thinning, and Sheldon wore delicate steel-rimmed glasses. Both men exuded a placid, genial self-confidence that put Jasper at ease. If you didn't know better, you would have pegged them for senior accountants at a Big Four firm rather than two of America's wealthiest industrialists.

"Have a seat, please, Mr. Marshall." Sheldon motioned him toward a large, comfortable armchair, and the Hafts settled into an overstuffed sofa. A pile of file folders sat on the glass coffee table in front of Sheldon. Jasper's attention was captured by a vividly colored mural mounted on the wall above the brothers.

"You're familiar with Thomas Hart Benton?" asked Sheldon.

"I've seen some of his paintings in museums, yes. Also a lot of reproductions, but never anything that good."

"It's not a reproduction, actually," said Sheldon pleasantly.

"Oh, I'm really sorry—"

"Not to worry." He laughed. "We inherited the painting from our father. He bought it long before the price of these things shot through the ceiling."

"We're very glad you took us up on our invitation," said Richard. "We know you're busy, and we look forward to speaking with you."

"Well, I'll admit that I'm very curious as to why I'm here."

"We'll try to get directly to the point, although there are some facets of this situation that are a bit complicated." Sheldon cleared his throat. "My brother and I have been following your organization, Mr. Marshall, and we like what we see. We're very impressed with your operation."

"Thank you very much."

"How many members do you have now?"

"Slightly fewer than a thousand. Around nine hundred."

"I thought it was more than that, but no matter. We have an intuitive feeling that you share many of our values and convictions."

"That may well be, sir."

"We might disagree on some specifics, but I think the three of us sense that the country is heading in the wrong direction. There are many policies of the current government that are contributing to this. But what we see when we look at the American landscape today is a nation that has lost its way—a place that once thrived on individual initiative and entrepreneurship, and which is now being weakened from within by dependence on the federal government. And for all that dependence, the government is sloppy and wasteful, a poor steward of our resources."

"That sounds about right to me."

"Now, we're aware that you live in Southern California, and we know that you've been involved in many of the issues surrounding our southern border. We know you have spoken out about the dangers of illegal immigration."

"It's a delicate issue, sir."

"Of course, it is. But when we look at it, we see many disturbing things. There are highly skilled engineers, technicians and computer scientists who can't get visas, who are subjected to a lengthy and very expensive process before they can enter the United States. At the same time, there's a wave of immigrants pouring across the Mexican border every day, illegal and unskilled. I think we're both aware that the government is subsidizing these people and footing the bill for their families."

"That sounds on target, yes."

"As you say, Mr. Marshall, it's a delicate issue," said Richard. "We're not insensitive to the plight of these people. And we're not against immigration: our great-grandfather came here from Germany in 1880, but he did so legally. And we're certainly not opposed to hardship cases, people who face real dangers and persecution in their native countries."

"Our feeling," said Sheldon, "is that the border has become unbelievably porous because the current administration has hampered the agents patrolling it. It's not a particularly nice thing to say, but we think the Atalas government supports illegal immigration from Mexico because they know those immigrants will ultimately become citizens. And when they do, they certainly are not going to vote Republican."

The three men shared a laugh.

"So I'm wondering, sir—"

"You're wondering where I'm going with this, and how it relates to you."

"Yes."

"As my brother said, we're impressed with you and your organization," said Richard. "We believe you stand for old-fashioned values of decency and responsibility. As far as we can see, you support the re-introduction of those values back into society, but in a compassionate way."

"Generally speaking, sure."

"But I think it's probably fair to say that you're hampered by a lack of money."

"Pretty much so. I think we could have a much greater impact, but nobody's ever heard of us."

"Precisely. That's why we'd like to make an investment in you and your operation."

"Really?"

"Let's look at the situation on our southern border for a moment," said Sheldon. "It stretches for nearly two thousand miles. There are forty-five legal border crossings, with 330 ports of entry. Yet we have something like 500,000 people coming across illegally each year. There's some dispute about the numbers, particularly how many are caught or turned away, but the general consensus is that we're netting at least 200,000 illegal immigrants annually. Now, we know that those people aren't climbing into the family Buick and heading to one of the forty-five stations. They're coming across rivers, climbing over mountains in rural areas, or being transported in trucks by professional guides."

"True."

"Most people don't realize that the Border Patrol only controls about 700 miles of our border with Mexico, and they're only empowered to intercept immigrants over about

130 miles of that land. We constantly hear about the 17,000 Border Patrol agents, but most of those people are sitting around at legal crossings, waiting for the Buicks. So the first thing we need to do is expand the enforcement zone for those agents."

"How do you intend to do that?"

"We have the machinery in place now," said Sheldon affably. "It's working its way through Congress. Either we'll get formal legislation, or some committee will pass a resolution."

"That's quite an accomplishment."

"It's just the beginning. After we've expanded the enforcement zone, though, the reality is that there won't be more than a few hundred agents clustered in one place. That's not enough to do the job. They'll need some backup, and we think that's where you'll be able to come in."

"I'm not sure I understand."

"Say we step in and fund your organization so that it expands rapidly. We isolate the four or six most vulnerable spots on the border, the places with the highest illegal traffic. We double the amount of manpower, thus more than doubling the number of arrests. But we do it in a sensible, peaceful way."

"Let me get this straight," said Jasper, "and please correct me if I'm wrong. You want me to expand the Angels of Democracy, place men on the Mexican border and arrest illegal immigrants?"

"No, no," said Sheldon patiently. "You won't arrest them. You'll be functioning in exactly the same way as you behave now—as Good Samaritans, people who enhance the fabric of the country by assisting law enforcement and promoting harmony."

"How many people are we talking about?"

"We've targeted six crucial areas," said Richard. "These are places with the highest volume of illegal immigrants and the lowest number of Border Patrol agents. Assume for a moment that you hire two hundred Angels of Democracy to assist each of those areas. The impact will be tremendous."

"Sir, with all due respect, this is going to cost a fortune. You'd have to pay those guys at least forty or fifty thousand dollars a year. On top of that you'd have to train them, give them uniforms, equipment and a headquarters to work out of. That's at least $75,000 per person in expenses. You're talking $18 or $20 million per location, multiplied by six."

"Actually, you're pretty close. We've done some studies on this." Sheldon reached for one of the file folders on the table. "The estimated figure is $17.3 million per year for each new location. It would drop significantly after that, because you have a one-time cost in material."

"Still, this would cost well over $100 million the first year. That's a lot of money."

"Mr. Marshall," said Richard, "we could raise the money tomorrow by selling that painting on the wall above my head, the one you like so much. But don't worry. We're as fond of it as you are, so we wouldn't sell it. Rest assured that we have the resources."

"Even so—"

"We understand you might be a bit overwhelmed," said Sheldon. "But remember that we've considered this very carefully, and we think we've chosen the right person. I'm curious to get your gut reaction."

"Sir, I just don't know. I wasn't expecting this."

"I imagine not."

"Where am I going to get two thousand new members from?"

"We have people who will help you screen them. They'll have to be chosen very carefully. We don't want anyone who just mustered out of the armed forces, no ex-police officers, or people of that nature—no one who is currently sitting around listening to the police radio for entertainment. We want them to be moral, upstanding citizens like yourself."

"I understand."

"And again, they won't be arresting anyone. At the most, they'll be detaining people until the agents can arrive. In the worst-case scenario, though, they're entitled to make a citizen's arrest in that situation, because they're witnessing a crime."

"I'm not too sure about that, sir."

"That's what our lawyers tell us, and we have some pretty good ones."

"What do you plan to do with all these people after they're arrested? There won't be enough space in the jails to hold them."

"That's a good question," said Sheldon. "We've thought about that carefully, and we have a specific plan. It won't affect you, since your involvement will end once the immigrants are apprehended, but we'll share it with you at some point."

"Will I have to give up control of the organization? The Angels of Democracy is really my baby."

"Another good question. You will be an equal partner with us. Legal agreements will be drawn up to that effect. You should do very well for yourself, but I want to make one thing clear: This isn't charity. We're going to expect results. That's how we run Haft Industries. Employees who produce profits for the company are rewarded handsomely, while executives who drop the ball are sacked."

"I understand."

"Of course, we'll expect you to continue to be the leader of the movement. We know you have the magnetism to do it. Your role will primarily consist of traveling and speaking. Inspiring the troops."

"Thank you."

"Here." Sheldon handed a book to Jasper Marshall. "I want you to read this. It's a book I wrote for internal company consumption, titled *The Principles of a Free Market Economy*. It will give you a precise view of who we are and what we do. This book outlines how we've built a business with annual revenues of $125 billion, not to mention personal fortunes that exceed the assets of most countries."

"I'll definitely read it, thanks."

"Well, Mr. Marshall." Sheldon Haft looked at him carefully. "Do you have any other questions we might be able to answer?"

"If we go forward with this, where do we go from here?"

"We'll have the lawyers draft an agreement that will spell everything out. You can review it or have your own attorney do so—that's what I'd advise." He smiled. "If you can't afford an attorney, as they say, one will be provided for you. After we get everything on paper, you'll sit down with Kevin Lapham, our Director of Political Operations. Most of your direction and guidance will probably come through him. We'll communicate via phone and email, but it's probably best if we keep our face-to-face meetings to a minimum."

"I can understand that."

Lapham had first appeared on the Hafts' radar in the early 1980s, when the brilliant young economics professor had been plucked out of Columbia University to serve on Reagan's Economic Advisory Council. His advocacy of free markets and opposition to government regulation appealed to the brothers, who regarded him as one of the architects of the nation's financial recovery. They hired him immediately when Reagan left office in 1989. Lapham spent a hugely successful decade coordinating the growing Haft empire, making certain that each new division saw eye to eye with the regime in St. Louis. As the brothers became more immersed in politics, Lapham made the transition to overseeing the complex web of interest groups funded by Sheldon and Richard. His primary mission was to make certain that their money was well spent, and that the ideological objectives of the Hafts were translated into reality.

"Even so," said Sheldon, "we'd like to get rolling on this as soon as possible. This is an important project for us, and we feel that you're the right man for the job."

"Sir, I'm honored that you selected me, and look forward to working with you."

Jasper Marshall shook hands with the Haft brothers. He somehow managed to get out of the office, down the elevator and into the waiting Hyundai, where he sat wordlessly for nearly thirty seconds as he and Joe Guthrie stared at each other.

"Well?" Guthrie asked finally. "How did it go? You look like you're in a state of shock."

"Fasten your seat belt, Joey. We could be in for a bumpy ride."

Chapter 10

"In just a moment," said the CNN anchor, "President Atalas will be stepping to the podium in the East Room of the White House to deliver his remarks on Cuba. As we know, the Senate Foreign Relations Committee met yesterday and voted by a margin of 11-8 to deny sending the administration's Cuba treaty to the full Senate for approval. That vote handed the President the first foreign policy defeat of his second term. What can we expect to hear from him tonight, John?"

"Well, most observers think he'll be somewhat feisty," said the commentator. "Remember, last November the President was reelected by a solid plurality. He undoubtedly feels that he earned some political capital by that victory, and obviously has an agenda to enact. At the same time, he doesn't have a majority in the House, and only controls the Senate by a razor-thin margin. And as we know, there are many Republicans in both chambers who are still committed to obstructing him."

"Many pundits are predicting that he will take executive action on Cuba, thus bypassing Congress entirely. What do you think of that possibility, John?"

"I think it's very likely. I believe that what the President will do tonight will be to take a page from the Reagan playbook and go over the heads of Congress to talk directly to the American people. Remember that his popularity is still remarkably high, an average of 55 percent approval in most recent polls—lower than the numbers he came into office with four and a half years ago, but still impressive. I think both he and his advisors are banking on his ability to connect with the public. And remember that he is one of the most effective speakers of modern times, someone who definitely has the ability to deliver a rousing and effective address. He—"

"John, I have to stop you there, because the President is approaching the podium now."

"My fellow Americans," said Khaleem Atalas, "I come before you tonight to discuss some of the current foreign policy initiatives of my administration, and what those initiatives may mean for this nation and the world."

Atalas wore a dark blue suit with a red tie, with an American flag pin displayed prominently in the lapel; he seemed serious but relaxed.

"On February 3, 1962, President John F. Kennedy issued an executive order enacting a trade embargo with the island nation of Cuba. This action effectively blocked all imports from Cuba, and imposed severe economic, commercial, and financial hardships on the country.

"President Kennedy had some very good reasons for applying this embargo. At the time, Cuba was a sworn enemy of the United States. They were a Communist nation closely allied with the Soviet Union, and they were also part of a global network dedicated to both the spread of Communism and the deterioration of America's influence around the world. Located a mere ninety miles from our southern shores, the country was to serve as a staging ground for Soviet nuclear missiles just eight months later—a situation that precipitated the Cuban missile crisis and almost brought us to the brink of nuclear war.

"Some of you watching tonight remember those events very well. Others, like myself, weren't even born when the trade embargo was enacted. Many things have changed over the past fifty years. The world is now a very different place. The Soviet Union no longer exists, and in place of the global Communist conspiracy we have a handful of states still clinging weakly to the philosophy of Communism."

Atalas looked earnestly into the camera—or appeared to. In reality he was looking at Joel Gottbaum, who had thought the speech was too long and who was urging him with hand motions to speed it up. Several miles away in Northwest DC, Judith Wallko walked into the den and sat down next to her husband, who was listening intently.

"Well?" she asked. "Any surprises?"

"Of course not," said Chet Wallko. "He's a one-man band—a miracle worker who can perform the work of all the branches of government."

She smiled. "Well, I guess that's why he was elected."

"He wasn't elected," said her husband. "He was anointed from on high."

The President's speech continued.

"The one thing that hasn't changed much is the effectiveness of the sanctions imposed five decades ago. They have not brought about a transition in the brutal regime that rules Cuba, nor have they altered the thinking of the Cuban leaders to any significant extent. Over time, the only accomplishment of the sanctions has been to keep the Cuban people in a state of poverty and misery. In addition to lacking freedom of speech and assembly, they have one of the lowest standards of living in the hemisphere. Let me be clear that the United States stands for democracy and opposes Communism and other totalitarian regimes. But we also stand for compassion, decency, and the right of all children to be well-fed, properly housed, and effectively educated.

"The sanctions have had fifty years to work, and they have not worked. It is time to bring them to an end.

"Therefore, tomorrow morning I will sign an executive order revoking the trade embargo with Cuba. I have also instructed our able and diligent Secretary of State, Bethany Hampton, to begin talks aimed at normalizing relations with the nation of Cuba. This is not a political move, but rather a humanitarian one. It will be beneficial to the U.S. economy, but will have a far greater impact on the welfare of Cuba. It is time to bring the people of Cuba into the 21st century so they may begin to enjoy material prosperity and a decent standard of living. Then, and only then, can we begin the difficult task of restoring their basic human freedoms.

"Yesterday, as many of you are aware, the Senate Foreign Relations Committee defeated a motion to bring our Cuba treaty to the full Senate for a vote. The treaty was the product of a great many hours of intensive effort by the State Department. It was balanced and fair. It held the Cuba government accountable for their policies of repression, yet it also held out the promise of an upward path for the Cuban people. I cannot criticize the good intentions of those Senators who voted against it, and I cannot impugn their patriotism. However, I certainly take issue with their actions yesterday.

"I have received many blessings in this life—good health, excellent opportunities, a loving family, and some would say a great measure of luck." He smiled. "The one thing I haven't been blessed with, obviously, is a compliant Congress. I respect our disagreements in many areas. But I will not stand by while they condemn the Cuban people to another generation of poverty and neglect.

"Long before I was a President or Senator, before I entered public life, I moonlighted as a university instructor to make some money to pay off my own student loans. And I taught constitutional law. So I'm one of those rare politicians who hasn't just read the Constitution, but actually studied it. And here's how I read it in this case: the role of the Senate is to advise and consent on foreign policy, not to make it. The responsibility for making that policy resides in the President of the United States. As long as I'm President, I intend to continue to make that policy—not just when it involves our safety, security, and prosperity, but also when it touches on the compassion that distinguishes us as a people. I'm proud of that compassion, and I will nurture it whenever I can.

"I thank you for your time tonight, and I hope that I've given you an insight into my forthcoming actions. God bless you, and God bless the United States of America."

"What do you think?" asked Judith Wallko.

"I think if there was a second Cuban missile crisis," said her husband, "this guy would give the Russians an aerial map so they could bomb Indianapolis."

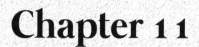

Chapter 11

"Democratic trash heap," said the voice at the other end of the phone. "Which pile can I direct your call to?"

"You asshole," said Kevin Lapham. "Don't gloat."

"I'm currently nine for nine," said Chuck Gardiner. "I think I'm entitled."

"Remember what the Greeks said about hubris."

"Don't know about that. They do make a mean gyro, though."

Gardiner was the head of the Special Operations Unit, a loosely knit group of freelance agents who reported directly to Lapham. Although he was one of the most highly paid members of the Haft organization, he wasn't actually an employee. Most of his compensation was transferred in cash by shell companies and deposited directly into offshore accounts. Sheldon and Richard Haft weren't even aware of who he was.

"Seriously, that was nice work."

"Nothing to it, really—it was like shooting fish in a barrel."

"If it was so easy, maybe we should be paying you less."

Gardiner chuckled. "Try it."

Six months earlier, the representative from Rhode

Island's 2nd Congressional District had announced his retirement due to illness. A special election was called. The Republican candidate was a committed conservative, but the Democrat was a problem: a former prosecutor and family man who advocated a strong national defense. Gardiner's agents followed him along the campaign trail and discovered that the man had a penchant for tall, black and muscular female prostitutes. They photographed three or four women leaving the candidate's hotel room in different cities, then paid the escorts for statements. The Democrat initially refused to quit when the evidence was presented to him, but quickly withdrew when the information was made public. He lost in a landslide, and his wife filed for divorce.

"Those statements were a thing of beauty, though," said Lapham. "How'd you get them?"

"Are you kidding? We took all that money you complain about paying us and waved it under their noses. Another ten grand apiece, and they would have sworn that they had slept with Khaleem Atalas."

"Life is full of missed opportunities."

"Doesn't matter one way or another to me. I think all politicians are twisted. You know that."

"Well, I hope you at least got a blow job out of it."

"I never mix business with pleasure."

"A joke," said Lapham. "Apparently you don't mix a sense of humor with your personality, either."

"Enough bullshit. What do you have for me next?"

"I'd like to meet sometime soon and discuss a project we have on the back burner. I need your input on a few points."

"Sketch it out for me."

"Not over the phone, no. This one is super top secret— we have it coded into the deep freeze."

"Whatever. It's your nickel. When do you want to do this?"

"I'll be swinging by Chicago next week. Maybe we can link up at the private aviation terminal at Midway."

"Why don't you come into the city for the day and let me show you a good time?"

"Here's why: when you're paying me, I'll come into the city and socialize with you. Meanwhile you can drag your ass out to the airport."

"Whatever you say, boss."

"I think this will intrigue you."

"The man of mystery," laughed Gardiner. "I love it."

Chapter 12

As 8:00 a.m. approached, Chet Wallko sat in his inner office with Linda Buckmeister, his Administrative Assistant, finishing their morning briefing. Buckmeister was his closest confidential advisor and had been with him since his earliest days in the Congress. She was from a working-class family just outside of Gary, Indiana, and had worked nights to put herself through law school. The pair usually met right after dawn to review the situation abroad and the political conflicts at home. The bulk of their conversation revolved around the Senator's overnight security summary—a compilation of intelligence put together for him by the CIA, which was less detailed than the Presidential Daily Brief but contained a range of items useful to the Foreign Relations Committee. Their conversation shifted to the constant backbiting on the Hill. The last five or ten minutes of their meetings were always reserved for ripe tidbits of gossip, something they both enjoyed.

"So," Linda smiled. "What did you think of the President's speech last night?"

"Rousing. Truly inspirational. After listening to it I jumped to my feet, saluted the flag, and ran off to bed."

"I'll just bet."

"Did it have any impact?"

"The snap polls show the public in a fifty-fifty split. Basically, the reaction was several notches below his popularity numbers."

"Well, no wonder. You have all these old farts out there like me who still remember that Cuba is supposed to be the enemy, not our ally." He paused. "You know, Gottbaum sat right there in that chair and told me Cuba was just the prelude to an opening with Persepostan. He said it was 'small potatoes'—his words—and would prepare the public for a nuclear treaty with the terrorists."

"He actually told you this?"

"Sometimes, these guys aren't as smart as they think they are. And they're riding high at the moment."

"That won't last. Reality will catch up with them."

"The question is whether they'll recognize it when they see it. But there's nothing better than a person who telegraphs his future moves to someone who disagrees with him on just about everything. Any other scuttlebutt?"

"Yes, in fact—I have something I need to raise with you."

"Shoot."

"I'd like to block out some time next week for a presentation by two consultants."

"Fabulous!" said Wallko. "You know how much I love consultants. Let's set a time so I can find something else to do."

She smiled. "I think this is important. I met with them last week, along with a group of junior staff. They have some very intriguing information—stuff I think you should hear."

"Who are these guys?"

"Their names are Lester Schmidt and Roger Dalborn. They've been doing some work for the Democratic National Committee."

"Well, that's interesting in itself. I didn't realize anyone over at the DNC was willing to give me the time of day."

"These two are freelancers. They have no formal connection to the Committee. They were hired to do a study, and they seem to have stumbled onto something."

"All right." He yawned. "If you think it's important, I'll do it. Worst case scenario, I can always watch hockey on my iPhone."

"I'll bet you won't be disappointed."

• • • • • • • • • • • • • • • • • • •

George Bindleman was everything a judge would want in a law clerk: smart, energetic, aggressive, and visionary. He graduated at the top of his class at Stanford and served on the law review. After clerking for a U.S. Appeals Court Judge, he had snagged the most prestigious possible position for a young lawyer in America: a clerkship with Paul Gilliam, Chief Justice of the Supreme Court.

Today, however, his mentor wasn't entirely happy with him. Gilliam thumbed through the pile of thick folders presented to him by Bindleman and shook his head.

"These cases are garbage, George."

"That's true, sir. I believe I told you that going in."

"Most of them have no legal basis beyond the plaintiff thinking that *Democracy Unchained* is unfair. There's really nothing in any of them that's actionable—they all read like little kids complaining because the schoolyard bully is pushing them around."

"Agreed."

"We have to do better than this."

"With all due respect, sir, we've looked at 75 or 100 thus far, and they've all been more or less the same."

Bindleman may have signed on with Gilliam as a steppingstone to an illustrious career, but he had grown to know him as a human being. He viewed the man with compassion. His close-up look at Gilliam caused him to reject the prevailing view within the profession: that the Chief possessed a brilliant legal mind that had come unglued after the death of his wife. Bindleman understood that his boss was just as tormented by voting in the majority in the *Democracy Unchained* case as he was by his personal grief.

"It's not enough to complain that the situation is unfair," said Gilliam, "because we can stipulate that it's inherently unfair. The First Amendment implies blanket protection of speech. While it doesn't explicitly say so, most people read the guarantee as a freedom that applies to everyone. In *Democracy*, the Court equated money with political speech—I don't think we can go back and revisit that principle, but we can most likely attack the fairness issue. Free speech shouldn't be a contest to see who can yell the loudest."

"I follow your reasoning, sir."

"So we have to keep going until we find the right case."

"Any idea of what that might be?"

"You'll know it when you see it," said the Chief. "It's not going to be blatant, necessarily—let's not hold out for a situation where a Neo-Nazi with a $5 million war chest is running against an Eagle Scout with no money. Just remember that the basic issue is fairness."

To an outsider, the process of a Supreme Court Justice searching for ideologically appropriate cases might have seemed bizarre, if not unethical. The Court received roughly 10,000 petitions each year and chose to hear fewer than 1 percent of those cases. Frequently, though, Justices felt strongly about points of law that they thought should be either reinforced or overturned, and it wasn't unusual for them to shop for cases that fit their agenda. The process was then relatively simple. The Justices met regularly to sort through the volume of petitions that flooded their offices, and they relied on the Rule of Four: if four of them felt the case held enough potential merit or impact, it was put on the docket.

"Sir," said Bindleman, "maybe we're going about this the wrong way. The First Amendment clearly states that Congress shall make no law abridging freedom of speech. It says nothing about the courts. There might be a legislative remedy to this."

"Maybe so." Gilliam smirked. "But that remedy would come in a different era. I don't know if you've looked at the ideological makeup of the House recently, but I wouldn't count on a solution coming from that crew."

"Not right away, no."

"And in any case, we certainly couldn't lobby for it. Remember that pesky separation of powers."

"True." Bindleman grinned. "But it's something to think about."

"You think about it." Gilliam rose and shook his clerk's hand. "I appreciate all your efforts. In the meantime, just keep looking."

Chapter 13

J asper Marshall and Joe Guthrie watched as the Gulfstream G650 landed at LAX. The plane taxied toward them and came to a stop in front of the Private Jet Terminal.

"I guess that's him," said Jasper.

"Nothing like making a statement."

"I expected it to be bigger, I guess."

"That's just Lapham's plane. I'm sure the Hafts ride around in something more appropriate, like the Goodyear blimp. Or maybe the space shuttle." Guthrie yawned. "This is like the good old days, when the peasants waited for the King to stroll down the red carpet and give them an audience."

"I wonder what he wants."

"Who knows? He'll probably look under our fingernails for traces of left-wing DNA."

The man who descended the stairs of the Gulfstream was shorter than they expected—no more than 5'6", with thinning silver hair and a sharp, chiseled face. He was nattily attired in a dark blue business suit with a matching burgundy tie and handkerchief. He moved with the assurance of someone who owned the world—and he was obviously not in the habit of smiling without cause.

"Jasper Marshall." The leader of the Angels of Democracy extended his hand.

"A pleasure. And you must be Mr. Guthrie."

"Don't hold that against me." Joe grinned. "You want to go inside?"

"No, we'll stay out here. Machines don't have ears."

He motioned them toward the shade of an overhang near the terminal.

"Very nice job thus far, guys," said Lapham. "We're right on schedule. Training is proceeding nicely, except for a few blips—agents out joyriding in ATVs, that kind of thing. All in all, though, it looks like a good crew."

"Well, your people screened everybody before we hired them," said Guthrie, "so we assume you filtered out the ax murderers."

Lapham ignored him.

"We weren't aware there was a schedule," said Jasper.

"There's no need for the two of you to be worrying about details." His manner was generous and affable, the attitude of a parent praising a child for a good report card. "We're coordinating the big picture. Generally, though, I'd say we're shooting for deployment in the spring. That's the season when public attention should be very high—people will be so bored after the monotony of the winter that they'll actually watch the news."

"How's that going to be handled?" asked Jasper.

"We'll start right here in Southern California, on your home turf. After a few weeks, when we see that things are going smoothly, we'll transition to another venue. We'd like to see both of you present for each deployment so you can monitor and psych up the troops."

"I'd love to know how you got the Border Patrol to go for this," said Joe.

"They're actually very pleased about it, Mr. Guthrie. They need all the help they can get, and they welcome the backup. But I can't stress to you enough that it has to be solely backup—your men can't engage in actual arrests or indulge in rough stuff of any sort. That's why we need the two of you present at each deployment." He smiled. "To intercept the occasional rogue agent wielding an ax."

"Got it."

"The other thing you have to remember, and this is crucially important, is that Sheldon and Richard Haft will not be associated with this publicly in any way. They will remain in the background. That's one of the reasons that your contact is coming through me."

"I don't know how you're going to pull that off," said Jasper. "They invested a fortune in this operation. I'm sure that money can be traced."

"The funding has been handled in such a way that it would take an entire team of forensic accountants to track it. I'm sure those teams exist somewhere, on someone's payroll, but it won't be an easy job. To be honest, I'm not sure how much it matters if people realize where the money is coming from. But when the press asks you about it, which they will, please say that you received thousands of small donations from public-spirited citizens who were concerned about the immigration problem. You are simply here to help. You are the Angels of Democracy, after all. Is that clear?"

"Yes."

He took a business card from his breast pocket and wrote something on the back.

"Here you are, Mr. Marshall. I'm giving this to you in the strictest of confidence. This is the name and cell phone number of someone you can call in case of emergency—if it's the middle of the night, say, and you can't reach me. If you find yourself in a sticky or unpleasant situation, try to call me first."

"Charles Gardiner," said Jasper, staring at the card. "Okay."

"I want this card to stay in your office safe. Do not carry it around with you, where others might see it and intercept the number."

"Who is he, may I ask?"

"He's someone you can rely on to fix any problem that might come up." Kevin Lapham shook hands with the pair, displaying the faintest suggestion of warmth. "Thanks very much for coming out here to meet me. This was a pro forma get together, so we could at least encounter each other and put a face to the name. We'll continue to communicate via phone and email, and we'll meet again shortly after the first deployment. But I want to stress that the two of you are doing an excellent job, and we appreciate it." He looked from one to the other. "Any questions?"

"Off the subject," said Joe, "but just something I'm curious about: what do the Hafts have against illegal immigration that would cause them to make this kind of investment?"

"Absolutely nothing," said Lapham. "Their real interests lie elsewhere."

Chapter 14

Lester Schmidt and Roger Dalborn followed Linda Buckmeister into Senator Wallko's inner office. The three men shook hands, and Wallko motioned them to a pair of chairs directly across from his desk.

"Have a seat, gentlemen."

"Thanks for seeing us, sir," said Schmidt. "We appreciate it."

"Well, let's set the ground rules. Linda told me you had something interesting. If that turns out to be the case, I look forward to hearing it. But if you start feeding me a line of crap, I'm going to toss you out."

"Agreed." Dalborn grinned. "We've been thrown out of worse places."

"We have a PowerPoint presentation for you," said Schmidt. "Mind if we take just a moment and set up?"

"Go for it."

Dalborn pulled down a portable projection screen while Schmidt fiddled with a laptop. They nodded at Linda, who dimmed the lights in the office. Schmidt clicked on the first slide.

"This is a list of contributions made by Sheldon and Richard Haft during last year's presidential campaign," said Schmidt. "As you probably know, they use a complicated series of foundations and front groups to channel money to candidates, even though the *Democracy Unchained* decision made it legal for them to make those donations."

"I was aware of that, yes."

"You'll also note that it's quite a lengthy list. The Democratic National Committee hired a team of forensic accountants to track these donations. The total comes to somewhere between $400 and $500 million—$433 million thus far."

"That's the figure that's usually tossed around."

"After the reelection of President Atalas, the DNC wanted to continue to monitor the Hafts' financial dealings in politics. They were curious to see whether the brothers would continue to remain active. So they kept the majority of those accountants on the payroll." He clicked to the next slide. "What they discovered was very curious. The Hafts took a break of about three months after the election, and then the donations started up again. Here's what they've found to date. You'll see that the list is much shorter, since there are no political campaigns in place at the moment. But the amounts are significant: roughly $78 million thus far, and we think the real total may turn out to be twice as much."

"So where's the money going, if there are no candidates?"

"As far as we can tell, the main recipient is an organization called the Angels of Democracy."

"Never heard of them."

"Most people haven't," said Dalborn. "They're headquartered in Pasadena and have about a thousand members. There are some branches in major cities around the country, but most of the manpower is centered in Southern California."

"Are they a militia group?"

"Not as far as anyone can tell. They seem to focus primarily on doing good works. They do assist the police in patrolling neighborhoods and keeping order at public events, but they've been careful not to lay claim to any police powers. I don't even believe they're armed." The next slide appeared on the screen. "This is their Supreme Commander, Jasper Marshall."

Wallko laughed out loud. The picture showed Marshall in the white robes of a Templar knight, emblazoned with a red cross on the breast of the tunic. Around his neck were numerous sashes, chains and medals, and he held the helmet of a Medieval warrior in his hand.

"This guy had better hope he doesn't fall into a swimming pool," said Wallko. "He'd sink right down to the bottom with all that paraphernalia and drown."

"It's admittedly funny," said Dalborn. "But this is his ceremonial garb, worn maybe once or twice a year. The rest of the time, he dresses like a normal person."

"What's the obsession with the Knights Templars?" asked Wallko.

"The Angels of Democracy take them as an inspirational model," said Schmidt. "They try to emulate their standards of piety, the fact that the Templars always stood up for the underdog."

"If memory serves, the Templars didn't end up very well. I believe most of them were arrested, tortured and killed."

"I think you're right. But remember, this is just a model to inspire good behavior among their membership. These guys are basically harmless."

"So you're telling me that the Haft brothers may have funneled $150 million into this bunch of clowns running around in funny uniforms?" Wallko smiled. "That doesn't make much sense, guys. I don't agree with the Hafts on everything, but they're certainly not stupid."

"That's the way it appears."

"Where's the money going?"

"Here's a rough breakdown." Schmidt advanced to the next slide. "The Angels of Democracy have started a huge membership drive. In recent months, they've opened a half-dozen recruitment centers. These places are located in the southern sectors of California, New Mexico, Arizona, and Texas. The only common denominator is that they're all fairly close to the Mexican border. They seemed determined to enlist thousands of new members. A lot of the money is being put toward salaries, uniforms, training and equipment. They're purchasing dozens of Jeeps and other four-wheel drive vehicles."

"So you think it has something to do with immigration?"

"That's the most likely conclusion," said Dalborn, "but we're not sure. It could be a false scent."

"You mentioned salaries. I had the impression that these guys were volunteers."

"The initial group was, yes," said Schmidt. "But the new hires appear to be going on the payroll."

"And the Hafts are footing the bill for all this?" Wallko shook his head. "I'm sorry, but it still doesn't sound right. Could this be a smokescreen—I mean, are these guys a front group for something or someone else?"

"At this point, sir, we just don't know. But I can tell you that there are people watching it very closely."

"You said something about equipment. What are they buying, other than vehicles?"

"An assortment of stuff," said Dalborn. "Mostly surveillance related: night vision goggles, infrared equipment, voice sensors."

"But no weapons?"

"Not firearms, no," said Schmidt. "But we believe these guys will be carrying tasers, which are legal for civilian use in most states."

"That's just great."

"There's one more thing, sir."

"There always is. Go ahead."

Schmidt clicked again, and a picture of what looked like a tent city appeared on the screen.

"This is a camp that's being constructed about forty miles north of Nogales. It's an aerial shot, but if you look closely, you'll see that it's a very large facility. This one will hold at least ten thousand people, and it's one of three being built at the moment. The tents appear to be filled with bunk beds. There's a series of prefab buildings which we suspect may house washrooms and kitchens."

"Where'd you get these photos?"

"This was taken by a CIA drone. We have a series of them, if you'd like to see them."

"I like you guys, but I have to tell you that you're on very thin ice here. I can just see the headline in *The Washington Times: Democratic National Committee Authorizes Aerial Surveillance of Right-Wing Groups*.

"There's nothing illegal about this, sir," said Schmidt. "It's all kosher. The DNC took some of their concerns to the Department of Justice, and the DOJ requested the aerial surveillance. We have no idea what these camps are for. As far as anyone knows they could be terrorist training locations, so the CIA was totally justified in photographing them."

"Listen," said Wallko. "As I told you, I don't always see eye to eye with the Haft brothers. But they're not terrorists, regardless of what that article in *Rolling Stone* said."

"No one has any idea if these camps are definitely linked to their involvement with the Angels of Democracy. But everybody seems to agree that they're worth monitoring."

"Well, you were right." Wallko looked at Linda Buckmeister. "This is definitely interesting."

"Thank you, sir," said Dalborn.

"And I assume you have some definite proof of a link between this Marshall character and the Hafts?"

"Absolutely," said Schmidt. "About three months after the election, Marshall and his second in command, Joe Guthrie, visited the Hafts in St. Louis."

"How do you know this?"

"We had people check all the commercial airline manifests between southern California and Missouri during that period. The two of them flew on JetBlue. They rented a car at the St. Louis airport. When they turned in the vehicle, it had less than 100 miles on it. It's 39 miles from the airport to Haft Industries. We figure the rest of the mileage was driving to and from a hotel, out to dinner, that sort of thing."

"Damn, you're good."

"We have good people."

"Still, that doesn't make sense. If the Hafts wanted to meet with those guys, why didn't they send a plane for them? Why have them fly commercial, knowing it could be traced?"

"We assume it was a mistake. Maybe they're getting sloppy."

"No, no. Sheldon Haft doesn't make mistakes. If he had them fly commercial, there was a reason for it. It was part of a plan. Just like all the donations to the Angels of Democracy, and the pictures of the tent cities you just showed me—if the DNC discovered it, that means the Hafts wanted it to be discovered."

"You probably know more about this than we do, sir. We're just doing the detective work."

"Well, good job." He rose and shook hands with them again. "I'd like you to stay in touch and keep me in the loop on this. Linda will give you my cell phone number so you can keep me updated."

"Will do, sir."

"Excellent." Wallko smiled. "And don't start taking aerial shots of my house, either."

Chapter 15

Khaleem Atalas and Bethany Hampton sat in very different postures on opposite ends of a sofa in the Oval Office. The President leaned backward in a relaxed pose, a pillow propping up his half-recline. Hampton sat erect on the edge of the cushion, as if wearing a back brace. She cradled a set of files on her lap and occasionally referenced them as they talked.

"So," asked Atalas, "what have your preliminary discussions been like with the Cuban diplomats?"

"Very smooth thus far—no glitches. They're very pleasant and polite. It's a different culture, obviously."

"I would imagine. My guess is that you'll be called to testify before Congress about this."

"Testify about what, for God's sake? All we're doing is exploring options to normalize relations."

"Well, you know how they feel about me." The President flashed his trademark toothy grin. "Their theory is that if you keep turning over the ground, you'll find a snake sooner or later."

"They'll have to look awfully hard to find one here, sir."

"Agreed. And Bethany, please stop calling me 'sir,' at least when it's just the two of us."

"You know the theory—if you do it in private, someday it'll slip out in public. It's just out of respect for the office."

"Understood. If you do get called, just continue to stress all the points we've emphasized thus far. The existing policy has had fifty years to work, the policy has failed, and it's time for a change. There will be enhanced communication and a limited amount of trade and tourism. Overall, the thaw in relations is a win-win for the Cuban people, something that will improve their standard of living and help bring them into the 21st century."

"I know the drill."

"What does your husband think of this?"

"He's all for it. Truth be known, he probably wishes he had done it himself. But he would have been afraid of the political blowback, for one thing. And of course, by his second term he was so deep in scandals that he had less and less time for foreign policy initiatives."

"He could have pulled it off. He's one of the most skilled politicians I know." Atalas grinned again. "Along with you, of course."

"Thank you, sir. I'm afraid I wasn't quite good enough."

"Well, I was a lucky guy. Don't forget that." Five years earlier, Atalas had defeated Hampton in a bitter primary contest, practically coming out of nowhere to win the Democratic nomination. "Things could easily have turned out differently."

Bill was the only one who saw it, she thought. *He kept warning me about this guy, and I ignored him. Had I listened, I'd be sitting here now, but Atalas wouldn't be Secretary of State. Housing and Urban Development, most likely.*

"You mentioned political blowback," she said. "Are you concerned about Florida next time around?"

"Not really. Joel believes that none of the Miami Cubans were ever going to vote Democratic anyway, and I think he's right. Do you agree?"

"Absolutely. There might be a few demonstrations when we open the embassy, but I'm sure no one there will be under sixty."

"Speaking of opening the embassy." The President fiddled distractedly with his pants cuff. "Are we closing in on a date?"

"Sometime in the late spring, I would think."

"Let's keep it formal but low-key. No big contingents of U.S. personnel—just you and a small group of aides. On their side, the Cubans will be very careful who they allow to attend."

"Agreed."

"How are we coming along on the back-channel talks with Persepostan?"

"It's agonizingly slow. The gist of their position is they want us to immediately lift all the sanctions, give them foreign aid, and allow them to continue with their nuclear program."

"Shit, let's give them something nice for Christmas, too."

"We have the edge on this. The sanctions are killing their economy. They can still keep a lid on things, but the situation is dicey when they look five or ten years down the road. The majority of the population is under twenty-five, and they have no jobs and no future. The leaders of the original revolution are now older than dirt."

"I'm told their biggest employers are the army and the secret police."

"That's correct, and that's part of the problem. They'll have to sell any deal they make to the army, and those guys aren't going to junk several decades of nuclear research. The only things the clerics have going for them at this point is the complete blackout on information from the outside world, and their ability to arrest anyone who looks at them the wrong way."

"Sounds like it's not going to be easy."

"Not in the least. Our only hope for any meaningful concessions is to keep the sanctions in place for a while, or even tighten them."

"I want you to keep trying."

"I will. But you know that the Israelis will go crazy over any type of deal, no matter what it is."

"What else is new?" The President shrugged. "They go crazy about something roughly once a month."

"And don't expect the Gulf states to be thrilled, either. Particularly Saudi Arabia."

"Things are different now. We're very close to being self-sufficient on energy. And not only are we hardly importing any oil from the Gulf, but the price has dropped dramatically. These guys don't have the money and the leverage that they were able to use on the Cane family. I'm confident that I can handle the Saudis."

"I'm sure you can."

"The real problem, when you look down the road, is Persepostan. They're supporting the New Caliphate in Sumeristan, and they're determined to completely destabilize the region. At the same time, they're resolute about getting a nuclear weapon. We can't bomb their nuclear program out of existence, because we can't figure out where half of it is, and the half we know about is buried so far underground that we'll never get to it. So the only solution here is to have some sort of treaty with them and work from within on slowing down their nuclear ambitions—even if it means easing the sanctions and allowing the regime to tighten their control on things."

"Well, I'll keep trying. Just don't expect anything in the immediate future. And if we do get any sort of movement, it's likely to be crumbs. Initially it won't be anything to base a treaty on, and it certainly won't be anything that Congress would swallow easily."

"Just stay with it. You're doing a hell of a job, and I appreciate it."

"Thank you, sir."

Not as good a job as you would have done as HUD Secretary, you arrogant piece of crap.

• • • • • • • • • • • • • • • • • • • •

George Bindleman settled into an armchair in the Capitol Hill townhouse of Ken Breslaw, one of his oldest and closest friends. Back in college, the two had been known as The Odd Couple, displaying an improbable bond between a raging liberal and a third-generation conservative. Bindleman had gone to law school after graduation while Breslaw headed directly for the Hill, where he worked for a variety of organizations funded by Sheldon and Richard Haft. He was currently Assistant Director of Americans for a Free Society— and widely regarded as a man to watch.

"So what's up?" asked Bindleman. "Obviously it's something momentous, since you didn't want to meet in public."

"I just thought we'd be more comfortable here, given the delicate nature of the discussion."

"Nice place." He glanced around at the paneling. "I see that working for the Antichrist is profitable."

"Genuine Chesapeake Bay hardwood." Breslaw grinned. "You know there's nothing I love more than the opportunity to cut down a few trees."

"Don't keep me in suspense."

"Seems like we're constantly realizing that we have more in common than we thought. We actually see eye to eye on a number of important issues."

"I don't recall, but I'm sure stranger things have happened."

"Take *Democracy Unchained*, for example. I know you think it was a disaster."

"Was and is. Looking at the last election, it gave your employers the license to spend a boatload of money. Didn't help, though."

"No, it didn't, but they would have spent that money anyway."

"Probably so." Bindleman stirred his drink. "But you're correct. The decision wasn't in anyone's best interest. Gilliam wouldn't vote for it today, if he had the chance to revisit it."

"You may be surprised to learn that there are people on the other side who feel the same way. People at the very top of the food chain, in fact."

"No way. You're bullshitting me."

"Not at all. The decision is irrelevant to the Hafts—as I said, they have the machinery to spend money and influence the system either way. It may be helpful to a lower-level conservative donor, but it doesn't really affect them in the least."

"Well, you're probably right, and that's interesting to know. But *Democracy Unchained* is now law, and we can't reverse it. Don't think we're not trying. We just can't find a case that gives us the right loophole to seize on."

"God, you guys are thick." Breslaw shook his head. "The loophole is right under your nose, and you don't see it. Maybe you're looking too hard."

"Sure. And you know what it is?"

"We think we do. Mind if I enlighten you?"

"You expect me to believe that you're going to give away the store? I may be a Democrat, but I'm not stupid."

"I'm a patriot, George, just like the Hafts." He winked. "Pull your chair closer, buddy, and listen up."

Chapter 16

Kevin Lapham walked into the private jet terminal at Midway and shook hands with Charles Gardiner. "Chuck, shall we go for a stroll?"

"It's raining."

"You won't melt."

Lapham borrowed two umbrellas from the desk agent and the men walked out onto the tarmac. Gardiner had the gait of an ex-athlete, as well as the self-assurance of someone who could easily walk through brick walls. A former Army Ranger, he had put himself through college after mustering out of the service. Lapham was fond of referring to him as the "thinking man's thug:" a guy who was comfortable supervising both roughnecks and philosophers.

"Tell me, have you given any thought to your golden years?"

"I'm not retiring," said Gardiner. "Certainly not yet. Unless you're firing me."

"Absolutely not. But if this next operation pans out, you'll be able to hang it up and relax on a beach in Costa Rica."

"Nah, there's too many people like me in Costa Rica. What have you got for me?"

"As I told you, this is top secret. We're not having this conversation."

"Okay. I'll pretend I don't know that you're building three tent cities near the Mexican border."

"How the hell do you know that?"

"Give me a fucking break. Those camps are secured at night by a handful of minimum-wage security guards. Any Marine just out of boot camp could crawl in there on his belly and photograph the entire place."

"And I gather you've done this?"

"Don't worry about me. Worry about the people you don't want to see it. For your next trick, do something really subtle. Parade a dozen elephants down Michigan Avenue at high noon."

"The camps aren't confidential. Anybody could be building them. And it's not illegal, either."

"Keep it up, and you're going to attract media attention."

"Maybe that's what we want."

"And what about these jokers riding around in their Hummers, playing with their night vision equipment?"

"They're in training."

"Training for what?"

"None of your business. Let's focus on the part of this that concerns you. Sometime in the next year, we'd like to see the Vice President leave office."

"Are you kidding? The guy was just reelected."

"This is true."

"If you want me to get some dirt on him, that's going to be a tall order. The way I hear it, he's a Boy Scout."

"There has to be something. There always is.'"

"Damn, I don't know. The guy doesn't even drink. He's married, and from all accounts takes it seriously. Not only is he probably too old to screw around, but it's not like he has tons of spare time."

"Well, there has to be something. We'd like to see him out of the picture."

"No way." Gardiner stopped walking and stared at Lapham. "You're not telling me to take him out, I hope? Because that would cost so much that I'd be able to buy the entire country of Costa Rica."

"*Of course* I'm not suggesting you take him out. I doubt that it's possible, and it's certainly not desirable."

"Anything's possible."

"All right, look: there's a long-range plan in place that I can't divulge to you. It's too delicate, and there are too many moving parts. But for the scenario to work, he has to bow out of the picture. There must be a way to make that happen."

"Boy." Gardiner shook his head. "I'd like some of whatever they're smoking out in St. Louis."

"I never said this was coming from St. Louis."

"Sure. You're just wandering around the country, making all this wild shit up."

"Yes and no. Things get handed to me in the broadest possible terms. The thoughts are ideological and speculative, not concrete—at least not in this case. It's a very broad agenda, and the gulf between idea and actions is frequently very wide."

"Spoken like a true politician."

"So why don't you nose around a bit, see what you can find out? The usual research rates will apply."

"Sure. I'd just love to get inside the head of someone who has the leisure time to dream up this stuff."

Lapham slapped him on the back. "After you become President of Costa Rica, you can tell me what it's like."

• • • • • • • • • • • • • • • • • • •

Peter Schoenfeld poked his head into the office of Kenneth Jablonski, *The Washington Post* National Editor.

"Morning, Kenny. You wanted to see me?"

"Close the door, please."

Jablonski sat with his feet up on the desk, shuffling through some copy. His office was a large glass cubicle with a panoramic view of the newsroom. "If you ever get to be a fucking editor, God forbid," he had once told Schoenfeld, "never let them give you a glass office. You won't be able to pick your nose whenever you want to."

"Have a seat."

"Sure. Let me maneuver my chair to get a better view of your feet."

Jablonski sat up with difficulty. He weighed nearly 300 pounds and was sweating despite the glacial temperature in the building.

"What do you have for me?"

"There's something going on down near the Mexican border."

"I'm listening."

"Here." He pushed a copy of *The New Patriot* across the desk, folded to reveal an ad in the back. "Read this."

The Angels of Democracy Aren't Just Looking For a Few Good Men, ran the headline.

We're looking for men who are morally upright, patriotically motivated and want to serve the national interest.

Are you between the ages of 21 and 35 and ready to take on a challenge? Do you enjoy helping others while serving your country at the same time? If so, we have a mission for you that will make you even prouder to be an American than you are right now.

We're presently recruiting full-time agents for a career assisting segments of our law enforcement community. The salary and benefits are competitive, but the spiritual rewards are even greater. To apply, you must have a valid driver's license, be physically fit and totally free of any criminal record...

"I gathered this was a militia," said Schoenfeld, "until I got to the part about assisting law enforcement. What's this all about?"

"Who knows? All I can tell you is they're hiring thousands of people. Or agents, as they like to call them."

"It looks like they have all their bases covered: Tijuana, Juarez, Presidio, Nogales. Who are these guys?"

"Don't ask me." Jablonski grinned. "You're the fucking reporter."

During the Cane administration, Jablonski and Schoenfeld had been responsible for one of the most lethal combination punches in American journalism. After George Cane's ill-advised invasion of Sumeristan, the situation on the ground unraveled rapidly. Dozens of American servicemen were being killed daily by a combination of snipers and improvised explosive devices. Robert Hornsby, Cane's Vice President and the former Director of Central Intelligence, determined that the insurgency was being fueled by Husam al-Din, who had four terrorist training camps in Northern Kabulistan. He convinced the President to launch an air strike and obliterate the camps. The surprise raid was successful, and Cane crowed about it as a proactive security triumph. About a week later, a *Post* stringer on the ground discovered that the camps had been bogus sites set up by Husam al Din to dupe the Americans. He supplied Jablonski with pictures of lifelike dummies strewn all over the rubble of the destroyed camps, and the editor had gleefully splashed them all over the front page. The incident culminated in Salman Al-Akbar's famous Christmas video, in which the terrorist leader taunted the American government while sitting next to one of the dummies.

Jablonski's scoop may have embarrassed the administration, but Schoenfeld's came close to dealing it a lethal blow. From a confidential source, he obtained a purloined copy of the Presidential Daily Brief for April 21, 2001, which indicated that the Cane White House had been aware of a possible terrorist attack but had done nothing to prevent it. The resulting series of stories further degraded the credibility of the war-torn President in the public's mind.

"You want me to go down there and check it out?"

"Do some snooping around first. But there's something else." Jablonski handed him a sheaf of photographs. "There's some sort of weird construction going on north of the border, in three different locations. I have no idea of what it is, or whether it's related to these Angels of Democracy."

"Hmm." Schoenfeld studied the pictures. "How'd you get these?"

"They're a little fuzzy, admittedly. They were taken by a freelancer with crappy equipment. But whoever is building this project is making no secret of it. The perimeter guards are the Bozo Brigade from Pinkerton—just about anybody can drive around at night and take shots like this with a telephoto lens. The problem is, we don't know what any of this means."

"Maybe it's a concentration camp for left-wing journalists."

"Hopefully so—I could stand to lose some weight. But do me a favor and look into it. Could be your next Pulitzer."

"My oh my. Where will I find the space on my wall?"

"Kiss my ass," said Jablonski cheerfully.

Chapter 17

The buzzer sounded on Joel Gottbaum's desk console.

"Yes?"

"Jorge Mendoza is on the line for you, sir."

"God almighty." Mendoza was the chairman of the National Council of Criollos Unidos, the largest and most influential organization lobbying for Hispanic rights. "I can see it's going to be one of those days."

"Shall I tell him you're tied up?"

"No, I'll take it." He pushed the button on the speaker. "*Buenos dias,* Jorge. How are you?"

"Good morning, Joel. Your question is a very curious one."

"Okay, I'll bite: why is that?"

"I would be feeling much better if you could tell me that we were making progress on the Path Bill. But I never seem to get that news from you."

"We're doing everything we can, Jorge."

"Is that so? The bill has languished now in committee for nearly an entire year, with no vote—not even a committee vote, much less a roll call on the floor of the House."

"Obviously, I'm aware of that. But I think you realize that we've had a number of other issues to deal with."

"Yes. You've been very busy legitimizing the Communist government of Cuba."

"Jorge—"

"But Latinos in this country don't get the same level of consideration."

"We both know you're not being fair. The President went to the wall for you last year by introducing the bill."

"And we also went to the wall for him. We had an unprecedented and very successful voter turnout drive. I can say in all modesty that Hispanic support played a significant role in his reelection."

"That's true, and we appreciate it."

"Perhaps so. But we would also appreciate it if you could expend just a little bit more energy in trying to get this bill passed, or at least attempting to bring it up for a vote so that everyone is forced to take a stand."

"That's exactly what we're doing. The legislative team is working very hard on it."

"They're hired hands, Joel. Congressmen know they don't have to listen to them."

"What exactly would you have us do? What would make you happy?"

"We'd be grateful if the President would at least give the appearance of getting behind this. He could make some phone calls, lobby Congress personally. It would have a large impact."

"You're well aware that he normally doesn't do that. That's why we have legislative aides, and they're some of the best in the business."

"It seems to us, Joel, that he does get involved from time to time, but only when he feels passionate about something. Perhaps that doesn't apply here?"

"Give me a break. You know that's not true."

"If this keeps up, it will be very difficult to rally the same level of support for a Democratic presidential candidate the next time around."

"Threats are unbecoming to a person of your stature, Jorge."

"Joel, Joel. Of course I am not threatening you. I would merely suggest a different course of action, one which will benefit both of us."

"Care to elaborate?"

"I believe people in your line of work would call it realpolitik. Take the pragmatic view. Be powerful, be coercive. Make grand statements."

"I think we both know that bill isn't going to pass."

"Of course it won't pass. But why don't you light a fire under your guy and have him at least get excited about it? Have him wave his arms around. Have him throw his chest out for a change and hint that he might start issuing executive orders. Then my people might leave me alone for a while, and in turn I can leave you alone."

"I'll see what I can do."

"I appreciate it, gringo. *Vaya con dios*."

• • • • • • • • • • • • • • • • • • •

Several days later, Curt Bassen reached for a toothpick. He was concluding his weekly private lunch meeting with Khaleem Atalas.

"I think we've covered most of the major stuff, Curt," said the President. "No further Senate fallout on Cuba?"

"They're pissed off, of course, but they'll get over it. Most members of the Foreign Relations Committee were expecting the executive order as soon as they voted the treaty down."

"I would think so."

"They'll make some noise about it in the press, but that's as far as it'll go."

"Good."

"Any progress on Persepostan?"

"They've indicated to Bethany, in general terms, that they want a framework of understanding before they commit themselves publicly to sitting down for negotiations. Their initial demands are completely ridiculous, as you'd expect, but she'll whittle away at the list. She's pretty tough, as you know."

"True. And after all, they like blondes."

Atalas grinned. "I don't think she's dumb enough for them. I'd love to be a fly on the wall while they try to iron out a preliminary understanding, though."

"Has her timetable changed at all? I believe you said you thought she'd resign 18 to 24 months into the second term, so she could focus on another presidential run."

"I still think that's about right. I told her I'd like to see the Persepostan deal wrapped up before she leaves, but that's not hard and fast. If you recall, the North Vietnamese dickered for years over the shape of the table before they finally agreed to talks. She's done a great job, so I need to respect her future plans." He paused. "You're still not considering taking a whack at it yourself?"

"I'm still leaning negative," said the Vice President. "I'd probably be too old for two terms, to begin with. And I just don't know if I want to ask my family to go through it again."

"If you change your mind, let me know. I'll be with you."

"I appreciate it. Anyway, Bethany should do much better next time around, since she won't have you to contend with."

"It wasn't me. They were too arrogant, and she got blindsided."

"That sounds about right."

"Anything else?"

"A couple of things." Bassen glanced at his notes. "I got a call from Jorge Mendoza. He's apparently been bugging Joel as well. They'd like to see some action on the Path Bill."

"Wouldn't we all. The bill is a non-starter. Mendoza's a sharp guy, I'm sure he knows that."

"Of course he does. But he's looking for you to make some noise about it publicly, so he can get his supporters off his back."

"What does he have in mind?"

"The usual routine. Have a meeting with the Speaker. Call a few dozen Congressman. Make some stirring public statements. It would be useful for him if we gave the impression that we're pushing as hard as we can on it."

"Okay," said Atalas, scribbling on a note pad. "I can do that."

"Talk about your own immigrant background. That always resonates with the public."

"True."

"Just don't mention that you learned Spanish at Andover."

The President grinned. "It was Exeter. They have a great foreign language lab."

"Speaking of which: I assume you're following this business going on down at the Mexican border?"

"I've been briefed on it, of course. I asked them to put you in the loop as well."

"What are your thoughts?"

"I don't have any, to tell you the truth. The FBI is monitoring the situation, and they've checked out these Angels of Democracy pretty thoroughly. They're convinced the group is harmless, and that's good enough for me."

"I'd like to know where their money is coming from."

"Who knows? Probably an ongoing right-wing bake sale."

"Even so, let's keep it on the radar. I don't have a good feeling about it."

"Tell you what: if you're concerned, you keep it on your radar. I don't have time to be following the activities of every kook fringe group out there. There are so many real threats that I can't worry about a bunch of frustrated vigilantes running around in weird uniforms." He grinned again. "Although, who knows? After we're retired, we may be doing the same thing."

Chapter 18

"**G**ood evening. I'm David Gregory of NBC News, and tonight we have the distinction of bringing you a very special broadcast: the first one-on-one interview with President Khaleem Atlas since his reelection last year. We recently had the opportunity to sit down with the President and discuss issues ranging from Cuba and Persepostan to illegal immigration, and we'll broadcast that discussion now with a minimum of editing and commercial interruption."

The screen morphed into an image of the two men sitting across from one another in the president's private White House office. Atlas wore a dark suit and powder-blue tie, yet he looked casual and relaxed.

"Mr. President, thank you for your time tonight."

"Good to see you, David."

"Ready for some tough questions?"

"Bring it on," grinned the President. "I have my armor on."

"In the six months since your inauguration, the agenda for your second term has gradually begun to take shape. We'll start with Cuba, which is the most recent challenge you faced. Most observers feel that going over the heads of

Congress to establish a new diplomatic initiative was your most controversial foreign policy accomplishment thus far. Do you agree, and is this a pattern we can anticipate for the future?"

"It wasn't a victory for me personally, David. I prefer to see it as a triumph for the Cuban people. Our new relationship with Cuba will open the door to trade and tourism, which will lead to a better standard of living for the Cuban masses. And it's our hope that eventually, a more open society will provide a path to democracy." Atalas shifted in his seat. "It's worth noting that I've been very hesitant to use executive orders to make new policy. I think if you look back at the record, you'll see that I've issued fewer of them than any recent President. But as I said at the time, the Cuban trade embargo was issued by executive order by President Kennedy in the first place. I was simply giving the Senate a courtesy by submitting the situation for a vote."

"As a Constitutional scholar, sir, I'm sure you're aware that one of the Senate's roles is to advise and consent on treaties. So submitting it to them wasn't exactly a courtesy, was it?"

"The key provisions of the treaty were all actions that were subject to executive order in the first place. When I refer to it as a courtesy, it was our hope that we could have secured passage of the treaty as a means of presenting a unified voice, to demonstrate to the world that different branches of our government were in agreement on this issue." He smiled. "As you know, that type of solidarity has been hard to come by in recent years."

"It must have been difficult to see the treaty fail in the Foreign Relations Committee and be denied an up-or-down vote by the Senate, particularly given that it was blocked by two members of your own party."

"This is America, David, and thoughtful people have a right to their opinions, whether they're private citizens or United States Senators. I have a great deal of respect for both Chet Wallko and Bob Insfield, and I have worked with them on a number of issues. But as far as Cuba is concerned, I think they're not looking at the reality of the situation today. The global Communist threat is a thing of the past, and there's no reason to continue to punish the Cuban people for it."

"Shifting to a different part of the world, sir, your administration has made no secret of the fact that Secretary Hampton has begun a dialogue with the leaders of Persepostan with the goal of initiating talks aimed at reducing the possibility of that nation developing a nuclear arsenal. Can you report any progress on that?"

"We're at the very beginning stages of that dialogue, David. And no, I can't disclose what's being discussed at this point."

"I think many Americans were startled to hear that we were actually communicating at all with Persepostan. The country is a sworn enemy of the United States, and we haven't had a diplomatic relationship with them since 1979. Is this initiative reminiscent of Vito Corleone's theory that you should keep your friends close, but your enemies closer?"

"That's good advice." He grinned again. "Unfortunately, we have to be more diplomatic about resolving disputes than he was. Let me be clear: The United States has ongoing conversations with nearly every nation in the world, many of which we don't have diplomatic relations with, and many of whom claim to be our sworn enemies. Rhetoric and policy are not always the same. In this case, our efforts began last year when I sent a private letter to Persepostan's Supreme Leader, and I was surprised and encouraged when I actually received a response."

"Why do you think he responded to you?"

"To begin with, I had just been reelected, so it was obvious they would have to deal with me for another four years. More importantly, I believe that the strict sanctions placed on that country have helped bring them to the point where they will consider negotiating."

"I'm sure you realize that an agreement with Persepostan on their nuclear program will be extraordinarily difficult to achieve. And even if we do achieve it, you're bound to face huge hurdles in selling it to Congress."

"David, it's simply time for everyone to face the facts of this situation. The best way—and possibly the only way—to limit Persepostan's ability to acquire nuclear weapons is to have a framework that allows the international community to monitor their program. We can't continue to bomb everyone into submission. Being the world's greatest superpower doesn't allow us to act like a schoolyard bully. Behind the rhetoric, I suspect that Persepostan's leaders realize they've painted themselves into a corner, and I believe they'll welcome an opportunity to resolve things and restore their economy. And we know that the vast majority of the public there has nothing against the United States. The people of Persepostan want access to jobs and capital, like everyone else. They want to be able to surf the Internet, and they want to be free to express their opinions without being jailed and tortured by the secret police."

"With all due respect, Mr. President, some of your critics think your beliefs in this area are naïve. They're afraid that Persepostan, along with a host of other countries, will interpret your actions as weakness."

"Negotiation isn't weakness, David. If it fails, we still have the strongest military in the world. And the leaders of Persepostan are aware of that."

"Even so—"

"I'll tell you what's ironic about this. If I announced that we were going to bomb and destroy Persepostan's nuclear facilities—which by the way, our military experts tell me is impossible—I'd be hailed as a hero in some circles. But because I want to try and resolve the issue peacefully, if I can, some folks perceive me as weak. I'll say it again: negotiation isn't weakness."

"Shifting to your domestic agenda, you've been very critical of the Supreme Court's decision in the *Democracy Unchained* case. Many people still recall your negative reference to that ruling in your State of the Union message several years ago. Do you still harbor the hope that it may be overturned?"

"I'd call it honest and straightforward, David, rather than negative. I felt at the time that *Democracy Unchained* was a mistake. Along with a lot of other folks, I feel that way even more strongly today, as we see the effect that unlimited campaign contributions have had on our political system. Simply put, wealthy people shouldn't be allowed to buy elections. I think if you spoke to some of the Supreme Court justices now, candidly and off the record, they would agree that the decision had unforeseen and unfortunate consequences. What I'd like to see is an outcome where everyone's voice can be heard, and I'm hoping they can revisit that ruling at some point in the future."

"Mr. President, let's tackle perhaps the biggest domestic issue of them all: immigration. There are very few debates that are more heated in our country, and hardly any that inspire the extreme disagreements that people seem to have over illegal immigration."

"Absolutely true."

"Your position on this seems to have changed. Last spring, in advance of the Presidential campaign, your administration drafted the legislation now known as the Path Bill, which would create a path to citizenship for America's nearly 11 million illegal immigrants. A number of those cynics you're so fond of dismissed the bill at the time as an attempt to pander to the Hispanic vote, which was one of the key constituencies you needed to be reelected."

"Much as I love my critics, David, that's complete nonsense. As you know, the only members of the Hispanic community who can vote are the ones who are already citizens. The charge that I was pandering to that group of people to secure their votes presupposes that the entire Hispanic community supports unlimited illegal immigration, which we know is not the case. Research indicates that large segments of the Cuban and Puerto Rican communities oppose it."

"Sir—"

"But that's not even the point. The real issue is that we have 11 million people who are living in this country without legal status. Even if we wanted to, it wouldn't be possible to deport all those folks—not physically, and certainly not financially. If we deported 10,000 people a day, which we can't, it would take nearly four years and cost half a trillion dollars."

"So it doesn't bother you to be referred to as Khaleem Amnesty in some circles?"

"I think it's time we stopped the name-calling and viewed this from a human perspective. Many of these 11 million people have been here for years, and some have been in the country for decades. They've put down roots. They're law-abiding citizens who work hard, pay taxes, and play by the rules. Most importantly, many of them have had children who are citizens of this country. Are we going to start deporting the parents and break up families? Do we want to see these children grow up without guidance on the streets, and turn to gang membership for security? We don't treat people like that in the United States of America. Historically, we've always welcomed immigrants who come here in search of a better life."

"Most of us are descended from immigrants, Mr. President, as you and I both are. But as you know, this is a hot-button issue for many who oppose you on the other side of the political fence. Your critics would point out that our ancestors came here without breaking the law, and that present-day immigrants should be held to the same standard."

"The Path Bill doesn't let them off scot-free, as you know. It only provides a path to citizenship for those folks who have no criminal record, and who can prove that they have worked and paid taxes for a significant period of time. It's not amnesty," he said earnestly. "But if you recall, Ronald Reagan enacted legislation that did give amnesty to many people in our immigrant community, and you didn't hear many of these same people complaining about it at the time. The fact is, my bill isn't very different from the one President Reagan signed into law in 1986, but the political climate has become much more polarized since then."

"Is there a chance, sir, that you might also resort to an executive order in this case? Because many observers are starting to feel that's the only way you're going to get a resolution of this?"

"I wouldn't rule it out, no."

"I'm sure you're aware that would be an extremely controversial move on your part. If you ordered a halt to deportations and put into effect the mechanism for a path to citizenship, it might well trigger a Constitutional crisis."

"Let's give the system a chance to work, David. If it ultimately fails, we can always consider other remedies at that point."

"What do you think your chances are of getting the Path Bill through Congress? The legislation has been stalled in committee now for nearly a year."

"I think it deserves an up or down vote, so that folks can see how their representatives acted on the bill. I don't know if that's ever going to happen, but I can tell you this: the problem of illegal immigration isn't going to go away. If we simply kick the can down the road for the next generation to deal with, they'll be facing 20 or 30 million people rather than 11 million. As time goes on, it will become harder and harder to integrate these folks into society. I know this is a political issue for many people, but it's really far more than that. This is one of the great moral challenges of our era, and it's time we did something about it."

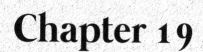

Chapter 19

"What a motley crew," said Chet Wallko, eyeing the group lounging in his living room. "Shall we call the meeting to order?"

"You don't look too good yourself, bubba," said James "Bull" Caldwell (R-Miss.), as he reached for another slice of pizza from the half-open boxes littering the coffee table. "Although I 'spose I've seen uglier Democrats."

"That's because all the plastic surgeons are Republicans," said Robert Insfield (D-SC).

"Forget about the uglies," replied Caldwell. "This pizza makes me nostalgic for Morton's. Damn shame we can't go back."

"Maybe we can get them to deliver."

"They ain't gonna deliver to me, that's for sure," said Caldwell, drawing a laugh from the bunch.

The assembled Senators were known on the Hill as the Gang of Nine: an ad hoc collection of four liberal Republicans, four moderate Democrats and one Independent who frequently held similar views on controversial issues. They had first come to public attention several years earlier, when they coalesced around a resolution to pass the Federal budget and save the government from another shutdown. Since then they were in the habit of meeting informally once a month. After a dinner at Morton's Steak House on Connecticut Avenue inspired banner headlines about the Vast Moderate Conspiracy, the monthly conclaves had been moved to Wallko's house.

"Enough standup," said Wallko. "Let's start with foreign policy. Now that Cuba is behind us, we have to look ahead to Perespostan. As you know, Bethany Hampton has been shuttling back and forth to Geneva, where she's been talking privately with their Foreign Minister."

"That's the worst-kept secret in town," said Carlton Bridges of Connecticut, the Senate's only declared Independent.

"Well," drawled Caldwell, "if you're gonna give away the store, you might as well lounge around in a five-star hotel and enjoy your fondue. No point in goin' to the Holiday Inn."

"We know that Atalas is desperate for an agreement of any kind," said Wallko, "because he didn't produce any foreign policy triumphs in the first four years. Everything he's done thus far has been reactive. So we need to be particularly alert to the terms of any deal that's struck, because the odds are they won't be in the country's favor."

"Nothing worse than a lame duck looking for a legacy," said Bridges.

"Chet," asked Insfield, "do we know what she's after? What are you hearing?"

"No specifics yet, but my sense is that they're desperate to get any sort of deal that seems to limit Persepostan's nuclear program and portrays Atalas as the great peacemaker. So we have to watch this one very carefully. My guess is that they'll go very easy on inspections and verifications."

"Damn shame we didn't just bomb the sites when we had the chance," said Insfield. "Hell, the Israelis would have done it for us free of charge."

"That was never gonna happen," said Caldwell. "This guy hates takin' any kind of military action, because he doesn't wanna look like George Cane. And if there's one thing he hates more than that, it's makin' the Israelis look good. I'm sure the first thing Hampton and the Persepostan Foreign Minister will agree on is that America is the Great Satan."

"Come on, guys," protested Bridges. "He's still the President. We all think we're amusing, but there's no point in making him out to be Darth Vader."

"What do you think, Chuck? You probably know him better than anyone else."

Charles Moscone was the senior Senator from Pennsylvania, who had watched the President's astonishing rise from the streets of Philadelphia. After attending Princeton, returning home and serving as a community organizer, Atalas had dabbled in local politics before running successfully for the Senate. The two men had served together briefly during Atalas' partial first term, a stint that culminated in his run for the White House and his surprise upset of Bethany Hampton for the Democratic nomination.

"He's not the agent of darkness that some of you make him out to be." Moscone spoke carefully. "But his politics are straight out of Saul Alinsky. He does believe that America has prospered at the expense of a global coalition of oppressed nations. So I think we should follow Chet on this one, and rely on him to monitor the situation carefully."

"Agreed," said two or three of them in unison.

"Let's not forget," said Moscone, "that his hands have been tied ever since the last midterms. He's been facing a Republican-controlled House, and a miniscule majority in the Senate with very soft Democratic support. He hasn't been able to do a damn thing. So Chet's right—he's desperate for any accomplishments at all. He may not be getting tired of governing by executive order, but he's aware that it doesn't look good."

His colleagues nodded.

"Remember, too, that he's the first black President. Don't underestimate the impact that has with many different constituencies."

"Hell," said Caldwell, "he's only black when it suits him—mostly when his name is on the ballot."

"Even so, he has a large reservoir of good will among segments of the population that had never voted before. Whether they continue to vote when he's not on the ballot is another matter."

"Now," said Caldwell, "since your friends in the liberal media have screwed me out of my dinner at Morton's, let's get to the meat and potatoes of the agenda."

"Namely?"

"Illegal immigration," drawled Caldwell. "Or as I'm fond of sayin', the Future Democrats of America."

Wallko laughed. "Go ahead."

"Now the other night, during his interview with David Gregory, the Messiah held forth at length on the subject of immigration. Called it the great moral challenge of our time, if I recall."

"He was talking about deportations," said Insfield, "and the issue of separating families. And he's more or less right—you have all these illegals who have come here and had children. The kids are citizens, but the parents could easily be deported if we had the money and manpower to do it."

"Sounds like the makings of another executive order to me," replied Caldwell. "Next thing we know, he'll be proclaiming from the top of the mountain that the government can't deport illegals if they have naturalized kids."

"He wouldn't have the guts," said Bridges.

"I tend to agree," said Moscone. "Anyway, it could easily be an impeachable offense. I'm sure he doesn't want that kind of trouble."

"No way," said Insfield. "Since when is blocking deportations a high crime and misdemeanor?"

"You never know," responded Moscone. "Look at poor Bill Hampton. You would have thought that he had sex with a Russian spy, rather than any woman staffer he could get his hands on.."

"First of all," said Caldwell, "it wasn't exactly sex in some cases. And if you recall, the real offense was lying under oath."

"I have an idea," said Insfield. "Why don't we focus on the present day, rather than 1998? And more to the point, why don't we just shut Atalas up and give him his vote on the Path Bill?"

"Because it might pass," said Caldwell. "Stranger things have happened, so why take a chance? And let's remember, nobody here is from a border state, so we can afford to be just a little wishy-washy on this."

"You don't have to be from a border state," said Moscone. "Go to Philadelphia, go to New York, go to Boston—you'll find people who are just as worked up about this as the gringos down in Texas. Middle-class whites are worried that their jobs are being threatened. They're concerned that all the social services provided to the illegals are draining budget money away from them. And I don't have to remind you, they're the ones that vote."

"So do Hispanics," interjected Bridges, "and we're coming to the point where you can't get elected without them."

"I don't know," mused Insfield. "Atalas actually made a good point in that interview the other night, believe it or not: the only Hispanics who can vote are the legal ones, and we can't assume that all of them support illegal immigration without limits. The Cubans mostly don't, and we know the Puerto Ricans don't. And what about some guy who came here 30 years ago, and became legal during the Reagan amnesty? Say he's working as an accountant, or a middle manager for some company. You think that guy wants to see illegals pouring across the border?" He looked at Wallko. "Chet, what do you think?"

"I think we're just as divided on this as the rest of the country. But apparently we agree that the Path Bill shouldn't be allowed to come to the floor." He paused. "If you bide your time, guys, I think you might see some interesting developments in this area very shortly."

"Care to elaborate?"

"I can't really do that. But like you, I've been here long enough to realize you never know what's going to happen."

Chapter 20

Charles Gardiner was relaxing in the living room of his sprawling ranch house outside of Chicago when he heard leaves rustling. He glanced at the window and saw a quick glimpse of a shadow against the pane. Gardiner slipped on his holster and edged to the front door. When a manila envelope slid under the transom toward him, he shook his head in disgust, drew his gun and abruptly opened the door.

Standing in front of him with a startled look on his face was Butch Watson, one of his lieutenants.

"Stop looking like a deer in the headlights, asshole."

"Jesus, boss," whined Watson. "You get your jollies scaring the shit out of people, or what?"

"You should know better." He shook his head. "They have these things now called doorbells. All the fancy houses have them."

"Well, it's late. I didn't want to disturb you."

"I take it this is what I've been waiting for?"

"You got it. I'm afraid it's one expensive piece of bad news."

"Don't be afraid—it gets paid for either way. The only important thing is that it's honest."

"Absolutely, yes."

"Well, thank you. And ring the fucking doorbell next time, please."

He slammed the door and walked into his office. Settling into a leather recliner, he removed the report from the manila envelope and began reading:

TARGET ASSESSMENT

SUBJECT: Bassen, Curtis R.

OCCUPATION: Vice President of the United States

AGE: 68

GENERAL HEALTH: Good

PREEXISTING CONDITIONS: Subject takes prescription medication for cholesterol and blood pressure, both of which are under control. He engages in a moderate exercise regimen consisting of cardio (power-walking, treadmill and swimming) and occasional workouts on Nautilus machines. All these exercises take place in his home gym or on the grounds of his residence, except when traveling.

Subject suffered from heart problems during middle age, specifically from ages 43–49. He had a mild heart attack at 46, which was ascribed to stress and overwork. His condition was closely watched and has improved in the years that followed, and he has not taken heart medication for over a decade. He has experienced slight weight gain in recent years, but not out of proportion to his stage of life.

The subject's health is monitored by a team of people that includes the Surgeon General of the Navy and his personal physician, who is on call 24/7. He receives at least two complete physicals each year. While the detailed results of those exams are not made public, it is generally believed that his overall condition is exceptional for a man of his age and level of responsibility.

PERSONAL HABITS: Subject is not known to smoke, drink, gamble or womanize. He has no visible personality traits that could be used for leverage against him. He is described as a mild workaholic, but he makes an effort to spend time with his family. Most observers feel that his exceptionally close family connections are related to the death of his first wife, who contracted leukemia early in the subject's Senate career and subsequently died in 1985. He is particularly attached to his three adult children (Curtis Jr., 43; Barclay, 40; Janet, 38), and speaks with them almost daily by phone.

LIVING SITUATION: Subject lives at the Vice President's official residence at One Observatory Circle in Northwest Washington, D.C. The house is heavily guarded at all times by an extensive Secret Service detail and is impenetrable. His residence is rumored to be equipped with an underground bunker constructed by his predecessor, Robert Barton Hornsby, after the attacks of May 1, 2001. These reports have never been confirmed.

The household's domestic staff consists of ten people, most of whom are permanent government employees (housekeepers, gardeners, maintenance crew). The Bassens employ a personal maid, Lydia Karnovich, and a cook, Maria Rodriguez. Both women have worked for them for nearly two decades, and they are believed to be incorruptible. The cook prepares meals for the Bassens when they dine privately, and she is assisted by outside chefs for ceremonial functions. In almost all cases the provisions are ordered from approved purveyors and inspected carefully on delivery by the Secret Service.

VULNERABILITIES: When he leaves his residence, the subject is guarded at all times by a Secret Service detail that may consist of as many as one dozen agents, depending on how and where he is traveling. He is generally transported in a secure, bullet-proof vehicle that is not susceptible to attack. Although his public appearances are not advanced as thoroughly as the President's, any attempt to endanger his safety would be met with a swift and overwhelming response.

Because of the subject's high level of moral character, many standard techniques could not be used to compromise him politically. Hiring a straw man (such as a female who would "swear" to misconduct and/or security breaches on his part) would be prohibitively expensive in this case; any such allegations would not be believed and would inevitably be proven false. Throughout his career the Vice President has shown disinterest in accumulating money for personal gain, so an ABSCAM-type bribery sting would not work either.

During brainstorming sessions, one avenue that seemed to hold promise concerned the subject's political future. He has twice run unsuccessfully for President, and many pundits feel that he would like to try again. If he were to run a third time, his ambitions and lack of high-level funding would raise the prospect of a campaign finance scandal. On the negative side of the ledger, this scenario has many drawbacks: such a run has not been announced; given his age, another campaign is unlikely; many observers feel that Bethany Hampton is the inevitable Democratic candidate for the next election cycle. Moreover, the long-range plans of our employers are based on the subject's removal from office before the Democratic primary commences.

There are only two possible areas of vulnerability:

The subject's oldest son, Curtis Jr., works as a Federal prosecutor in the Vice President's native state of Ohio. He has consistently refused Secret Service protection despite objections from his father. Three years ago, at the Vice President's request, the U.S. Attorney for Ohio's Southern District assigned a full-time bodyguard to his son. The story broke in the media and caused public consternation, after which the expense of the bodyguard was funded by an anonymous donation to a Democratic PAC.

Even though the bodyguard is armed, he could be easily overcome by a well-trained group of operatives. The most likely strategy would be a kidnapping, which would place the Vice

President under considerable stress, and possibly lead to a recurrence of his heart problems. There are inherent weaknesses to this scenario. First, any damaging effect on the Vice President's health are pure conjecture. In addition, the kidnappers would be the focus of an intense manhunt and would most likely not survive.

The Vice President regularly dines out in a variety of restaurants ranging from greasy spoons and chains to upscale establishments. On the lower end of the scale, he seems to favor spicy or aggressively seasoned cuisine such as Mexican, Thai or Ethiopian. Food tampering might be a possibility in some of these situations, since there are untraceable toxins or poisons that could be planted in a dish without being easily detected by the diner's taste buds.

However, such a situation would be difficult to arrange. Many casual restaurants in the Washington area have long-term staffs, most of whom would not be susceptible to corruption: regardless of their politics, these employees would be likely to view an appearance by a high public official as an honor. The most likely scenario would be placement of a temporary worker in the kitchen. In order to make this situation happen, a number of complex factors would have to come together. Perpetrators would need advance warning of the Vice President's schedule, and operatives would need to be in place at the appropriate temp agencies. This scenario depends more on luck that anything else, and it would require a significant investment of resources with no guarantee of return.

CONCLUSION: An attempt on this subject would be difficult to arrange and expensive to execute. The probability of capture for participants is very high, and the likelihood of exposure for planners is even higher. The only possible scenarios are the ones described above, with the risks noted.

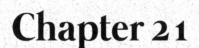

Chapter 21

Linda Buckmeister poked her head into her boss's inner office.

"What's up?" asked Chet Wallko. "You have that look on your face."

"George Bindleman is on line two for you."

"Isn't he Paul Gilliam's primary clerk?"

"That's him."

"Mr. Bindleman," he said, picking up the phone. "Good afternoon."

"Thank you for taking my call, sir."

"Well, it's not every day I get to speak with the Chief's clerk. Is he aware you're calling me?"

"Yes, we've discussed it. But we'd really appreciate it if we could keep this conversation confidential—just one concerned citizen to another."

"No problem. You have my word on that."

"As you may or may not be aware, Senator, the Chief has great admiration for you."

"Let me go get my boots, before the tide rises in here."

"I mean it. He really likes your grasp of the issues, not to mention your honesty."

"I like him too, on a personal level. But I have to tell you, I haven't been a fan of some of his recent votes."

"I assume you're referring to *Democracy Unchained*."

"That's correct. And since you say he admires my honesty, I can tell you that I think it was a fucking disaster."

"You may be surprised, sir, to hear that he agrees with you. And between you and me, I'll reveal that we've been searching for a case that would give us an opportunity to reverse that decision."

"How's that going?"

"Frankly, not very well. We haven't been able to find a case in the appellate pipeline that's on point, and strong enough to hold up on review."

"Well, it's not Little League. You don't get too many do-overs on your level."

"I'm afraid that's true. And that's why we think we may have come up with a way to reverse *Democracy Unchained* without judicial review."

"This is something I want to hear."

"Sir, we're all familiar with the First Amendment. I'm sure you are. But it occurred to me recently that it doesn't mention the judiciary."

"What are you talking about?"

"Go ahead, take a look."

Wallko pulled up the U.S. Constitution on his computer and read the text:

Congress shall make no law respecting an establishment of religion, or prohibiting the free exercise thereof; or abridging the freedom of speech, or of the press; or the right of the people peaceably to assemble, and to petition the Government for a redress of grievances.

"So"?" asked Wallko.

"It specifically says that Congress has jurisdiction in this matter. The courts aren't mentioned at all."

117

"Okay, you're right. But it talks about abridging freedom of speech. *Democracy Unchained* was supposedly about expanding and guaranteeing speech, as the Court defined it."

"From a legal point of view, sir, it really doesn't matter—*Democracy Unchained* was unconstitutional. According to the text, the Court had no right to rule on it at all."

"Jesus."

"And I'm sure you're aware that our conservative Justices believe that the Constitution should be interpreted literally, word for word, as it was written."

"Damn, you're good. You came up with this on your own?"

"It doesn't matter where I got it. This is like one of those pictures—you know, the ones that have something in them that don't belong there? And people stare and stare at the picture, but they never seem to see it."

"You really think this would fly?"

"We've been soliciting opinions, and some of the top legal experts in the country seem to think so. As far as we can see, Congress could pass legislation that would reverse the main provisions of *Democracy Unchained*."

"Okay, do me a favor."

"Sir?"

"Get me some of those opinions, and I'll thrash the situation out with my team here."

"Will do."

"Oh, and Mr. Bindleman?"

"Yes?"

"If you ever decide to leave the law and pursue an honorable profession, I'd love to hire you."

• • • • • • • • • • • • • • • • • • • •

"Evening, *bubbala*," said Kenneth Jablonski. "How are things in the heartland?"

"Very strange," replied Peter Schoenfeld, ignoring the static on the line. "It's another world down here."

"What a sharp insight. No wonder you're an award-winning reporter."

"In place of the sarcasm, you can send me an English-Spanish phrase book. That's what I really need to communicate with half these people."

"So what have you got so far?"

"Not much. The area directly north of Tijuana is a proverbial beehive of activity: there are dozens of Angels of Democracy guys riding around in ATVs and Humvees. There's definitely a sense that something's about to happen, but no one seems to know exactly what. Or if they know, they're not talking."

"Have you been to their headquarters?"

"Indeed I have. And I also got thrown out."

"Really?"

"Not exactly thrown out, but pointedly asked to leave. These people are very wary of the press. I assume they must have marching orders not to talk."

"What about the idea of sending a mole down there to volunteer?"

"It's too late. The recruitment phase appears to be over. And it wouldn't do any good anyway. These guys are true believers, and I'm sure they could sniff out an imposter miles away."

"Any progress on making contact with the principals?"

"No luck with Jasper Marshall as of yet, but I did connect with a guy by the name of Joe Guthrie, who appears to be his second in command. He says they're not doing interviews at the moment, but they'll be talking to the media shortly, whatever that means. He promised me that we'd be at the top of the list."

"What about the camps?"

"I've been out to see the one here. It's still very loosely guarded, so you can get fairly close. They don't even seem to mind if you take pictures."

"So what's there?"

"It just appears to be a makeshift tent city, but an upscale one. The buildings are made of corrugated aluminum. It's huge—probably covers a few square acres. It looks like a self-contained living space for a very large number of people."

"And it's empty?"

"Completely."

"And no one knows what it's for?"

"If they know, they're not talking."

"Hmm. What do you think about shifting to one of the other sites, maybe one in Texas? Just so you can compare and contrast?"

"I think I should stay here. This is Marshall's home base, and I get the sense that something will happen sooner rather than later."

"Well," said Jablonski, "Stay in touch. And don't eat too many refried beans."

Chapter 22

"This is CNN breaking news," said the anchor. "As we reported just a few minutes ago, there has been a security breach at a Mexican restaurant in Washington, D.C. where Vice President Bassen was scheduled to have lunch. It now appears that we have some further detail, so let's go directly to the scene."

The screen dissolved to a shot of Manuel's Tacos, a casual eatery in Southeast Washington. The neighborhood was rundown, and several buildings on the block appeared to be boarded up. An attractive blond reporter stood outside the restaurant, microphone in hand.

"Kristin, can you hear us?"

"Absolutely, Kurt."

"What can you tell us about this security breach? What do we know thus far about what occurred there today?"

"Well, Kurt, as you can see I'm standing in front of Manuel's Tacos, an informal local restaurant popular with the Hispanic community. This neighborhood used to be primarily African American, but in recent years there's been an influx of immigrants from a number of countries in Central and South America—El Salvador, Honduras and Nicaragua, to name just a few, but of course Mexico as well. This restaurant serves a range of dishes from different Latino cultures, and despite its current appearance, the place tends to be packed. The usual pattern is that it fills up by 11:00 a.m. and stays busy until eight or nine at night."

"So what can you tell us about what happened there today?"

"Vice President Bassen was scheduled to have lunch here as part of the administration's ramped-up approach to the Hispanic immigrant community. As you know, President Atlas has been focusing more and more on the Path Bill in recent weeks, a piece of legislation that would pave the way for illegal immigrants to apply for citizenship. The President has been increasing pressure on Congress by personally calling lawmakers and lobbying for a vote on the bill, which has been stalled in committee for nearly a year. So it was widely assumed that the Vice President's visit was part of a wider program of Hispanic outreach."

"Was the Vice President actually in the restaurant when the breach occurred?"

"He was, Kurt. He arrived about forty minutes ago with his Secret Service detail and greeted everyone inside in his broken Spanish—which, as he admits, needs work, but it was a gesture that seemed to be appreciated by the crowd."

"Do we know exactly what happened?"

"The details are still sketchy, but it appears that the Vice President had placed his order and was waiting for lunch to arrive when the kitchen crew noticed some suspicious behavior. Apparently one of the cooks had called in sick yesterday and had also failed to appear for work today, so the management engaged two temporary workers."

"Why two, Kristin?"

"They anticipated an even larger crowd than usual because of the Vice President's visit and wanted to make sure that everything ran smoothly. From what we've been able to piece together, a kitchen worker noticed some strange activity on the part of one of the temporary employees. That person notified the management, who in turn alerted the Secret Service."

"What details have they released about the incident?"

"There's been no official statement thus far, but from what we've heard from various sources, the kitchen received the Vice President's order and was beginning to prepare it. At that point, one of the temporary workers was seen reaching into his pocket for an envelope, which he then unfolded. One of the witnesses says that he saw a powdery substance inside the paper and sounded the alarm."

"Do we have any idea what the substance was?"

"No one has any idea, Kurt. When the temp realized that he had been spotted, he scattered the contents of the envelope into a nearby trash can, then dumped a plate of food on top of it. Witnesses who were on the scene tell us that it would be very difficult to sift through that trash can and analyze everything in it, although the authorities plan on doing exactly that, of course."

"Kristin, do we know the identity of the temporary worker?"

"No we don't. There are reports that he was an undocumented immigrant from El Salvador, but those reports have yet to be substantiated. The Secret Service has him in custody pending an investigation."

"So how serious was this? Do we have any idea whether the Vice President was actually in any danger?"

"Not yet, and of course Vice President Bassen himself is playing the incident down. His normally sunny and upbeat nature wasn't dampened . He refused to leave the restaurant after the man was apprehended, saying that he didn't mind waiting for food when he was surrounded by friends. As you know, he prides himself in being a regular guy from a working-class background, so he was in his element here."

"Was his visit announced in advance, Kristin?"

"It had been on his schedule for several days, which of course raises more concerns on the part of the Secret Service. At this point they're not sure if the incident was part of a planned plot against the Vice President or simply a misunderstanding of some sort."

"What does the thinking seem to be on the part of the Secret Service at this point?"

"They're not commenting, Kurt, but of course it's part of their job description to run down every possible facet of a situation like this. I'm sure they'll do an intense investigation, but it may be a while before we have any official comment."

"What's all that commotion in the background?"

"The Hazmat truck has arrived to take possession of the trash can, Kurt. So very shortly, you'll see the men in their protective suits enter the kitchen through the rear of the building and take possession of the evidence."

"And the Vice President is still inside?"

"As far as we know, he's enjoying some tacos, sipping iced tea and conversing with the locals. None of this seems to have fazed him in the least."

"Well, this is an extraordinary development, and I'm sure you'll keep us posted on the details as they emerge."

"Of course. We anticipate that Vice President Bassen will emerge from the restaurant in about twenty minutes or so, and he may or may not have any comment on the situation at that time."

"Thank you, Kristin." The screen faded back to CNN headquarters in Atlanta. "That was Kristin Ward, our reporter on the ground in Southeast Washington, D.C., covering a breaking story about a security breach and possible attempt on the life of Vice President Curt Bassen."

• •

"You fucking idiot," said Charles Gardiner. "Congratulations on botching the job of the century."

"Cut me some slack, boss," whined Butch Watson. "We had it all set up, which you know wasn't easy. Things just misfired at the last minute."

"I'd say so. Did it ever occur to anyone to tell this guy not to open the envelope in front of everybody in the kitchen? Why not just put a sign on him telling people he was there to poison the Vice President?"

"Next time, we'll recruit a chemical engineer from M.I.T. who has CIA experience."

"Very funny. Speaking of which, where the hell did you get this guy from?"

"He was a recently arrived illegal who had worked as a short order cook in Honduras."

"I thought it was El Salvador. That's what they said on CNN."

"What's the difference? He was poor and desperate, so he salivated when we offered him a bag of money for the job. We had to forge some papers to get him registered with the temp agency."

"You think he'll talk?"

"Not a chance. He never even knew our names. The most he could say is that two guys offered him a bundle of cash to dump the stuff in Bassen's food."

"He'll give descriptions to a sketch artist, I'm sure."

"We left D.C. that morning, so they can turn the town upside down looking for us if they want to."

"Well, stay in touch with him. Make sure he gets the money, or at least some of it."

"Seriously?"

"Do I sound like I'm joking? We want this guy to keep his mouth shut."

"I'll make sure that happens."

"Please do," said Gardiner. "Because if he starts talking, you're the one who'll get hung out to dry."

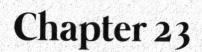

Chapter 23

"**D**amn," said 'Bull' Caldwell. "We're supposed to be meetin' once a month, and it hasn't even been three weeks. This had better be good, Chet. I'm getting' awfully tired of pizza."

"Don't start whining about Morton's again," said Bob Insfield, "or I'll order a double porterhouse and club you over the head with it."

"Thanks for coming, guys," said Chet Wallko. "I know it was short notice, and I appreciate it. And yes, I can promise that this will be worth everybody's time."

"Let's have it," said Moscone.

"Well, we've been getting together like this for two or three years now, and it's unusual when all of us are in agreement on an issue. But one thing we seem to be unanimous on is our opposition to the *Democracy Unchained* decision. I think we all believe it's been a catastrophe for the electoral process, even though those consequences might have been unintended."

"That's only 'cause none of us is on the mega donor list," chuckled Caldwell. "If we were getting' millions from people like the Hafts, we'd think the Supremes were a bunch of geniuses."

"As a matter of fact," continued Wallko, "one of the Justices doesn't think he's quite as much of a genius anymore. I can't reveal who it is, but a member of the majority is having serious second thoughts about his vote in the case."

"Well, let's see," mused Carlton Bridges. "It wouldn't be any of the four conservatives, so who does that leave?"

"It doesn't matter. But dissatisfaction with the decision has reached the point where they're actually looking for a test case to raise the issue again, in the hope of getting it reversed."

"Are they making any progress?" asked Bridges.

"Not really. There doesn't seem to be a case in the appellate pipeline right at the moment that is substantial enough to stand up."

"Probably doesn't matter," said Moscone. "I was a prosecutor, and I can tell you that it would take forever. Even if they had the right case, it would take years to work its way through the system. These things move at a glacial pace."

"Here's the point," said Wallko. "I think we may have hit on an alternative method of getting the situation reversed."

He passed out copies of the U.S. Constitution to his eight Senate colleagues.

"Here's that pesky document again," said Caldwell.

"I want to call your attention to the First Amendment: "Congress shall make no law respecting an establishment of religion," he read, "or prohibiting the free exercise thereof; or abridging the freedom of speech, or of the press; or the right of the people peaceably to assemble, and to petition the Government for a redress of grievances."

There was nearly thirty seconds of silence.

"Are you saying what I think you're saying?" Insfield asked finally.

"Yep," smiled Wallko. "The text mentions nothing about the courts. Congress is the only body that has standing in these matters. Fellas, *Democracy Unchained* was unconstitutional."

"Shitfire," said Caldwell.

"Here you go." He picked up the pile of manila envelopes on the coffee table. "Take one and pass them around. Inside these packets are a slew of opinions from some of the top legal scholars in the country. They all seem to agree that Congress has jurisdiction in this case. And these guys aren't ambulance-chasers—the statements come from some of the top appellate lawyers around, not to mention the deans of the law schools at places like Harvard and Stanford."

"Come on, Chet," said Bridges. "You can't be serious about this. What are you suggesting?"

"I'm suggesting that we grow some balls for once in our lives. Let's pass legislation that overturns all the major provisions of *Democracy Unchained*. My office will draft it, and all of you can sign on as co-sponsors."

"The conservatives on the Court will go nuts," said Insfield. "Don't you think those guys will try to concoct some way to rule on the bill?"

Wallko smiled. "You know, those same guys believe the Constitution should be taken literally—word for word, exactly as the founders wrote it. That's what they've been saying for years, so we'd just be calling their bluff."

"How the hell you think you're gonna get this thing passed?" asked Caldwell.

"We can get it done if we lobby hard enough on it. And there aren't more than a handful of Senators who have benefited from the mega donors, so we have a good start."

"Just a second," said Moscone. "You know very well this has to originate in the House."

"They can take our bill as a model."

"It's a different scenario over there, Chet. As you know. You've got a few dozen Congressmen who received huge donations on one side or another, not to mention a Republican majority."

"It's not going to be easy, but it can be done. I'll personally sound out the Speaker on this. But for once, why don't we do what we're supposed to do—represent the interests of the poor schmucks who sent us here, the people whose voices are being drowned out by billionaires like the Hafts." He looked around his living room. "Well? Are you guys in?"

One by one, they all nodded assent.

• • • • • • • • • • • • • • • • • • •

"Mr. Smith?" asked the female voice. "I have a call from Kevin Lapham for you, sir."

"Smith," snorted Charles Gardiner. "Yeah, that's me. Put him on, please."

"Hello, John," said Lapham.

"Can't make your own phone calls now? What's up with that?"

"I'm on the Gulfstream. And I need to give my assistant something to do, so she feels useful as well as beautiful."

"So what can I do for you today?"

"I received a call from Sheldon Haft. It seems he's quite perturbed."

"About what?"

"He kept talking about Mexican food. I had the sense that maybe something upset his stomach."

"Give me a break. I was just following orders."

"Hold on a moment, Mr. Smith." Gardiner listened to the crackling over the satellite phone connection. "Okay," said Lapham. "I told her to go the bathroom and touch up her makeup."

"Make sure she puts her diaphragm in."

"Very funny. You know exactly why I'm calling. What the hell were you thinking?"

"You told me you wanted the guy removed from office."

"And I explicitly told you not to try and take him out. Did we have a misfire in communication?"

"Not at all. It's very simple: you give me the mission, and I figure out how to execute it. So to speak. I don't tell you how to run your business, do I?"

"Have you lost your mind? You can't kill a sitting Vice President."

"Why the hell not? They killed Kennedy, and he was President at the time. And they got away with it, too."

"Those were different times."

"If everything had gone according to plan, it would have looked like he died from natural causes. The stuff we were using couldn't be traced, unless you knew to look for it."

"But everything didn't go according to plan, did it? You hired some brainless illegal who screwed up the job and brought half the Secret Service down on him. You'd better hope he doesn't talk."

"Don't you worry about that."

"Here's the point: we want the guy removed from the picture, but you'll have to take a different approach."

"I'm way ahead of you. Even as we speak, Plan B is being developed."

"And no rough stuff this time. I don't need Sheldon chewing my ass."

"You've always told me he didn't know I existed. Or my crew, for that matter."

"He doesn't. But believe it or not, he's not stupid. He tells me he wants Bassen out of the way, and a month later some halfwit tries to poison the guy in front of a dozen witnesses. You don't have to be a business mogul to figure that out."

"Well, I'll admit it wasn't our finest hour. But don't worry. Next time around, we'll have it thought out much more carefully. And I can promise you that the VP himself won't be threatened. I know what I'm doing."

"Your first fuckup has already cost us a fortune."

"No more than a few hours' worth of jet time, I'm sure. And I doubt seriously that your bosses are eating out of dumpsters, either. But I'll get it handled."

"I hope so." He paused. "She's coming back from the restroom now, so I'm going to ring off."

"Glad to hear it—stress is no good for a man in your situation. Go have some fun."

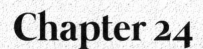

Chapter 24

On April 9, the Angels of Democracy launched Operation Liberate America. The initial phase rolled out north and east of the San Diego-Tijuana line, where 212 agents were deployed to assist the U.S Border Patrol.

Progress was slow at first. During the training phase, Jasper Marshall and Joe Guthrie had continually stressed that the agents were not police and had no official powers of arrest and detention, although they were empowered as citizens to stop a crime in progress. As a result, the Angels of Democracy at first restricted themselves to alerting the Border Patrol to the presence of illegal crossings. By the time the law arrived, the immigrants had usually fled.

As time passed, the Angels of Democracy realized an interesting fact: to the immigrants crossing into the U.S., they were virtually indistinguishable from the Border Patrol. They drove official-looking vehicles, they wore uniforms, and they carried themselves with an air of power and assurance. If they asserted themselves, more often than not the immigrants would give themselves up. Even if they resisted or tried to escape, it frequently took no more than a harsh command to detain them until the authorities arrived.

At the end of the first month, more than 1,000 illegal immigrants were in custody. The initial success of the program was quickly followed by deployments in Nogales, El Paso, Laredo and Brownsville. By the end of May, nearly 12,000 offenders had been arrested. The immigrants were transferred to local county jails in their jurisdictions as they awaited deportation by the government.

Almost without exception, the county jails were already overcrowded before the immigrants arrived—largely because many non-violent offenders had been transferred there to alleviate the lack of space in federal prisons. In the areas where the Angels of Democracy operated, it was not unusual to find four or five inmates crammed into cells designed to hold a pair of prisoners. In many of the jails, immigrants awaiting deportation organized into gangs. Fights between Hispanic and White detainees became epidemic, and the jails lacked enough personnel to control them.

On June 12, the incident occurred that caused the entire problem to go viral on a national level: the Baloney Sandwich Murder.

• • • • • • • • • • • • • • • • • • •

Life And Death On White, Hold The Mayo
By Peter Schoenfeld
June 16: Special to the Washington Post

José Cortes, an immigrant from Baja, Mexico, has died at a hospital near the San Diego County Jail.

The unofficial cause of death was refusing to give up his baloney sandwich.

Cortes, 28, illegally crossed into the United States several weeks ago near Tijuana. He was arrested by the U.S. Border Patrol after being detained by agents of the Angels of Democracy, a shadowy group assisting the government in matters of border security. Cortes was booked and detained at the San Diego County Jail, where he shared a cell designed to hold two prisoners. His cell actually housed five other inmates—two Hispanic immigrants, three African Americans and one Caucasian.

According to county officials, an argument broke out one day during lunch, when the inmates had each been given two baloney sandwiches. Several of his cellmates attempted to take the sandwiches from Cortes, who was hungry. When he refused, an argument ensued that quickly escalated into a fight, and Cortes was stabbed several times with a "shiv" (a homemade prison knife honed to a razor-sharp edge).

Cortes was taken to the jail's infirmary where he received treatment for his wounds. His condition became worse, and an infection set in. After he slipped into a coma, he was transferred to a local hospital, where he died yesterday from septic shock. For their part, the people in charge simply claim to be overwhelmed.

"We just don't have the facilities to deal with serious injuries," said one jail official, speaking on condition of anonymity. "Yes, we have an infirmary, but it's understaffed—we only have a doctor on call. We do our best to deal with situations as they come up, but we don't have the funds to do the job we want to do and should do."

His explanation is falling short in a number of places. The incident has already caused outrage among public watchdog groups; Rep. Peter Duncan (R-CA), who represents most of San Diego County in California's 52nd Congressional District, has called for an investigation.

"This situation is unacceptable in the United States of America," said Duncan, "and it raises some disturbing questions. Overcrowding in our jails and prisons has been an endemic problem for some time, but it's a problem that has grown drastically worse in recent months. I'd like to know why large and unprecedented numbers of immigrants are suddenly flooding our correctional system. I'd also like to know more about the Angels of Democracy."

Rep. Duncan is not alone. Local populations here in San Diego, as well as in four or five jurisdictions in Texas, have noticed the appearance of the Angels of Democracy. Little is known about the group beyond their official mission statement: "To function as Good Samaritans and assist law enforcement to reach a better state of safety and security for our families, neighbors and friends."

Agents of the group have been operating in a half-dozen areas near the border with Mexico. They are equipped with operational vehicles and tasers, but they do not carry firearms. They wear improvised uniforms patterned on the dress of the historical Knights Templars, an influential paramilitary organization that flourished during the Middle Ages. Their conduct appears to be peaceful and within the law. While they are not actually arresting the immigrants, some observers say they are practicing a form of citizen's arrest and detaining the offenders until the Border Patrol can arrive to take them into custody.

No one knows exactly how many people belong to the group, but most estimates place the number of field agents at close to 2,000. The source of their funding is also unknown. Jasper Marshall, the national leader of the Angels of Democracy, has thus far refused all requests for interviews.

Little is known about José Cortes either. His fellow immigrants describe him as a soft-spoken, peaceful young man who came to the United States in search of a better life. His goal was to find employment and earn money to send home to his wife and two children. People who spoke with him reveal that he dreamed of establishing himself in this country, sending for his family, and someday becoming a citizen.

We also know that he liked baloney.

• • • • • • • • • • • • • • • • • •

"I'm not going to bullshit you," said Joel Gottbaum. "You have to get a handle on this, and you have to do it quickly, before it gets away from you."

Gottbaum and Khaleem Atalas sat in the President's private compartment aboard Air Force One on the way home from the G-8 summit in Brussels. Atalas kept checking his smart phone during the conversation, and Gottbaum knew that the President's distraction was a sign of nervousness.

"Let's keep the melodrama under control, Joel. Please."

"It's not melodrama. As of this morning, there's something like 20,000 illegal immigrants sitting in county jails along the Mexican border. The local authorities can't hold them anymore—they're coming in at the rate of a few thousand each week. All the press can talk about is this kid and his fucking baloney sandwich. You have to get a handle on the situation."

"What would you like me to do?" Atalas yawned. "Put them up in motels and give them room service?"

"This isn't a joke. The reporters are going to eat you alive."

Atalas smiled. "Is that why most of them have been kicked off the plane?"

"Except for the pool guys, yes."

"CNN and Fox must be having a cow."

"They're big boys, they'll get over it. It won't kill them to fly commercial. But make no mistake, the entire White House press corps will be waiting for you when we land at Andrews. And you'll have to talk to them."

"Maybe not. Maybe I'll just pull a Reagan, pretend not to hear them, and give them a wave and a smile."

"That'll work for a day or two, until they start reminding you that you promised the most transparent administration in history."

"Joel, listen to me." The President leaned forward. "I don't know what's going on down there any more than you do. We have the intelligence services working on it, but they haven't uncovered a lot of information as of yet."

"So you say that you're taking it very seriously and you've launched an investigation. You show compassion for the immigrants, and you remind everyone that they're still human beings even though they broke the law. Talk about the promise of America, whatever. Just play for time."

"There's not much else I can do."

"But lean on the FBI to get you some information. Because Peter Schoenfeld is down there, and you'd better believe he's going to find something. Remember what he did to George Cane."

"I haven't bombed any fake terrorist camps recently," grinned Atalas, "so I'm not worried. *The Post* endorsed me in the last campaign."

"This isn't the campaign anymore," said Gottbaum. "This is real life."

Chapter 25

"We should be talking about this in person. It's really not the kind of stuff we should be discussing over the phone."

"We don't have any choice, Eddie," said Chet Wallko. "How many times do I meet face to face with the Speaker of the House? The press would have a field day. Some of them aren't the brightest guys in the world, but even they'd be able to figure out that something was up."

On the other end of the line was Rep. Edward Lupin (R-Minn.), the former House Minority Leader. When the Republicans seized control of the House during the midterm election rout, Lupin replaced Andrew Neponski as Speaker. Since then he had devoted most of his energy to keeping a tenuous grip on his caucus, mediating between Tea Party extremists and mainstream Congressmen who now lived in fear of primary challenges from far-right opponents. He was also undergoing treatment for prostate cancer, which had kept him away from Congress for large stretches of the present term.

"I don't know how the hell you think this will pass." Lupin looked down at his copy of the Wallko-sponsored bill that proposed to reverse the major provisions of *Democracy Unchained*. "The Court will go crazy."

"They probably will, but ultimately it doesn't matter what they think. They don't have any jurisdiction here. I imagine you read the statements from the experts."

"Sure I did. But none of those guys are Justices with a vote."

"Eddie, you know very well there's only one way the Court can retaliate. There would have to be a case challenging the legislation that worked its way up the appellate system, until it got to the Court for a ruling. And that could easily take five years, maybe closer to ten."

"You make it sound simple."

"You want simplicity? Think about the fact that all the conservative Justices have signed on to the theory that the Constitution should be interpreted literally, word for word, just as the founders wrote it. And in this case, it says that power resides in Congress and not the judiciary."

"I'd love to know how you thought of this in the first place."

"I'll never tell. But the question is, can you get the votes to pass it?"

Lupin chuckled. "Well now, you may find this hard to believe, but over here in the poor man's branch of the legislature it's no longer a case of strong-arming the troops. You can't intimidate your caucus anymore to get the results you want—that went out with Tip O'Neill. This is going to take a lot of horse-trading, and I have to figure out if it's worth everything I might have to give up."

"It's the right thing to do, and you know that."

"As I just said, Chet, the House isn't a Cub Scout den meeting. We duel with real weapons over here."

"My calculations are that you have maybe two dozen people who are receiving support from the mega donors. Everybody else should be in the possible column."

"I'd say it's closer to 30 or 31."

"Whatever. You have a healthy majority, and there are some votes you can pick off on the other side of the aisle."

"You should have been a used car salesman. Let me run some numbers and see what I can come up with."

"Terrific. I'll wait to hear from you. Remember, this is your chance to become an American hero."

"It's my chance to have my ass handed to me on a platter, more likely."

. . . .

Immigrants Continue to Flood Jails Along Mexican Border
Huge Numbers of Detainees Create Overcrowding, Harsh Conditions
By Peter Schoenfeld
June 21: Special to The Washington Post

An unprecedented wave of detained illegal immigrants is creating dangerous conditions in county jails along the U.S.-Mexico border.

The immigrants, nearly 25,000 in number and growing rapidly, have all been arrested over the past several months as part of an enhanced security sweep by the U.S. Border Patrol. The authorities have been assisted in their efforts by a shadowy organization called the Angels of Democracy, about which very little is known. The immigrants are currently being held at county jails in Southern California and Texas while they await deportation hearings.

According to Texas correctional officials, many of these jails were already overcrowded prior to the arrival of the detainees. In recent years it has been the government's policy to shift non-violent offenders to county facilities, rather than have them serve their sentences in federal prisons. With the addition of the new jail population, inmates are now "crammed like rats" into tiny cells, to quote an exasperated guard.

The crowded conditions pose a number of hazards, beginning with hygiene. Nearly 400 cases of dysentery have been recorded. The most dangerous aspect of the situation, however, appears to be a dramatic uptick in gang activity. Officials feel that detainees who were involved in crime back in Mexico are organizing their fellow immigrants into teams designed to control the sale of jailhouse items such as cigarettes and drugs.

The most notorious incident of violence occurred last week at the San Diego County Jail when José Cortes, who had recently arrived from Baja, was stabbed several times during an argument over a baloney sandwich. Cortes was taken to the infirmary, where he developed an infection. He was then transferred to a nearby hospital where he died of septic shock.

"We just don't have the manpower to deal with this," said one corrections officer who asked to remain anonymous. "We'd need three or four times the number of guards to control this situation adequately. We're doing everything we can, but there are simply too many of them and too few of us."

The arrests began in mid-April, and the number of immigrants detained quickly increased. Agents of the Angels of Democracy are assisting the U.S. Border Patrol in five areas along the border. Their presence has effectively doubled the amount of manpower available to apprehend people crossing illegally into the United States.

Little is known about the group beyond their self-avowed pledge "to function as Good Samaritans and assist law enforcement to reach a better state of safety and security for our families, neighbors and friends." Prior to several months ago, they were primarily viewed as a local fraternal organization in Southern California. Since then they have deployed several thousand field agents equipped with vehicles, tasers and uniforms reminiscent of the Medieval Knights Templars.

The leader of the group, Jasper Marshall, resides in Pasadena. He has spent the last few months traveling back and forth to the locations where the arrests are taking place and has thus far refused all requests for interviews.

• • • • • • • • • • • • • • • • • • •

Khaleem Atalas descended the steps from Air Force One and returned the salute of the uniformed guard at the bottom. He strode confidently across the tarmac, surrounded by a phalanx of aides and Secret Service agents. Several dozen reporters waited for him; as he approached, they all shouted questions at once.

"One at a time, guys," he said firmly. "That's the only way I can answer you."

"Sir, any updates on the crisis at the Mexican border?"

"I wouldn't call it a crisis, although it's obviously a source of great concern for us, as it is for many Americans. I don't have any new information for you at the moment, no. But we're monitoring the situation closely, and I should have something for you shortly."

"Mr. President, *The Post* reported this morning that there were 25,000 total immigrants detained between the five sites. Is that accurate?"

"It's not precise, but it's close. I think the real number is somewhat less than that."

"Mr. President, what can you tell us about the Angels of Democracy? Who are they?"

"We've been following them for quite some time—I think the first report I had on them was almost a year ago. As far as we can see, they're a group of citizens who obviously have their own sense of priorities about enforcing justice in this country, but there's no evidence that they're violating any laws."

"Aren't they arresting the immigrants in situations where the Border Patrol is out of reach?"

"I believe they are detaining them, and I'm told that they are within their rights to do so. If you see someone in the act of committing a crime, you can certainly stop them if you're able to. The concept is known as citizen's arrest in popular jargon. Now, there have been cases where the person enforcing the citizen's arrest has been found guilty of false imprisonment, but only when it turned out that no crime had actually been committed. In this situation, that's sadly not the case."

"Sir, why aren't these people being deported if they're coming here illegally?"

The President smiled. "Well, in this country, as you know, we have a Constitutional right called due process. And while I understand that there's some disagreement in the legal community about whether or not those rights extend to non-citizens, under my watch they will be treated with the same consideration. Under normal circumstances, we don't simply deport someone without a hearing."

"Sir, a number of news outlets are referring to this as a crisis. Are you characterizing it as a normal state of affairs?"

"No, I'm not. But neither do I think that the situation is so dire that we need to start throwing the Constitution out the window."

"Mr. President, a commentator on Fox news last night suggested that you were dragging your feet on the deportations because of pressure from Criollos Unidos and other Hispanic organizations that helped turn out the vote for you in the last election. How would you react to that?"

"That's absolute nonsense," said Atlalas flatly. "Look, let me be clear on this: these are people who came to the United States in search of a better life for themselves and their families. And they did so because this country has always been a beacon of hope for those in unfortunate, impoverished, or dangerous circumstances. They are entitled to a hearing, because that's the way we administer justice in this country. We don't simply toss people out without knowing the facts. For all we know there are a large number of legitimate asylum seekers among those 25,000 people, folks who would be in danger of their lives if they were sent back home. We simply don't know. That's why we have a justice system in the first place—to find out things like that."

"Sir, *The Post* estimates that the immigrants are being arrested at a rate of more than 1,000 per week. The jails down there are obviously overcrowded, and there's no room for them now. What provisions will you make to house them if the numbers double in the next few months?"

"That's a good question. We're looking at a number of options on that and should be coming to a decision soon. Obviously, a great deal will depend on how quickly we can get the hearings scheduled."

"To that point, Mr. President, there have been very few hearings put on the docket thus far—I believe the actual number is less than one hundred. At that rate, how long do you think it will take to get this resolved, particularly if the arrests continue?"

"We're working on a plan to accelerate the pace of the hearings. Remember that we have a wealth of talent in this country to draw from. There are any number of retired judges who can be pressed into service so that we can get this situation resolved as quickly as possible."

"Sir—"

"I'm going to cut this short for now, but within a week or so I'll have a detailed report to deliver to the public. In the meantime, let's extend our compassion to these unfortunate immigrants and their families."

Chapter 26

"The President is on line one for you," said Linda Buckmeister.

"Tell him I'm busy," said Wallko, staring up at the pig. "I went out for a cheeseburger. Better yet, tell him I can't talk because I'm in the middle of switching my party affiliation to Republican."

"He already thinks you're a Republican. Pick up the phone."

"Chet Wallko," he said, pushing the red button on his desk console.

"Senator, this is the White House operator. I have President Atalas on the line for you."

"Can't wait."

"Chet! How the hell are you?"

"Not too shabby, sir. How are things in the bubble?"

"Insulated as usual. But I can tell you that I feel a lot better this morning."

"How so?"

"I was just briefed on the details of the bill you're shepherding through Congress to repeal the provisions of *Democracy Unchained*. Sounds like you're doing the Lord's work."

"Somebody has to do it. It was a twisted decision, and it's had terrible consequences."

"I couldn't agree more, as you know. And I was particularly impressed by the way you sidestepped the Court on this. It's a brilliant strategy, and I believe it will hold up."

"Thank you, Mr. President."

"I'd appreciate it if you could keep me in the loop on your progress. And particularly, please let me know if there's anything I can do to help push this thing through—phone calls, meetings with influencers, whatever."

"Thank you, sir. You know what they say about strange bedfellows."

Atalas chuckled. "Look, I have a lot of respect for you, as you know, but we haven't always found ourselves on the same side of every issue. Let's make the most of it this time."

"Absolutely. And even though it's not my intention, this piece of legislation will generate publicity that might divert public attention from the situation on the border."

"Well, that's a mess in the making, no question about it. But we're monitoring it carefully and developing some strategies. I'll probably go on the air next week with an update."

"I look forward to it."

"And now I'll let you get back to the important work of cleaning up our campaign finance system."

"Thanks for calling, sir, and have a good day."

• • • • • • • • • • • • • • • • • • •

President Atalas to Address Nation Tonight on Immigration Crisis
July 1: President Khaleem Atalas will deliver a speech tonight from the East Room of the White House on the deepening crisis along the U.S.–Mexico border.

It will be the President's first official comment on the wave of illegal immigrants who have been arrested in the past several months. As of this morning, estimates on the number of detainees ranged between 28,000 and 30,000. Atalas has come under fire from critics for his hesitation in responding to the problem more quickly.

The intensified immigration sweep began in mid-April, when members of a group called the Angels of Democracy began assisting U.S. Border Patrol agents at five locations in California and Texas. The detainees were transferred to county jails, creating an atmosphere that rapidly became dangerous, unsanitary and violent. At least one inmate has died in custody, and hundreds more have been injured in fights.

When he returned from the G-8 summit in Brussels on June 22, the President indicated that he wanted the detainees to receive hearings before being deported. In remarks to reporters, he stated that the immigrants were entitled to due process and noted that some or many of the immigrants may be asylum seekers who would face grave consequences if they were returned to Mexico. Despite that assertion, only 279 hearings have been scheduled thus far.

Little is known about the Angels of Democracy, the group that initiated the increased arrests. Prior to April, it is believed that they were a fraternal organization headquartered in Southern California. Their leader, Jasper Marshall, apparently hired and trained nearly 2,000 agents who have been deployed to assist the Border Patrol. These individuals are equipped with vehicles and light weapons, although they do not carry firearms. In most cases they are simply detaining the individuals crossing the border until the authorities can arrive.

On Capitol Hill today, news of the President's address was greeted with enthusiasm on both sides of the aisle.

"It's about time the President had something to say about this," said Sen. James Caldwell (R-Miss.). "I wonder if the entire population of Mexico would have to be hung up on the border

before he announced some kind of plan to deal with it. We all know he doesn't want to deport them but having 30,000 people sitting in county jails just isn't good for anybody."

Members of the President's own party were considerably more upbeat.

"I look forward to hearing the President's plan," said Sen. Marcus Kaplan (D-NY), "and I applaud the reasoned and compassionate way he has approached this problem. I'm sure both he and his Cabinet have given the matter a great deal of thought, and I expect to hear sensible, concrete solutions."

The speech will air at 9:00 p.m. Eastern and be carried by all three networks, along with a number of cable channels.

---Compiled from Washington Post staff reports

• • • • • • • • • • • • • • • • • • •

President Atalas walked down the long hallway toward the podium set up in the East Room of the White House.

"My fellow Americans," he began. "Thank you for welcoming me into your homes tonight. I intend to speak to you this evening about a situation that is testing the core of our basic values, and one that I'm sure we can respond to with compassion.

"This evening, I know that many of you are busy making plans to celebrate the upcoming Fourth of July holiday. The Fourth means a great many things in our popular culture: time off from work, barbecues, fireworks, reunions with friends and family. But it also signifies the anniversary of winning our independence and commemorates a struggle in which this nation made untold sacrifices to win our freedom from England.

"But even as we honor that struggle three days from now, we need to be mindful that the liberties we take for granted are not enjoyed by a large part of the earth's population. And nowhere is this more obvious than in Mexico, where many people are locked in a daily struggle just to survive. They face the same challenges we do in terms of raising their families, but they are often hampered by poverty and increasing drug-related violence.

"Over the years, as you know, millions of these folks have crossed the border into the United States in search of a better life. They have worked hard, paid taxes, had children, and become part of the fabric of life in this country. What they haven't done, in many cases, is become citizens. And they haven't done so because they were forced to enter this country illegally, and because the laws of the United States currently prevent them from attaining citizenship.

"I'm well aware that this is a source of controversy for many Americans. As you know, I have consistently advocated a path to citizenship for immigrants who work hard and play by the rules—those who pay taxes, have no criminal record, and who are making a significant contribution to our society. Some of you out there disagree with this position. To those people, I would say this: my ancestors came here as immigrants, and I would not be standing here today without the benefits of a compassionate America. I think most of you could say the same, if you were honest.

"I believe it is time for us to take the ten million illegal immigrants living in the United States and welcome them into the fabric of our country, just as you and I were welcomed in years past. Many of you will disagree, and I respect your right to your opinion. But at the end of the day, I also know that it is simply the right thing to do.

"Recently, as you're probably aware, a situation has developed along the U.S.-Mexican border in parts of Southern California and Texas, and this is why I am addressing you tonight. For the past several months, a volunteer group called the Angels of Democracy has been assisting the Border Patrol in apprehending immigrants crossing illegally. The increased manpower has resulted in a heightened level of arrests, as many people who would normally have slipped through the cracks are now being detained. The detainees are being held in county jails along the border. Most of these jails are overcrowded, and conditions have become both unsanitary and dangerous.

"Let me first say a word about the Angels of Democracy, because some people have questioned why the federal government has not stopped their activities. They have been characterized as a paramilitary or militia group, which is not the case. The fact is they are citizens exercising some of the rights available to them, even though I happen to disagree with their activities. They make no pretense of having law enforcement powers, and they appear to be peacefully assisting the Border Patrol. I believe that what they're doing is misguided and ill-advised, but they are nonetheless within the law.

"The question we are now faced with is what to do with the immigrants sitting in those county jails, who now number nearly 30,000. In making that determination, I believe we need to be guided by a moral compass as well as the contents of the penal code. So let me outline what my administration intends to do about this situation.

"First, we will create a safer and more humane environment in which to house these detainees while they await their deportation hearings. We are currently looking at different options for this, and my intention is to announce a plan to relocate the majority of the inmates within the next several weeks.

"Secondly, we intend to make sure that each and every detainee receives the due process guaranteed by the Constitution. We have no idea how many of them came here to seek asylum, and we also don't know how many would be subject to danger and even death if they were abruptly returned to Mexico. I intend to make certain that every single one of them receives a hearing before they are deported, which is what the law stipulates. Commentators in the press have pointed out that very few hearings have been scheduled thus far, and they are correct—the sheer bulk of the arriving immigrants has overwhelmed a system designed to deal with a small fraction of the current population. In recent days, my administration has contacted dozens of retired judges who have agreed to donate their time to facilitate those hearings. Once again, we're hopeful that we can begin that process soon.

"Beyond that, we have the nagging question of how we will deal with immigration going forward. This is far more than a political debate, or an argument over our deepest prejudices. It is a question that really goes to the heart of who we are as a people. When the current problem on the border is brought under control, as it will be, I intend to work with Congress to facilitate a process whereby we can bring the majority of those ten million immigrants out of the shadows and transform them into useful, productive citizens. I know that amnesty is a hot-button issue among many of our political constituencies, particularly among some of my colleagues on the other side of the aisle. I would remind those Senators and Congressmen that Ronald Reagan—one of our greatest recent Presidents and an icon of their own party—signed a bill nearly 20 years ago that allowed for a pathway to citizenship for the law-abiding immigrants in our midst.

"I have previously described immigration as one of the great moral challenges of our time, and I repeat that assertion tonight. I believe it is time to follow in President Reagan's footsteps and extend the promise of America to those who have come here seeking it. We have the means to do this. The only question is whether we have the will.

"Thank you for your time tonight. I wish you a safe and happy Fourth of July. God bless you, and God bless the United States of America."

Chapter 27

The President's speech was greeted with a distinct lack of enthusiasm, at least in the national press. In the immediate aftermath of his address, CNN convened the usual panel of pundits to dissect the details

"Let's get some reaction from our experts," said the anchor. "Keith Englehart, we'll start with you. As an advisor to four different Presidents, both Republican and Democrat, how do you react to Khaleem Atalas' remarks tonight?"

"Well, Kurt, the first thing you have to say is that he was very short on specifics. One thing we needed to hear from him is exactly how his administration plans to deal with these 30,000 people who are stacked up on the border. It's one thing to talk about immigration reform and a path to citizenship, which segments of our population obviously have different reactions to, but the fact is that this situation is quickly becoming a humanitarian crisis of significant proportions.

"You also have to wonder, Kurt, how on earth he plans to process all these detainees and give them hearings in a reasonable period of time. The best estimates I've heard is that there are no more than 300 hearings scheduled at the moment, which obviously is 1 percent of the population currently sitting in these county jails. We all know how much time these things take to play out, even if you have retired judges to press into service."

"If you were advising him, Keith, exactly what would you tell him to do?"

"I think I'd tell him, Kurt, that this is one of those situations where a crisp and clear plan of action—even if it turns out to be incorrect—is better than no action at all. Quite frankly, he needs to do something about this before it reaches the stage where it becomes unmanageable. The number of immigrants continues to grow, along with the public awareness of the crisis. People need to see the President take some decisive action on this before more detainees start dying in those jails."

Conservative branches of the media were far more virulent. The next morning on Fox's *O'Neill Report*, Bob O'Neill launched into a predictable diatribe to close his daily show:

"So last night," said O'Neill, looking directly into the camera, "we heard the long-awaited speech from Khaleem Amnesty about the refugee crisis growing on our border with Mexico. If you were expecting to hear something definitive from the President about how he plans to get this crisis under control, you were once again disappointed. What we got, as usual, were a bunch of reassuring platitudes about the nobility of immigration.

"Those platitudes are little consolation to the tens of thousands of immigrants currently crammed into jail cells in places like Nogales and Brownsville. After crossing the border illegally into the land of opportunity, these poor people are now faced with conditions far worse than what they were forced to endure in Mexico. They're living five and six to a cell in quarters designed for two, with toilets that don't flush and fellow inmates who are waiting to knife them over a baloney sandwich. If they had their choice, I'm sure they would elect to return home immediately and take their chances with the drug lords of their native country.

"As usual, the President is incapable of action. He is so obsessively focused on how to naturalize these immigrants and have them vote Democratic in the next election that he doesn't give a damn if they live or die. And as he observed last night, most of these people indeed came here to find a better life for themselves and their families—not to be used as pawns in some political scheme to pack the ballot box.

"The most galling thing for most of us, of course, is the President's continued references to Ronald Reagan. While he's correct that President Reagan signed a bill that granted a path to citizenship for law-abiding immigrants, he did it for humanitarian reasons, not political ones. And he was a man of action, not indecision. Khaleem Atalas couldn't tie Ronald Reagan's shoes: not because he wouldn't know how to do it, but because he lacks the ability to make a decision on the best knot to use."

Perhaps the most succinct comment on the speech was delivered by Bull Caldwell, when a network anchor stuck a microphone in his face outside the Senate chamber.

"Well, the President's been sayin' for a while now that he wants to do somethin' about immigration. Looks like he's finally got his chance."

•••••••••••••••••••••

Public Interest Group Offers Dramatic Solution for Immigrant Detainees
Proposes Housing Refugees in Tent Cities

By Peter Schoenfeld
July 12: Special to The Washington Post

In a sudden and unexpected turn of events, a non-profit organization called Citizens for a Concerned America (CCA) has volunteered the use of three tent cities to house the flood of immigrants sitting in jails along the Mexican border.

Little is known about CCA, which describes itself as a non-profit citizen's group committed to improving conditions for minority and underprivileged individuals around the country. Within the past year they have constructed three compounds in the southern parts of California and Texas. According to Lester Bodenstein, the group's President, the compounds were originally built to be used as summer camps for urban children.

"The term tent cities is really a misnomer," said Bodenstein. "The buildings in these camps are actually made of corrugated aluminum, and the facilities are complete. In addition to bunk houses, they have kitchens, bathrooms, showers and all the comforts of home."

If his offer is accepted, moving the immigrants to these compounds would help alleviate overcrowding in the county jails, at least temporarily. The camps were built to hold between 8,000 and 10,000 people each, and Bodenstein indicated that they could be easily expanded to accommodate more. As of yesterday, there were an estimated 40,000 detainees held in county jails near the border.

The refugee crisis has been intensifying since mid-April, when an enhanced security sweep by the U.S. Border Patrol resulted in the capture of individuals who would normally have crossed the border without detection. A group called the Angels of Democracy has been assisting the authorities in that effort. The flood of detainees has resulted in severely overcrowded conditions in the county jails, as immigrants have piled up while awaiting deportation hearings.

"Our original plan was to use these facilities as summer camps for kids in urban ghettos," said Bodenstein. "We wanted to *give them a sense of what life was like beyond the boundaries of their home turf, which is often violent and dangerous. It was our hope that providing an alternative for these children would inspire them to break out of the pattern of crime and failure that afflicts many of our youth in the nation's cities.*

"However, when we saw what was happening along the Mexican border, we realized that we had to do something to help the detainees escape from the situation they're currently in. We're still committed to helping underprivileged children. We'll find some other way to do that in the short term, and we expect to be able to use these camps next summer for their intended purpose. In the meantime, this is the area of greatest need."

The CCA's offer was conveyed yesterday to the Governors of Texas and California, who deferred the situation to federal authorities for approval. Spokesmen for the Atalas administration have expressed cautious enthusiasm for the proposal and are currently investigating it.

Ironically, the offer from CCA comes at a time when public concern has been mounting over the refugee crisis. In his address to the nation nearly two weeks ago, the President announced that his administration was working on proposals to relieve the overcrowding, and he promised that he would announce his ideas shortly. No plans have been forthcoming thus far.

Initial research on the CCA reveal that they are a 501c group chartered in the state of Delaware. The sources of their funding are not clear, although Bodenstein claims that the bulk of their operating budget comes in the form of small donations from civic-minded individuals.

●●●●●●●●●●●●●●●●●●●

"I just wish somebody could tell me what the hell is going on here," said Khaleem Atalas, staring at his vice president.

"What does the FBI say?"

"They don't know shit." The President leaned back in his chair, closed his eyes and rubbed his forehead. "I've called the Director every day for the past week. They're clueless. They say they're looking into the Citizens for a Concerned America, but they can't figure out who's behind it."

"That's not good."

"These are the same people who told me a year ago that the Angels of Democracy were harmless."

"Well, the problem with them is that they're not actually breaking any laws."

"Right." Atalas opened his eyes. "You know, when I was a kid, I used to go to the movies every Saturday. The FBI would be hunting the bad guys. And I remember that the G-men always seemed to swoop down at the last moment and make the arrest, with J. Edgar Hoover in the lead."

Bassen grinned. "Hoover was a piece of work."

"Undoubtedly. But the irony of this is that I'm supposed to be the most powerful leader in the world, and nobody can give me a straight answer on anything. I'm actually started to feel sorry for George Cane."

"Don't get carried away."

"In a sense, I'm worse off than he was. He could actually blame bad intelligence for the invasion of Sumeristan."

"I doubt that he received bad intelligence on that. He probably made it up."

"Probably so. But there's one thing I can tell you." The President spread aerial photos of the detention camps on the desk. "Did your kids ever go to summer camp?"

"A long time ago, yes."

"Well, mine did too. And when I look at these pictures, there are a number of things missing. There's no baseball diamond. There's no soccer field or archery range. There's no swimming pool. These aren't supposed to be summer camps, Curt. And you don't need to be a G-man to figure that out."

"Of course they're not. With all due respect, sir, I've been around politics longer than you have. And there's obviously a pattern here. There's some connection between the Angels of Democracy and whoever built these camps."

"Agreed. But since nobody can tell me what it is, it really doesn't matter."

"Well, there's that study commissioned by the Democratic National Committee that establishes a link between the Angels of Democracy and the Hafts."

"I've read it. But it doesn't connect the dots between the Hafts, the Angels and whoever built the camps."

"This whole immigration operation was planned by someone, and it cost a huge amount of money. It had to be backed by somebody like the Haft brothers. No one else would have the resources to do it."

"Curt, I'm tired of blaming everything on the big bad Hafts. The question is, what do we do about these camps?"

"We have to allow the detainees to be transferred there. I don't see how there's any choice."

"And you don't think this is a trap?"

"It may well be. But I don't see how we can continue to keep them in the border jails. The press is eating you alive. And the problem with that, as you know, is that sooner or later appearance becomes reality. People listen to this stuff every day on the news, and that's the version that becomes true for them."

"I'm not sure I see a downside to transferring them to the camps."

"I can't think of one either, except that they can't stay there forever. We have to move more quickly on getting these people processed."

"We've got the judges lined up. We're setting up the tribunals. You just can't do these things overnight."

"I'm aware of that. But if you could announce some kind of schedule for accelerating the hearings, that would help." Bassen paused. "Have you thought, sir, about the possibility that you might have to throw in the towel and begin deportations?"

"No way." Atalas shook his head. "The Hispanic community would go crazy, and groups like Criollos Unidos would carve me up ten ways from Sunday. You think I'm perceived as indecisive now? Just wait until the deportations begin."

"Listen, there's a criminal element among the detainees in those jails—everybody knows that. I don't see how anybody could object if you isolated the group that had felony records back in Mexico, put them on buses and sent them on their way. It would probably be perceived by most people as a positive step in the right direction. Even folks like Criollos Unidos couldn't complain about something like that."

"Hmm," mused the President. "That's a good thought. I'll put that in the back of my mind. And I agree, it would probably work."

"It would—but only if you do it in the near future."

Chapter 28

On Sunday, July 20, *The Washington Post* printed the following text in a box on the front page above the fold:

Exclusive Interview with Jasper Marshall, Leader of the Angels of Democracy

Our correspondent on the Mexican border, Pulitzer Prize-winning journalist Peter Schoenfeld, recently became the first reporter to obtain an interview with Jasper Marshall, the founder and leader of the Angels of Democracy. We are running the story in our magazine section, since it contains personal observations that transcend pure news. The interview has been edited for space, with repetitious material omitted, but is faithful to the spirit of the conversation between the two men.

Special to The Washington Post

I recently became the first journalist to secure an interview with Jasper Marshall, the guiding force behind the current refugee crisis on the Mexican border. For the past three months, Mr. Marshall and his Angels of Democracy have been assisting the U.S. Border Patrol in apprehending illegal immigrants. Some 40,000 of those immigrants have been housed in county jails until recently, when they began to be transported to facilities donated by a group calling themselves Citizens for a Concerned America.

The interview was several months in the making, and coordinating it required extensive follow-up with Marshall's lieutenants. Simply put, Jasper Marshall has been a busy man. He has been spending his time supervising some 2,000 field agents in five different locations throughout Texas and Southern California.

We met at the Angels of Democracy headquarters near Brownsville. Jasper Marshall entered the room alone and greeted me with a firm handshake. He is a pleasant and personable man who uses his genial manner to deliver a message that is radical and disturbing at times. Underneath his geniality, I sensed a quick intelligence and a genuine desire to help humanity, even if a number of people disagree with his methods.

Q. Mr. Marshall, the current refugee crisis on the U.S.-Mexico border has stimulated a great deal of interest in the Angels of Democracy. Please tell us a little bit about the group, how and why it started, and what its aims are.

I founded the Angels of Democracy about 12 years ago as a volunteer organization dedicated to improving life in America. In our mission statement, which has been quoted numerous times in press reports, we say that our primary goal is "to function as Good Samaritans and assist law enforcement to reach a better state of safety and security for our families, neighbors and friends." We can examine the details, and I'm sure you'll ask me about them, but that's it in a nutshell.

How many members are there?

We currently number around 3,000, many of whom joined within the past year. The original core of the group comprised around 800-900 members.

How many of those are volunteers?

Most of the original members were people donating their time and services. The majority of the recent recruits are being paid, which we think is fair given that their work is full-time.

*Where does your funding come from? You know, there are
people who have analyzed your operation from the outside and
have estimated that the amount of money needed to support current
activities on the Mexican border would number in the millions,
perhaps the tens of millions.*

The bulk of our operating budget comes from donations.
We've been very fortunate in attracting generous people who
share our beliefs and actually put their money where their
mouth is.

*Given the scope of your border project, you must have some
very large donors.*

We have both large and small donors, and everything
in between. With all due respect to you, some of the people
looking at us from the outside are members of the press who
do not share our belief system. If someone is confronting a
large and sustained body of opinion that conflicts with their
own beliefs, the first thing they're likely to think is that there's
a conspiracy afoot. For many people, that's the only way to
explain the tidal wave of feeling on the other side of the fence,
the only way they can accept it.

The fact is that many citizens in this country feel frustrated
and disenfranchised. These people are usually portrayed in the
press as militia members, gun nuts, or recluses on the order of
Ted Kazcynski. And I have no doubt that some of them are,
but I also think that number is very small, a tiny minority.
But it's comforting to people in the mainstream to paint those
who disagree with them as dangerous lunatics, because that
gives them a basis for dismissing their opinions. If you look
back through history, you'll see that there's a pattern for this.
Up until a few centuries ago, it was still acceptable to burn
heretics at the stake.

*I trust that none of the Angels of Democracy have been
burned at the stake thus far?*

No [laughs], but I'm sure there are people who would do it if they could.

What do you have against illegal immigration?

Only the fact that it's illegal, that the people sneaking across the border from Mexico are breaking the law. This is the point that always seems to get lost in the discussion. If you want to get technical about it, they're not immigrants at all—they're criminals. I think you referred to them before as refugees. The Geneva Convention on Refugees restricts the use of the term to people who emigrate because of fear of persecution based on their race, religion or political opinions, things of that nature. That's not the case here.

Don't you think that some of the immigrants crossing from Mexico are coming to the U.S. because they're afraid of the climate of violence created by the drug lords?

For some of them, yes. But it's up to them to tell us that. We have a procedure for those people to apply for asylum, which would probably be granted.

You seem to have made quite a study about this.

Well [laughs], I think you're saying that for a guy who spent most of his working life managing a Home Depot store, I'm surprisingly well informed. And that's really part of my point: there are many citizens out there who have taken the time to educate themselves about our system of government, and yes, they're very well informed, despite the fact that they may have worked at unskilled or blue-collar jobs. Appearances are sometimes deceptive.

I love Home Depot—I'm in there almost every weekend, working on one project or another. But you have to admit that very few people in your situation get to the point where they are leading a movement.

I have no idea whether I'm leading a movement. Here's what I think I'm doing: accepting donations from like-minded citizens and using that money to assist the U.S. Border Patrol in apprehending people crossing the border illegally. As of today, we have something like 40,000 detainees sitting in jail. These are people who normally would have slipped through the cracks and evaded the authorities.

I gather you don't subscribe to the theory that these immigrants are doing jobs that U.S. citizens wouldn't take?

They're primarily doing low-wage jobs, but there's no way to tell whether U.S. citizens would do them or not. All we know is that these jobs exist, and when illegal immigrants show up to apply for them, the jobs haven't yet been filled.

There's a group called the Concerned Citizens of America that has volunteered the use of three tent cities to house the detainees, and the process of transferring them has already begun. Are you familiar with this group?

I've heard of them, but I'm not familiar with them. But I think what they're doing is a humanitarian gesture that should be applauded, rather than viewed with suspicion. We seem to have lost sight of the fact that it's the responsibility of the federal government to secure the border, and it's certainly their responsibility to care for detainees in a humane way.

A lot of people are curious about your background, not to mention your politics. Do you mind if I ask?

I'm an independent, because I believe in examining each candidate's position carefully before coming to a decision, and I think that process is easier if you don't subscribe to a set political ideology. I'm from Pasadena, married, and have two children who are grown. As I said, I spent most of my working life managing a Home Depot store.

What were the Angels of Democracy doing for the first ten years or so, before you began your activities on the border?

Exactly what we're doing now—assisting law enforcement in keeping the peace. We functioned as volunteer and unpaid security at any number of public events, ranging from rock concerts to political rallies. We do not claim to have police powers, and frankly wouldn't want any. We only get involved if we see a crime being committed, in which case our role is to detain the criminal until the proper authorities can arrive. I know we've been described as a militia group, but nothing could be further from the case.

Well, you seem like an eminently reasonable man. So I have to ask you, as a reasonable man, what's the right thing to do with all these immigrants piling up on the border? Should they be deported?

I think we should follow the law. The President has said that they deserve hearings before being deported, which sounds fair. I believe he feels that some of the detainees may be asylum seekers, even though they didn't identify themselves that way and apply for asylum.

I'd like to go back to something you touched on earlier, when you asked what I have against immigration. My own ancestors were immigrants, going back three or four generations, and I'd bet that yours were as well—that's the case with most Americans. I think the President made this point in his last speech. But I'd also bet that your ancestors came here legally, as mine did. And I think we sometimes overlook the fact that America still accepts more immigrants than any nation in the world, close to a million each year. But those are people who have followed the law and come to this country legally.

If the current rate of arrests continues, we could have more than 100,000 people detained at the border by the end of the year. Many members of the public already view the situation as a humanitarian crisis. Do you feel even slightly responsible for that?

Not at all—that's like saying that police are responsible for crime, or that doctors cause disease.

Let's look at the facts. Most estimates put the number of illegal immigrants at around 600,000 annually. Roughly half of them come across the Mexican border. Up to this point, we've been apprehending a small fraction of those people. So I'd say yes, it's entirely possible we could have 100,000 in custody shortly.

Just looking at it from a logistical standpoint, what are we going to do with all those people?

I have no idea. I'd say it's the responsibility of our elected officials to figure out what to do with them. That's a responsibility they've largely been able to evade so far, because they haven't been willing or able to catch them.

I'd like to go back to the finances of your operation for a moment. Paying the salaries of 2,000 field agents is an enormous expense, not to mention their uniforms, equipment and vehicles. Where's all this money coming from? You must have some huge donors.

As I said before, we have any number of donors—large, small and everywhere in between. It's true that an operation like this costs a lot of money, and we've been very fortunate that there are many like-minded citizens who appreciate what we're doing.

I mentioned uniforms a moment ago, and I'd like to ask you about that. Most press reports describe your outfits as an adaptation of the Medieval Knights Templar.

That's correct, yes. We sometimes say that we are descended from the Knights Templar—not in any literal sense, but in terms of the way we view our role in society.

What is it about that particular group that appeals to you so strongly? Many Americans are probably unfamiliar with them and what they stood for.

The Knights Templar was a Medieval monastic order that flourished in Europe for more than a century, around the time of the Crusades. They eventually grew into a rich and powerful organization, but the Knights themselves were heroic figures. They took vows of both poverty and chastity, and they dedicated themselves to helping their fellow man. Eventually the authorities turned on them and destroyed the order, primarily because a number of governments were in debt to the Templars. We've essentially patterned ourselves on the noblest aspects of the order.

Do you view yourselves as being guided or inspired by God?

I think it would be a terrific world if everyone were inspired and guided by God. But in the sense that you're asking the question, the answer is no, not at all.

How do you see the future of the group? What will you do when your current work on the border winds down? I imagine you'll have to lay off a number of the new hires.

I can't say what the future holds, any more than you can. But we'd certainly hope to continue being useful to humanity.

Mr. Marshall, it's been an interesting conversation. Thanks for your time.

Thank you, I enjoyed it.

Chapter 29

"This is Fox News. Thanks for joining us this evening. As you can see, we're looking at a backdrop of the Senate chamber, where a vote will begin shortly on H.R. 3422, popularly known as the Restoration of Democracy Act. Let's go down to the Senate floor and check in with our correspondent on the scene. Chuck, what's the atmosphere like in the upper chamber tonight?"

"It's highly charged, John, because we haven't seen a piece of legislation like this in many years, if ever. As you know, this is a bill that repeals most of the provisions of the Supreme Court's so-called *Democracy Unchained* decision. That case declared campaign contributions to be the equivalent of political speech. It lifted most of the restrictions on donating to campaigns, saying that those restrictions violated the First Amendment. Since then, we've seen huge donors come forward in both ends of the ideological spectrum to take advantage of the situation, creating the impression in many voters' minds that the large donors were essentially buying elections."

"And Chuck, correct me if I'm wrong, but that Supreme Court decision reversed previous limits that had been set by the McCain-Feingold campaign reform act of 2002."

"Absolutely right, John. McCain-Feingold limited direct individual contributions to $2,000 and set a ceiling of $5,000 for direct donations to political action committees, or PACs. It also attempted to ban the use of corporate or union funds to sponsor political TV ads. In the wake of *Democracy Unchained*, many large donors who had previously been operating under the radar were suddenly able to open their checkbooks for the candidates of their choice. The most famous example on the right is the Haft brothers in St. Louis, but there have been substantial donors on the liberal side as well."

"So how would you characterize the impact of this legislation for the average person, Chuck?"

"Well, it's enormously significant. If you're a hard-working guy who can manage to scrape together $2,000 for your favorite candidate, your voice will be heard as clearly as that of a billionaire. So it really does level the playing field."

"And this has been a highly controversial bill from the beginning, hasn't it?"

"Indeed it has. As you know, the legislation was shepherded through Congress by Senator Chet Wallko of Indiana, who based the bill on his reading of the First Amendment. He pointed out that the text specifically refers to enforcement of freedom of speech as the domain of Congress, rather than the courts. According to that interpretation, *Democracy Unchained* was unconstitutional."

"He claimed he had many of the country's top legal scholars agreeing with him, didn't he?"

"That's correct. Wallko had affadavits from most of the major constitutional scholars, as well as the deans of our best law schools, saying that he was dead right in his opinion. And then, of course, we had the statement from Chief Justice Paul Gilliam, who went on record saying that the Court had basically been wrong. While Gilliam said that he felt the Court had the right to voice an opinion in the matter, jurisdiction plainly belonged to Congress. But the key moment, in the opinion of many people, was the stunning statement by the Haft brothers supporting the reversal of *Democracy Unchained*. That statement was really what gave Congressional Republicans the political cover to vote for it."

"Even with all that, it was a fight to get the bill through the House, wasn't it?"

"Absolutely, John—it was a squeaker. Remember that a number of the House members, on both sides of the aisle, had received substantial sums from large donors other than the Hafts. At the end of the day, though, campaign finance reform is a hard thing to oppose effectively."

"Apparently, we expect tonight's vote in the Senate to be a formality."

"Hold on a moment, John. Senator Wallko, chairman of the Foreign Relations Committee and sponsor of the bill, is making his way onto the floor. Let's see if we can have a word with him." The Fox correspondent fought his way through the scrum of reporters and zeroed in on Wallko. "Senator, how are you feeling tonight? I imagine it must be a mixture of excitement and apprehension."

"This is a great night for America, Chuck," said Wallko. "There's no other way to put it. Tonight, we're taking our electoral process out of the reach of the special interests and handing it back to the people. As far as apprehension goes, I'm actually very confident. We've been lobbying hard on this, and we believe we have the vote locked up."

"You received help from a number of quarters on that, didn't you, including President Atalas? It's our understanding that the President met personally with dozens of members of Congress from both parties."

"He was a great help, Chuck." Wallko smiled. "It was refreshing to be on the same team as the President, for a change. He worked very hard to make this happen, and we're grateful for that. Now if you'll excuse me, I have a few things I need to take care of before the vote."

"Absolutely. That's Senator Chet Wallko, the mastermind behind the bill nicknamed the Restoration of Democracy Act."

"I think I see Vice President Bassen coming to the podium now, Chuck."

"Yes, here he comes. The Vice President, as the President of the Senate, will preside over tonight's proceedings."

"Ladies and gentlemen," said Bassen, banging the gavel and grinning broadly. "Please take your seats. The Senate will be in order.

"The business before us tonight is the legislation titled H.R. 3422, which has previously been passed by the House. If a majority of this chamber concurs, this bill will become the law of the land. The clerk will call the role."

"If you've just joined us," said the Fox anchor, "we're awaiting the vote on the so-called Restoration of Democracy act. The bill's sponsor, Senator Wallko, assures us that he has the votes needed for passage. And tonight, we're looking for a simple majority, correct, Chuck?"

"That's right, John. The bill will become law with 51 votes. If it were in danger of filibuster, or if there was a likelihood of a Presidential veto, the bullet-proof number would be 60, but neither of those situations apply tonight."

"As our viewers can see, the clerk has begun to call the role. Senators are responding by voice votes, which are being recorded by the clerk. And even now, we see Senator Wallko conferring with a few of his colleagues, presumably making a last-minute pitch for the bill."

"That's probably what he's up to John, but from the sound of it he doesn't need to worry. We seem to be on track for the bill to pass comfortably."

Less than five minutes later, the clerk handed the results to Bassen, who pounded the gavel enthusiastically.

"The bill passes by a vote of 55-45," he grinned, "and H.R. 3422 has become law."

• • • • • • • • • • • • • • • • • • • •

"Praise the Lord," said Sheldon Haft, his eyes fixated on the wide-screen TV.

Kevin Lapham and his brother Richard watched the roll call vote with him in Sheldon's penthouse office outside of St. Louis. "How does it feel to be on the right side of an issue for a change?"

"It can't hurt," said Richard.

"Good job, Dickie. This was the right move. At least it will allow us to go back to our strategy of gaming the system anonymously."

"I'm not too sure about that, sir," replied Lapham. "Virtually every national magazine has run a story on you over the past few years. It's going to be very hard to put the toothpaste back in the tube."

"People have short memories." Sheldon shook his head. "Thanks to Dickie's idea about this border deal, the public will be preoccupied for the rest of the year. Not to mention everything else that will follow." He looked at Lapham again. "Let's get the names of the Republicans who supported this, put them on the Christmas list."

"I'm on it."

"How are we coming along with the camps? Have all the detainees been transferred?"

"Just about, sir. In a few weeks from now, they'll start to look as crowded as the county jails."

"Good work. I read in the newspaper that this Bodenstein character said something about building additional bunk houses. Please make sure that doesn't happen."

"I've already talked to him about it, after that story came out."

"And for God's sake, make sure we don't hire any extra security."

"We won't, but I'm hearing that the government plans on assigning some people from Homeland Security to each camp."

"Let them go ahead. Our people who fly commercial tell me that DHS has made a complete botch of the airports, so they should be perfect for the job here." He turned off the TV. "I can't watch any more of this. Tell me, how are we progressing with Operation Veep?"

"The backup plan is in place. I just want to go over the details one more time before I sign off on it."

"Please do." Sheldon Haft got up and stretched. "I don't want any more screw-ups like the fiasco at the Mexican restaurant."

Chapter 30

*D*éjà Vu on the Mexican Border
Tent Cities Becoming Overcrowded and Dangerous
By Peter Schoenfeld
August 4: Special to The Washington Post

As the number of illegal immigrants detained on the U.S.-Mexican border officially tops 50,000, the improvised camps in which they are being held are becoming a breeding ground for crime and disease.

Use of the three tent cities was donated by a group called the Citizens for a Concerned America. According to Lester Bodenstein, the group's President, the compounds were originally built to be used as summer camps for urban children; they were described as self-contained living quarters complete with bunk houses, showers, toilets and kitchen facilities. They were designed to hold between 8,000 and 10,000 people each.

When the detainees were transferred to the camps several weeks ago, the installations were already full. The number of illegal immigrants arrested has continued to skyrocket since then, as a result of the enhanced security sweep conducted by the U.S. Border Patrol and the Angels of Democracy. At the time he volunteered the use of the facilities, Mr. Bodenstein stated that the camps could *"easily be expanded"* to accommodate more people. Construction of new bunk houses has not begun, and Mr. Bodenstein has been unavailable for comment.

Ironically, the immigrants were transferred to the camps in the first place because of dangerously overcrowded conditions in county jails along the border. Poor sanitation in the jails led to an outbreak of dysentery, and violence between inmates became common. In one incident, dubbed the Baloney Sandwich Murder by the tabloid press, an immigrant named José Cortes was knifed by another inmate during an argument over food. Cortes later died of septic shock in a nearby hospital.

Much of the violence that afflicted the inmate population in the county jails was gang related. According to corrections officials, immigrants who were involved in criminal activity back in Mexico quickly organized into teams designed to control the trading of contraband, including cigarettes and drugs. The overcrowded conditions quickly led to arguments and fights among the inmates.

Since they were relocated to the temporary camps, the pattern of gang violence has continued. Security is also an issue. Prior to the arrival of the immigrants, the camps were patrolled by paid security guards. When the inmates were transferred, the federal government assigned agents from the Department of Homeland Security to maintain order in the camps. The number of agents assigned to each camp has been described as *"woefully inadequate,"* in the words of one Texas official, and requests to the government for more manpower appear to have fallen on deaf ears.

The Post recently contacted the Texas State House to corroborate rumors that the Governor was thinking of calling on the government to declare a state of emergency in the camps.

"We have no plans to do that at this time," said a staffer in the Governor's press office. *"But if the number of refugees keeps increasing, we wouldn't rule it out."*

• • • • • • • • • • • • • • • • • • •

One evening midway through the August Congressional recess, Chet Wallko was relaxing at home when his wife poked her head into the den.

"Eddie Lupin is on the line for you."

"I'll be damned." He picked up the phone. "Eddie, how are things in Minnesota?"

"Well," said the Speaker, "at least it's not snowing."

"That's something, I suppose. How's your vacation going?"

"Right." He laughed. "Too bad the public doesn't know that we work harder at home than we do in Washington."

"Some of us do. Tell me, how are you feeling?"

"Like crap, thanks. They tell me it'll get worse before it gets better."

"That sucks."

"Chet, I've got something I need to put on your radar."

"Shoot."

"I'm on the phone every day with members of the caucus, as I'm sure you are. And I have to tell you there's a situation developing."

"I'm listening."

"Our guys are out there doing voter outreach, as I know your guys are. They're talking to constituents, doing a lot of town halls. And what they're hearing is disturbing."

"Let me guess: the public is angry about something. Probably they're angry at me, but the beauty of it is that I don't give a shit."

"Not you, Chet. And they're not exactly angry, either. But I have to tell you there's a lot of unrest about this situation down there on the border."

"Do tell?"

"People are horrified, to put it mildly. I know the press is probably to blame for the way they've portrayed this, but it doesn't look good. It looks like we've put the immigrants into concentration camps. These places are filthy, they're violent, they're overcrowded. Voters are coming to these town halls to voice their disgust. Women are crying."

"Well, I didn't put them there."

"Of course you didn't. But your guy did. And these people are truly outraged. This isn't your standard business of being pissed off at the government. The situation down there offends their sense of decency."

"First of all, he's not my guy."

"He's the leader of your party, like it or not. I assume you're still a registered Democrat."

"Come on, Eddie. You know I have no pull with this administration."

"I know that. But this isn't your garden variety outrage. Jews are horrified because these camps remind them of the Holocaust. JapaneseAmericans are uneasy because the camps remind them of the detention during World War II. The Hispanics are off the wall. It's not a good thing."

"Well, I agree. But I'm not exactly a policy maker in this crew."

"You need to hear this, Chet. A lot of these folks are calling for impeachment. And they're not fringe lunatics— they're honest, hard-working, ordinary voters."

"So they want Atalas impeached. I want a lot of things. Did I ever tell you that I always wanted to play shortstop for the Cubs? But I couldn't do it because my arm is weak, and I can't turn the double play quickly enough."

"Neither can the Cubs. This is no joke, Chet. These people need to blame someone, and the most obvious target is Atalas."

"I hear you. But I also think it's going to look different to Congress when they get back to Washington."

"Maybe so. But I can tell you this: if we come back from recess and we've got 100,000 immigrants in those camps, we've got a situation on our hands. Particularly if people keep getting killed over baloney sandwiches."

"Enough with the baloney sandwiches, please. The question is, what do you want me to do? And the real question is, what do you think I can do?"

"Probably not much. But if Atalas knows what's good for him, he should start sending these people back to where they came from."

"I don't think that's going to happen." He paused. "But I appreciate you calling. It sounds like we're going to have an interesting fall."

• • • • • • • • • • • • • • • • • • •

Rioting Breaks Out in Detention Camps Along Mexican Border
Immigrants Demand Due Process, Better Living Conditions
By Peter Schoenfeld
August 20: Special to The Washington Post

As many Americans indulge in the final days of summer and look forward to the Labor Day weekend, riots are occurring in the three detention camps along the Mexican border.

The camps—two in Texas and one in Southern California—are overflowing with illegal immigrants caught up in the security sweep being conducted by the U.S. Border Patrol and the Angels of Democracy. Since the arrests began in mid-April, some 65,000 immigrants have been detained. They were initially held in county jails along the border. Last month, after conditions in the jails became intolerable, they were transferred to the temporary holding facilities.

At the largest camp north of Brownsville, Texas, nearly 25,000 detainees are crammed into a space designed to hold 10,000. The bunk houses are not yet air conditioned, and temperatures have exceeded 100 degrees in recent days. Inmates have organized themselves into a movement they refer to as "La Lucha," which translates as "The Struggle." Enrique Gonzalez, leader of La Lucha, describes his group as a cross between a trade union for inmates and a revolutionary movement.

Within the past week, members of La Lucha have launched a hunger strike, and some of the more militant inmates have ambushed and beaten agents of the Department of Homeland Security, who were assigned to maintain order in the camps. After a series of large-scale brawls in the exercise yard, one of which sent 12 immigrants and three DHS agents to the infirmary, the Governor of Texas has dispatched a contingent of State Police and Texas Rangers to the site to quell the violence.

Use of the camps was donated by a group called Citizens for a Concerned America. Its president, Lester Bodenstein, claimed the camps were originally constructed as summer camps for underprivileged children. He also stated that more bunk houses would be constructed to house the ever-increasing flow of illegal immigrants. The additional facilities have not been built, and Mr. Bodenstein has been unavailable for comment.

"This is a disgraceful situation," declared Jorge Mendoza yesterday during a telephone interview. Mendoza is the head of Criollos Unidos, the largest and most influential organization devoted to Hispanic rights.

"If these prisoners were white and Caucasian, this would not be happening. They would not be subjected to these conditions, and they would have had their day in court long ago.

"President Atalas is getting ready to go on his annual summer vacation. Very soon he will be on Martha's Vineyard, playing golf

and snacking on ice cream. In the meantime, tens of thousands of brown people are rotting in concentration camps near the border.

"*Some time ago, the President promised that the detainees would receive due process. He assured us that they would receive deportation hearings to determine whether or not their individual situations qualified them for asylum in the United States. We now have over 60,000 prisoners, and we have had exactly 469 hearings.*

"*I call upon the President to be as good as his word.*"

The White House could not be reached for comment on Mendoza's statements.

Chapter 31

The documentary ran on PBS the weekend before Labor Day. It drew one of the largest audiences ever garnered by them nationwide, particularly considering the time of year. It also attracted so much attention in the press that it was aired again the following week. Media critics across the country called it "explosive," "painfully revealing," "gut-wrenching" and "searing."

Without question, it helped to solidify outrage against the administration's handling of the immigration problem on the border. Leading conservatives, who had been railing against public broadcasting for decades as a tool of the liberal conspiracy, were astonished at how far PBS went to discredit the way the President had dealt with the situation.

The title was *Faces of Despair: The Refugee Crisis in America.*

"I wanted to come to America," said the off-camera voice of a young man at the opening, as the camera panned across a desolate village in the Mexican interior. *"I wanted to make some money and help my family. But I also thought that if I worked hard and stayed long enough, I could become somebody.*

"I grew up in a small village outside Matamoros. I had three sisters and four brothers, and all eight of us slept on the floor of our

house, next to the stove." Pictures of a disheveled shack filled with filthy children flashed across the screen. White House spokesmen later charged that the hovel being shown was located in El Salvador and not Mexico, but it hardly mattered. People in the audience were probably already crying.

"My father worked as a migrant, and sometimes there was not enough food. We always thought that if we made it to America that our worries would be over.

"I left school after the sixth grade and worked twelve hours a day, saving money to come to America. When I had saved a thousand dollars, we found a coyote, a smuggler, who was willing to transport me for that price. I was loaded into the trunk of a car and driven across the border." The screen featured generic footage of cars driving across Texas sagebrush in the middle of the night. *"A few miles north of the border, we were stopped by some men wearing uniforms. They opened the trunk and found the three of us. They told us to wait there until the Border Patrol arrived. We thought they were police, so we did as we were told.*

"The three of us were taken to a jail near Brownsville and put in a cell. There were three other men in the cell, all older. They smoked cigarettes and had tattoos." As he spoke, there was a succession of pictures of the overcrowded cells in the county jails: PBS obviously had access to the archives of *The Washington Post* photographers. *"The men told us what to do from the beginning. They took our food and beat us up when we disobeyed them. All three of us got very sick.*

"After almost a month, we were herded onto trucks and taken to the camp north of Brownsville. Conditions there were better at first, but quickly got worse. There were few guards to control the gangs, people kept getting sick, and we were not allowed to bathe."

The documentary went on like this for a solid hour, portraying the camps as just a notch better than Auschwitz. It would be aired twice more between Labor Day and the end of the year. In the aftermath of the first showing, representatives from Amnesty International, the American Red Cross and the UN Commission on Refugees came to southern Texas. Clips from the film were shown on TV as parts of ads from humanitarian groups. It was, in the words of Joel Gottbaum, "a shitstorm tsunami."

• • • • • • • • • • • • • • • • • • •

President Cuts Vacation Short, Returns to Washington
Vows to Contain Refugee Crisis on Mexican Border
By Peter Schoenfeld
August 28: Special to The Washington Post

President Khaleem Atalas abruptly suspended his summer vacation yesterday, leaving Martha's Vineyard and returning to the Capitol to focus on the nation's refugee crisis.

"We need a swift and meaningful resolution to this situation," said the President, who was originally scheduled to remain at his rented vacation home until the Labor Day weekend.

"By returning to Washington, I will be able to confer with my Cabinet and top security agencies to work out a plan to ease tensions along the Mexican border. The immigrants living in the detention camps in Texas and California are enduring harsh conditions and dangerous circumstances. This situation has continued long enough, and it is unacceptable in the United States of America. We live in a complicated world, and we have many problems to deal with. We need to eliminate the distraction of the refugee problem so we can focus on some of the other pressing issues facing our country, and it's my intention to do this as quickly as possible."

As he left Martha's Vineyard, the President offered no specifics on how he planned to deal with the crisis, but top aides indicated that a plan would be announced within a few days.

Problems along the U.S.-Mexico border have worsened in the past week. Public awareness of the situation was heightened by a recent documentary that aired several times on PBS stations around the country. Titled Faces of Despair: The Refugee Crisis in America, *the film was narrated through the eyes of immigrants themselves, and it focused on conditions in the three temporary detention camps.*

Several days ago, a second riot broke out at the Brownsville camp, pitting inmates against agents of the Department of Homeland Security. DHS agents were assigned to maintain order in the camps when the immigrants were first transferred there, and officials have consistently complained that the number of personnel was too small to police the population effectively. A contingent of Texas Rangers and State Police has been assisting DHS for the past week.

According to confidential sources, the second riot was initiated by members of an inmate group called La Lucha, or "The Struggle." It began in the camp's exercise yard and quickly spun out of control, with as many as 100 inmates battling a combination of security forces. State Police used tear gas and water cannons to control the melee, and two detainees were ultimately shot in the fracas.

"We are not animals," said Enrigue Gonzalez through an interpreter. Gonzalez is the leader of La Lucha, and he claims more than 1,200 of his fellow inmates have thus far joined the struggle.

"We are human beings, and we demand to be treated that way. We will not stop until the U.S. government grants us the rights that we are entitled to as children of God."

In the aftermath of the PBS documentary, conditions in the camps have been condemned by Amnesty International, The American Red Cross and the UN Commission on Refugees, as well as Criollos Unidos, the nation's largest organization devoted to lobbying for the rights of Hispanics. According to most estimates, the number of detainees in the three camps now totals slightly more than 70,000.

• • • • • • • • • • • • • • • • • • •

Several days after returning to Washington from Martha's Vineyard, President Atalas held his first press conference in nearly three months.

The encounter with the media was carefully managed. The White House press corps received no advance notice of the event, which was announced only fifteen minutes before it started. Atalas also took a page from the playbook of another embattled President, Richard Nixon, and scheduled the press conference for 8:00 a.m., an hour when the most antagonistic reporters would either be still asleep or hung over from the night before.

The President walked into the briefing room a few minutes past eight, wearing a dark blue suit and a solemn expression. The room was empty save for a handful of wire service correspondents.

"Good morning and thank you for coming on short notice. I have a statement to read, after which I'll take just a few quick questions.

"I returned to Washington two days ago to take personal charge of the problems occurring on the U.S.-Mexico border. Since then, my time has been spent in consultations with the Cabinet, with the FBI and CIA, and also with those officials entrusted with the day-to-day supervision of our national security. I have also been in contact with a range of attorneys and humanitarian groups.

"As a result, I would like to announce the following five-point course of action:

"Effective immediately, I am declaring a state of emergency in both California and Texas. This declaration will allow me to use the full power of the federal government to help diffuse the tensions that have increased recently in the border camps. I want to make it clear to the governors of both states that they have a direct phone line to me, and that I won't refuse any reasonable request for assistance.

"Secondly, I am instructing both state governments to immediately activate their National Guard units and deploy them to the three detention camps. In conversations with both governors, I've indicated that a force of three to four thousand troops will be necessary to maintain order in each camp. Those troops should be arriving on site within a few days.

"I have also directed my administration to work closely with the humanitarian groups that have investigated conditions within the camps. We welcome their input, and we pledge our complete cooperation in working with them to assure more humane living conditions for the detained immigrants.

"Fourth, I am taking intensified steps to speed up the deportation hearings for detainees. I have previously stated that I believe each and every one of them is entitled to due process, and I'm still firm in that conviction. However, I also recognize that the pace of scheduling those hearings has been unacceptably slow. Consequently, I have ordered the Joint Chiefs of Staff to immediately submit to me a list of officers in the Judge Advocate General's Corps of each service who could be detached and ready to preside over deportation hearings. While it's true that there are differences between military and civilian law, it's also true that many of these judges have extensive experience in the civilian sector. I expect to have the list by the end of the week, and I will make sure the accelerated schedule of hearings begins as soon as possible.

"Lastly, I have asked the Army Corps of Engineers to conduct an investigation of each camp, and report back to me within the week with an estimate for expanding the living quarters, as well as improving the ones that already exist. The

Engineers are the finest group of contractors on earth, and they are eminently capable of building the required structures in a very short period of time. These improvements will go a long way toward making life much more bearable for the detainees awaiting hearings.

"I'll take a few quick questions."

"Mr. President, do we know how many detainees are currently in the camps?"

"As of this morning, the best estimate we have is close to 80,000."

"Sir, do you have any plans to begin deportations in the near future?"

"As I stated, I believe the immigrants are entitled to due process. The Constitution guarantees that right to American citizens, and we have traditionally extended it to those people in the country on a temporary basis. I've also said that we don't know how many of the immigrants are entitled to asylum. Before we start deporting these folks, we need to make sure that none of their lives will be in jeopardy if they are returned to Mexico."

"Sir, you've come under fire recently from a wide range of citizens and groups over the slow reaction of your administration to this crisis. I think many people would like to know what has taken so long to form a plan of action to deal with this?"

"Well, I've been in office for four and a half years now, so I've gotten used to being criticized—it comes with the job, and it's a rare day when someone isn't attacking me for something. In this case, we have a situation that came out of nowhere. No one was expecting it, and it took a while for people to understand the scope of the problem. Our initial efforts were focused on determining whether the actions of the Angels of Democracy were even legal, and I think most observers would admit that events moved very quickly in this case. But as I've stated before and just repeated, these conditions are not acceptable in the United States of America, and we will do something about it."

"Sir, when you left Martha's Vineyard a few days ago to return to Washington, you said the refugee crisis had become a distraction that was preventing you from focusing on other issues. Do you think that description might be found offensive by many people in the Hispanic community?"

"Let me be clear on this: we live in a very dangerous and complicated world. There is widespread starvation throughout South America, an AIDS epidemic in Africa, unrest throughout the Middle East, and Persepostan is trying to develop nuclear weapons. We need to be able to concentrate on those issues, and deal with them effectively in a way that insures the future of the planet. And, of course, we have problems in this country as well, and those problems will be addressed. But when I referred to the refugee situation as a distraction, I was trying to place it in a much larger global context."

"Mr. President, some of your critics are charging that your reluctance to deport the detainees is politically motivated. Since you're on record advocating a path to citizenship for illegal immigrants, some people have suggested that you have a vested interest in keeping them in the country. Bob O'Neill at Fox News even stated that your goal was to have the immigrants naturalized on the assumption that they would vote Democratic. What's your reaction to that, sir?"

Atlas forced a smile. "Gentlemen, have yourselves a nice day." He turned and walked out of the briefing room, ignoring the shouted questions that followed him.

Chapter 32

"This is CNN Breaking News with more information on the developing story we first covered about twenty minutes ago. Curtis Bassen, Jr., the oldest son of the Vice President, has been the victim of an unsuccessful assassination attempt. As we originally reported, the attack took place outside the Federal Courthouse in Dayton, Ohio, where Bassen works as a prosecutor. In just a moment we'll be going live to Samantha Olsen, our correspondent on the scene, who has been gathering information on this bizarre and shocking event.

"As far as we know, Bassen was shot in the attack but not seriously injured. He was taken to a nearby hospital, and we're awaiting word on his condition. The initial eyewitness accounts indicated that it was a lone gunman who approached Bassen as he was leaving work and suddenly drew his weapon. There are reports that Bassen's bodyguard shot the assailant as well.

"We have Samantha Olsen now, live at the courthouse in Dayton. Samantha, can you hear us?"

"Loud and clear, John. I'm standing here in front of the Federal Courthouse for the Southern District of Ohio, where Curtis Bassen, Jr. is employed as a prosecutor. About forty-five minutes ago, he was the subject of an attack by a lone gunman as he emerged from the building."

"Samantha, can you tell us what happened?"

"From what we've been able to piece together, John, Bassen was leaving work around five this afternoon, accompanied by his bodyguard. As they descended the steps of the courthouse they were approached by the gunman, who drew his pistol when he was approximately five feet away. According to bystanders who witnessed the event, the bodyguard reacted very quickly, but the gunman was able to get off one shot, and we believe that shot hit Bassen in the leg. The bodyguard then returned fire, shooting the assailant in the chest."

"What do we know at this point about the condition of the Vice President's oldest son?"

"He was taken to nearby Grandview Hospital and is currently being treated, but our understanding is that his condition is stable, and his injuries are not life-threatening. We believe that the bodyguard was uninjured."

"And what about the gunman, Samantha? What's his condition at this time?"

"EMTs were called, but he was pronounced dead at the scene."

"Do we know who he was at this point?"

"What we're hearing, John, is that the man carried no identification with him. This means that determining his identity will take a while, if that identity can be confirmed. Authorities will take fingerprints and run them through the national databases, but something will only turn up if he had a previous felony conviction, was in the military, or ever applied for a job that required him to be fingerprinted."

"Well it sounds miraculous that Bassen wasn't injured more seriously, given how close the gunman was when he opened fire. I'm sure that we can all be grateful for that."

"Everyone is certainly relieved, John. But as we assemble more information on what happened, the situation is starting to appear more and more suspicious. As I mentioned, the gunman was five feet away when he opened fire, but only succeeded in shooting Bassen in the leg. Either he was a poor shot, or his intention was only to inflict minor injury. According to some eyewitnesses, he seemed to actually aim for Bassen's leg. So more and more, it seems that perhaps this wasn't really an assassination attempt at all."

"That does sound very strange indeed."

"And, of course, we'll probably never know for sure at this point, since the gunman is dead."

"I presume the Vice President has been notified, Samantha? What are you hearing about that?"

"Vice President Bassen was in a meeting at the time of the incident, John, and we believe he was notified at once. We have reports that he is already en route to Andrews Air Force Base to fly to Dayton and be at his son's side."

"Has he issued any statement thus far?"

"Not that we're aware of, but everyone knows that the Vice President is exceptionally close to his children, and he's in the habit of talking to each of them almost every day."

"And his son was accompanied by a single bodyguard, is that correct?"

"That's right, John. As you may recall, Curtis Bassen, Jr. has consistently refused Secret Service protection, a situation which greatly concerned his father. About three years ago, the Vice President asked the U.S. Attorney for Ohio's Southern District to assign a bodyguard to his son. I'm sure you remember that there was considerable controversy about this, particularly after it was disclosed that the bodyguard was on the county payroll. Ultimately an anonymous Democratic donor came forward and offered to pay the bodyguard's salary."

"Do we have any idea what inspired the attack, Samantha? Was Bassen working on any high-profile cases at the moment, anything that might involve drug activity or organized crime?"

"Not that we know of at this time, although investigators will no doubt start examining those cases in detail very shortly. Unless we can find out who the attacker was, though, I'm afraid they'll be searching for a needle in a haystack."

"Any word from the White House yet, Samantha? Do we know if President Atalas will be issuing a statement?"

"He's been briefed on the situation, and we anticipate that he will have something to say about it this evening, but we have no definite word on that as of yet."

"Thank you, Samantha. We'll definitely be checking back with you periodically as you get information on this fast-moving story."

At 8:45 p.m. that evening, the President stepped to the microphone in the White House briefing room and made the following short statement:

"Good evening, ladies and gentlemen. As you're all aware, at about five o'clock today Curtis Bassen, Jr., the Vice President's oldest son, was attacked by a gunman as he left the Federal Courthouse in Dayton, where he works as a prosecutor. He suffered a gunshot wound to the leg and was taken to a nearby hospital, where he was treated and is currently recovering. The Vice President is at his side. As you also know, Grandview Hospital is also under lockdown and will remain that way for the next few days—not for security reasons, but to give the Vice President and his son the privacy they need at this difficult time. The White House should have an update on his condition for you tomorrow. In the meantime, we ask that you respect the family's privacy, and give them the time and the space to deal with the aftermath of this incident. Thank you."

"Mr. President, what is Curtis Jr.'s condition at this time?"

"He's reported as stable, and as far as I know he's doing fine. The bullet entered his right leg below the thigh and fortunately did not hit any bones. The doctors anticipate that he should be able to walk on crutches by the end of the week."

"How is the Vice President taking this, sir?"

"He's doing well, although there's no doubt that this was a traumatic incident for him. As you know, the family is extremely close."

"Sir, do we know the identity of the gunman?"

"We do not. As some of you reported, the man had no identification with him when he carried out the attack. Authorities are currently working to establish his identity."

"Mr. President, according to some of the eyewitnesses, the gunman seemed to be aiming for Bassen's leg. Given those reports, is it accurate to describe this as an assassination attempt?"

"I'll leave that determination to the authorities. Regardless of how they characterize it, it was an attack on a federal employee in the performance of his duties. Aside from the affection that we all have for Curt, Jr., he was also a representative of our federal judicial system. Had the gunman survived, he'd be facing some very serious charges right now."

"Sir, do you think this was an isolated act by a deranged individual, or do you suspect that there was a larger plot behind it?"

"I'm not going to speculate on that until we know that facts. But I think you're all aware of my position on gun violence, which I've made clear over the past four and a half years. Unfortunately, every few months I come to this microphone and talk about a shooting of some sort. I have repeatedly called for tougher gun laws and have repeatedly received no cooperation from those on the other side. It's past time that we did this in America, and there's no reason why we can't."

"Mr. President, turning to the situation on the Mexican border—"

"That's all I'm going to say at this time. Thank you and goodnight."

• • • • • • • • • • • • • • • • • • •

"How's Curt doing?" asked Atalas two days later, talking to the Vice President on a secure line.

"He's doing fine, sir. His leg is sore, but he should be up and on the crutches by tomorrow."

"That's great."

"I really appreciate your support on this. Thanks for running interference for me with the press."

"No worries. I figured the last thing you need was the buzzards circling you. I can tell you, though, that we'll probably have to lift the security cordon by tomorrow."

"I understand completely. It's been a great help, and I can't begin to thank you."

"How are you holding up?"

"I have no idea. You know how it is in a crisis—you put one foot in front of another and go forward. I'm sure it'll hit me later."

"Well, take some time off when you get back."

"Do we know who this guy was?"

"The FBI got a hit on him. I'm afraid it's the worst-case scenario—he was in the Army, served two years in Sumeristan."

"Jesus."

"It doesn't look good. They're working up a dossier on him now. But we're not going to release this to the press yet, because we don't know where it's going to take us. If we have to, we can always portray him as a deranged loner. There's certainly enough of those out there."

"That's the wise course."

"In the meantime, take care of yourself. I'll give you a call tomorrow."

"Thank you, sir."

Chapter 33

*H*ouse Republicans Drafting Bill to Mandate Deportation of Refugees
Illegal Immigrants Detained on Mexican Border Number Nearly 90,000

September 18

The Washington Post has learned that the American Values Caucus, a group of 53 Republican Congressmen who support conservative causes, is drafting a bill that would require President Atalas to deport the illegal immigrants currently held on the U.S.-Mexican border.

"The situation on our southern border has become intolerable," said Rep. Jeffrey Barrett (R-Texas), the leader of the caucus. "We have nearly 100,000 immigrants housed in conditions that are best described as inhumane. These are people who were arrested in the act of entering this country illegally. They shouldn't even be here in the first place, and our government certainly should not be footing the bill to take care of them."

Although some observers characterize The American Values Caucus as part of the Tea Party, the 53 members have no formal affiliation with that movement. They have consistently supported popular conservative ideas such as limited government and fiscal responsibility, and they have also campaigned to ban abortion on demand.

According to Barrett, the legislation would mandate President Atalas to immediately begin deporting the detainees and ease the refugee crisis. The President has repeatedly said that he supports due process for the immigrants, and he has taken steps to increase the pace of asylum hearings. Despite his efforts, fewer than 1,000 of those hearings have taken place thus far.

Current estimates of the number of detainees average around 90,000. Some of them have been in custody since April, when the U.S. Border Patrol began an enhanced security sweep aided by a group called the Angels of Democracy. The detainees are being held in three makeshift camps—two in Texas and one in Southern California—that were donated by Citizens for a Concerned America.

When the arrests began, the immigrants were initially detained in county jails along the Mexican border. Those jails quickly became overcrowded, unsanitary and dangerous, and the inmates were transferred to the makeshift camps in July. The flood of arrests continued, and the camps quickly became the site of gang violence and rioting. Three weeks ago, President Atalas declared a state of emergency and dispatched National Guard troops to restore order in the camps. The U.S. Army Corps of Engineers has set up temporary tents for the overflow detainees, and they are constructing prefabricated shelters that will be used as bunk houses. These are expected to be ready by next week.

Rep. Edward Lupin (R–Minn.), the Speaker of the House, indicated that he would put the bill on a fast track for a vote as soon as he received it. Given the large Republican majority in the House, the legislation is expected to pass easily. The details of the bill are not yet known, nor has it been established how much legal force the legislation would carry.

The White House has not released an official statement on whether it believes that the President would be bound to follow the dictates of the bill. Josh Rulander, President Atalas's Press Secretary, was quizzed about the subject at yesterday's daily briefing.

"It's too early to say," he commented. "We haven't seen the bill, obviously, and have no idea what provisions it will have in it. We also haven't determined whether there is any legal requirement for the President to follow its dictates. As soon as we know the details, we'll assemble a body of legal opinion on the subject, and we'll certainly litigate the matter if that becomes necessary."

For his part, Barrett refused to divulge any preliminary details about the legislation, beyond his repeated statements that the bill would demand the immediate deportation of illegal immigrants being held in the temporary camps.

"The President has said any number of times that this situation is unacceptable in the United States of America," said Barrett. "We agree with him 100 percent—probably the first time we've thought alike. But increasingly, it looks to us like we'll have to force him to do his job and deport these people. The White House may think that they're going to tie this thing up in the courts and stall for another five months while 100,000 more felons pile up on the border, but I'm here to tell them they won't be able to do that. If the House passes this legislation, it will become law. And if the President won't comply with the law, we have other means to get him to do so."

This story was compiled from Washington Post staff reports.

• • • • • • • • • • • • • • • • • • • •

"Good evening, and welcome to *60 Minutes*. I'm Scott Pelley. Tonight, we're going to begin with an interview with Jorge Mendoza, the head of the National Council of Criollos Unidos, which has been described as the nation's most influential group lobbying for the rights of Latinos. The interview took place at the headquarters of Criollos Unidos here in Washington, D.C.

"Mr. Mendoza, welcome to *60 Minutes*."

"Happy to be here. Thanks for having me."

"For those viewers who are unfamiliar with Criollos Unidos, why don't you tell us a little bit about your organization—what you stand for, and what you do."

"Certainly. We are the political organizing arm for Latinos and Hispanics who come from cultures all over Central and South America. As of last year, there were 55 million Hispanics living in the U.S., or nearly 20 percent of the nation's population. They come from many different backgrounds, but they face many of the same challenges. Our role is to lobby on issues that will help those 55 million people become part of the fabric of America.

"The term *Criollo* generally refers to anyone of Hispanic descent, but we invest it with a special, symbolic meaning. The original *Criollos* were people of Spanish ancestry that lived in Spain's overseas colonies from the 16th century onward. Despite the legitimacy of their birth, they were regarded as second-class citizens by those who had been born in Spain. We use this unfortunate analogy to refer to the plight of all Hispanics in the United States, whether they emigrated here legally or not, and we stand up for their issues."

"What are some of those issues?"

"Broadly speaking, we focus on civil rights: equality of opportunity in voting, education, health care, housing, and economic opportunity."

"And I would assume you're very involved with immigration as well."

"Absolutely. We are in favor of fair and nondiscriminatory immigration policies. We would like to see more people have the chance to enter this country legally. In cases where that did not occur, we favor a path to citizenship for undocumented immigrants. We would like to see these people integrate into our society and share in the American dream."

"To your knowledge, how many undocumented immigrants are there in this country?"

"Most estimates, Scott, place the total between 11 and 12 million. We encourage policies that will help them come out of the shadows and participate in all the blessings America has to offer."

"I believe your group actively supported President Atalas during his reelection campaign."

"We did. We funded an aggressive effort to turn out the vote among Hispanic and Latino citizens. Many of these people rarely participate in the democratic process because they feel excluded from it. They frequently believe that neither side truly represents their interests."

"Speaking of funding, where does most of your support come from?"

"Three-quarters of it comes from private donors, and we receive the rest in the form of grants from the federal government. Those grants enable us to continue with our health care initiatives and housing programs. Any political activities we engage in are always paid for by private contributions."

"So let me ask you this: As someone who supported the President for reelection, and who actively urged your fellow Hispanics to do so, are you happy with the results?"

"Unfortunately, Scott, the answer at this point is no. We gave our support to the President because he claimed to favor a path to citizenship for undocumented immigrants. He has said so many times since. But sadly, he has done nothing about it. While he did support the Path Bill, he hasn't used the power of his office to issue executive orders that would help those 12 million people become part of America. We consider this to be a great failure."

"I think you'd have to admit that given the current Congressional makeup, legislation such as the Path Bill didn't have much of a chance of passing."

"You may very well be right. But there is a difference between trying and failing and failing to try at all. Through the years and over the centuries, there have been many civil rights initiatives that took a long time to become reality in the United States. They ultimately succeeded because a number of visionary leaders kept proposing them and pushing for them. We thought we had such a visionary leader in President Atalas, but we were mistaken. The man is all talk and no action."

"Don't you think—"

"And while we're on the subject, Scott, let me point out that the President has been very actively engaged in lobbying for the civil rights of other minority groups. He simply does not seem as concerned with the welfare of Hispanics and Latinos."

"Mr. Mendoza, let's turn our attention to the situation on the Mexican border. I know you were down there recently, and you've been very vocal in your opinions about the refugee crisis. Can you share your thoughts on the situation with us?"

"This is one of the great humanitarian failures of the modern era, Scott. First, we have a President who is unable to act on behalf of the rights of undocumented immigrants, a cause he has repeatedly said he believes in. Then, we have a strange and shadowy group, the Angels of Democracy, who mysteriously show up and offer to help the Border Patrol arrest illegal immigrants. I've read estimates of the amount of money it took to back their effort down there, and most of the estimates are in the hundreds of millions of dollars. I'd like to know where that money came from."

"They claim that the bulk of it came in the form of small donations from concerned citizens, as you're probably aware."

"Scott, if the operation cost two hundred million dollars, as some suggest, virtually every adult in this country would have to give $10 or $20 to make it happen."

"But—"

"Let me just finish up this point. We have close to 100,000 immigrants rotting in these camps. Some of them have been in custody for nearly six months. They were first held in county jails, where conditions were crowded, unsanitary and violent. Then they were transferred to these camps, where conditions are now just as bad. And we have a President who is incapable of doing anything about it. He constantly says they are entitled to due process, but only 1 percent of them have received it thus far. If these were White people, Scott—if they were Caucasians—they would have received their legal rights long ago. And the outcry against their abuse would have been deafening."

"That sounds like a harsh judgement, and I believe you to be a fair man."

"I think it's more than fair. In fact, I think it's generous. We call upon the President to extend the promise of America to these people who yearned so desperately for it. It is the least he can do as a human being."

"Mr. Mendoza, you were the target of some criticism during your recent trip to the border because you met with an individual named Enrique Gonzalez. Gonzalez is the head of an inmate group called La Lucha, which I believe translates as 'The Struggle.' Both he and his group are widely seen as the force behind the recent riots in the Brownsville camp, which resulted in the National Guard being called in to restore order. Why did you meet with him, sir?"

"Because he is the voice of many inmates who cannot speak for themselves. While I don't agree completely with all of his methods, he has been successful in calling attention to the plight of his fellow immigrants who are being caged like animals in those camps."

"I believe that Josh Rulander, Press Secretary to President Atlas, has pointed out that Gonzalez had an extensive criminal record back in Mexico, which once characterized him as a terrorist."

"Throughout history, Scott, there have been people with messages that are revolutionary and unpopular. It is very easy to categorize these people as dangerous threats to the social order. And in fact, Gonzalez is a threat, because he's shining a spotlight on the way our society treats those who are less than fortunate. To be honest, I found him to be a passionate and thoughtful young man."

"What do you think of the legislation apparently being drafted by the American Values Caucus, which we understand would make it mandatory for the President to deport the detainees in the camps?"

"Like you, we have not seen the bill yet. But we are prepared to fight it. And for the sake of Khaleem Atlas, I hope he is prepared to fight it as well."

"That sounds like a threat."

"It is reality, Scott." Jorge Mendoza smiled and leaned forward in his chair. "I don't know if you've seen his poll numbers lately, but a majority of Americans condemn the President for his inaction in this matter. And I can tell you this: Presidents have been brought down for less."

• • • • • • • • • • • • • • • • • • •

Vice President Bassen Hospitalized with Chest Pains
Currently in ICU at Walter Reed
By Kenneth Jablonski, National Editor
September 30: Special to The Washington Post

Vice President Curtis Bassen was admitted to the Intensive Care Unit at Walter Reed Army Medical Center last night after suffering from chest pains.

The Vice President, 69, began complaining of discomfort in his chest shortly after dinner. Around 8:00 p.m. he was transported to the hospital and placed in the ICU in what officials describe as a "precaution." As we went to press, details of his condition had not yet been released.

"With a cardiac patient, it's not unusual to be put into intensive care until all tests are run and the symptoms are sorted out," said the Vice President's personal physician. "The fact that he's in the ICU doesn't necessarily mean that he has suffered a heart attack, but simply that we're acting with an abundance of caution. We'll have further information for you sometime tomorrow, after we get the results of the tests."

Bassen has a history of heart problems, but his condition was brought under control years ago by medication, and he has not experienced any problems for several decades. According to his doctors, the general state of his health is excellent.

In the absence of concrete information, commentators are speculating as to the possible cause of Bassen's sudden health issues. Some believe that his current condition may be related to the recent assassination attempt on his eldest son. Curtis Bassen. Jr., who works as a federal prosecutor in Ohio, was the target of an attack several weeks ago by a lone gunman. He suffered a gunshot wound to the leg and is recovering quickly, but sources close to the administration reveal that the incident placed a great deal of stress on the Vice President, who is exceptionally close to his children.

The White House briefing room was dark last night, and the administration has had no comment on the situation thus far. Bassen's team of doctors are scheduled to hold a press conference this afternoon, and hopefully will have more information on his prognosis at that time.

Chapter 34

"Give it to me straight," said Khaleem Atalas, closing his eyes and leaning back in the chair he brought with him from suburban Philadelphia to the White House.

"Okay," replied Joel Gottbaum. "You're in deep shit."

The President opened his eyes.

"Care to elaborate?"

"The natives are getting restless up on the Hill. I spoke to Eddie Lupin yesterday."

"Hell, I wasn't aware he even took your calls."

"He's a nice enough guy, but he can't control his caucus anymore."

"When did he ever?"

"This is different. The right-wing whack jobs are calling the tune up there, and the rank and file is constantly looking over their shoulders. These guys are watching every vote. They're terrified that some Tea Party bozo is going to challenge them in a primary, and they'll lose their seat."

"So I gather the bill is going to pass?"

"For starters, that's what I'm telling you."

"Do we know what's in it yet?"

"They're keeping it top secret, but it should be released in a day or two. According to Lupin, it's short and sweet—the immigrants are in violation of the law, and it's your responsibility to deport them."

"Can we litigate it? Have you talked to Gilliam?"

"I have, yes. He hasn't seen the bill either, but he did say that it was black letter law and the detainees were on the wrong side of it. Obviously the four conservative Justices would uphold it, but he's not sure one way or the other how he'd vote."

"What about the issue of due process?"

"The text of the Constitution is split on that, as I don't have to tell you. It's not certain how they'd choose to interpret it. But that's a long way off—we'd have to file suit, and the case would have to work its way through the system. Even if it were fast-tracked, it would still take a couple of months."

"Well, that would buy us some time."

"Maybe, maybe not. I'm sure the bill would be filled with timetables and deadlines."

"The deadlines would have to wait until we had our day in court. But from what you're saying, I gather I don't have a great chance if it goes up to the Supremes."

"I'd say it's fifty-fifty. But remember at least half the public is convinced that you've stalled around on this, and for all the wrong reasons—because you're in debt to the Hispanic lobby, because you want the immigrants naturalized so they can vote Democratic, or even worse, because you can't make a decision. On top of that, you seem to be forgetting that we have nearly 100,000 immigrants detained at the border, in facilities that the public believes are concentration camps."

"Do you have any suggestions?"

"If it were me, I'd deport the detainees who have criminal records. That would at least calm things down a bit. It would improve conditions in the camps, and it would be a move that would be hard for any reasonable person to argue with."

"Criollos Unidos would go beserk."

"Let them go beserk. You could still say that you support due process, but you're removing the criminal element for the sake of the others."

"I'm not going to do that—certainly not until the immigrants have their hearings, and we can determine whether or not they're qualified for asylum."

"May I ask what's taking so long? Because speeding up the hearings would be enormously helpful. I really thought that putting the military guys on it would accelerate the progress."

"I thought so too, but it's a mess. Every hearing takes forever. The detainees all need interpreters, for one thing. And if they're making a claim for asylum, which many of them are at this point, they have to give a detailed statement about the threats they'd face if they were sent back. And then we have to send investigators down there to check the statements out. It goes on and on."

"I have to warn you, they're talking impeachment in the House. And Lupin says these guys have constituencies at home that would love them for it."

"I don't think they have the guts."

"Do you really want to take the chance and find out?"

"All right." The President rubbed his forehead. "I'll have Justice look at the bill when it comes out, and they can advise me on whether we can fight it in the courts. If they agree with you that it's fifty-fifty, I'm going to go ahead and do it. An extra two or three months would give us the time to resolve this, regardless of what the Supremes say."

"Don't worry about the Supreme Court," said Gottbaum. "Worry about the court of public opinion."

• • • • • • • • • • • • • • • • • • • •

House Resolution 42—known as the Repatriation Act, or more popularly as the Deportation Act—passed by a margin of 265-170 on the day the total number of detained immigrants officially exceeded 100,000.

H. Res. 42

In the U.S. Congress, House of Representatives

The House finds and declares the following facts:

As of this date, there are approximately 100,000 immigrants housed in temporary structures on the U.S.-Mexican border. These individuals entered the United States illegally, and they remain in violation of this country's immigration statutes. A number of them have criminal records, and some of them may pose a terrorist threat which has not been adequately assessed.

The Fourteenth Amendment to the Constitution guarantees the right of due process to all citizens "born or naturalized in the United States," and excludes by omission those who have violated U.S. law by intentionally coming to this country without documentation.

We therefore establish the following provisions, to be known in the aggregate as the Repatriation Act:

The detainees currently held along our border with Mexico are to be deported as soon as possible and returned to their country of origin.

It is the immediate duty of the Attorney General, as the chief law enforcement officer of our nation, to ensure that the deportations begin in a timely manner.

It is the ultimate responsibility of the President, as our nation's chief executive, to verify that the deportations take place without any delay, whether that delay be administrative, procedural, or legal.

This act, when passed, shall become the law of the land in this matter, and the President shall be accountable to the House for its implementation.

Should any delay occur in the deportations, the House shall regard it as a dangerous and wanton disregard of the law, and this body will take all necessary steps to safeguard the nation's security.

Later that week, the bill passed the Senate by a vote of 58-42, with nine Democrats ignoring the President's lobbying efforts and voting for the legislation.

•••••••••••••••••••

Vice President Bassen Suffered Mild Heart Attack
Will Remain in Hospital at Least Another Week
By Kenneth Jablonski, National Editor
October: Special to The Washington Post

Vice President Curtis Bassen has suffered a mild heart attack, and will remain at Walter Reed Army Medical Center for at least one more week while his doctors decide on a course of treatment and rehabilitation.

"Tests have shown that the Vice President suffered a minor cardiac event," said Dr. David Connelly, Bassen's personal physician. "This was essentially a flare-up and extension of the heart problems he had several decades ago. He'll be kept in ICU for a few more days while we monitor his condition, then moved to a regular hospital bed. His overall health is very strong, and we anticipate a complete recovery."

Connelly said that Bassen had been treated for symptoms of heart disease earlier in his career, and that the condition had been brought under control with medication. He refused to speculate about whether his current heart attack had been brought on by the stress of a recent assassination attempt on his son, Curtis Jr., who works as a federal prosecutor in Ohio.

When asked if his health problems would prevent Bassen from serving out his term as Vice President, Connelly said:

"Certainly not. We anticipate a full and complete recovery, and in fact the Vice President will be placed on an exercise regimen by the end of the week. As I stated, this was a minor event, and in no way would be impediment to his remaining in office if he chooses to do so."

Bassen was rushed to Walter Reed Army Medical Center several days ago after complaining of chest pains. He has been attended by a team of cardiac specialists who performed a battery of tests, the results of which were made public today. The White House has been closely monitoring his condition and announced that President Atalas planned to visit the Vice President once he is moved to a regular hospital room several days from now.

"Our thoughts and our prayers are with Curt as he recovers from this minor setback, as we know he will," said the President in a prepared statement. "I have no doubt that he will achieve a complete recovery very quickly, and I look forward to beating him on the golf course again soon."

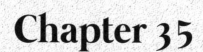

Chapter 35

"Thanks for coming, Dick." Khaleem Atalas sat down at his desk across from Richard Donovan, the United States Solicitor General.

"It's been quite a while since I've been here, sir."

"Since I nominated you, I believe. But we've talked on the phone a number of times."

"A few times, yes."

"Feeling neglected?" The President grinned. "Talk to my wife before you leave. The two of you can commiserate."

"I assume I'm here to discuss the case against the Deportation Act."

"Of course. Although it may be obvious, I want to make sure you understand how important this is."

"Go ahead, sir."

"This one's for all the marbles, Dick. What's at stake here is the power of the President to make crucial decisions on policy without meddling by the Congress. If this meddling is allowed to stand, it will have serious consequences for my successors in years to come."

"The constitutional issues aren't completely clear, as I'm sure you're aware."

"They're crystal clear to me. That's why I want you on this case all the way through, particularly if it goes to the Supreme Court."

"I'm not sure it will, sir."

"Well, run down the situation for me."

"This will be a short process, both because of the high profile of the case and also due to the urgency of the situation. We start out in the U.S. District Court for the District of Columbia, which is where you might catch a break—the justices are weighted on the liberal end of the spectrum and may see things your way, although that's not guaranteed. From there, whoever loses goes to the U.S. Federal Court of Appeals, and then to the Supreme Court, if they agree to hear it."

"I know all that. I'm looking for a reading on our chances."

"It's hard to say, sir. Certainly, if you do catch an early break that gets upheld on appeal, you're well on your way to dispelling any political problems you might have. But I'm not certain the Supreme Court will want to get involved in this. It's a no-win situation for them."

"Is there any way to rename this? Calling it *Khaleem Atlas vs. The Congress of the United States* sounds a bit too drastic."

"Well, there's no getting around the fact that it's drastic. At the very least, the folks on the Hill will see it as a turf war, and also as a war they don't want to lose."

"Do you think I have a shot of winning this thing?"

"I honestly don't know—the precedents are pretty evenly split. Congress does have the right to pass laws, after all, and you have the responsibility to steer the ship of state. So I think it totally depends on who they retain to argue the other side, not to mention the temperament of the judges who hear the case."

"Spoken like a true lawyer." Atlas paused. "Well, I'm going to leave this in your capable hands, and I know there's nobody better. I'm sure you'll do fine."

"I'll do my best, Mr. President."

"I'm counting on you."

• • • • • • • • • • • • • • • • • • •

After the President's ceremonial entrance to Walter Reid, and after the obligatory picture-taking sessions with the doctors and nursing staff, the two men were alone in Curt Bassen's hospital room.

"How're you doing, Curt?" asked Atalas after the door was closed.

"Not too bad for an old white guy. I never felt badly, to tell you the truth."

The President grinned. "Well, two things you can be sure of when they put you in Walter Reed: lousy food and ugly nurses."

"You got that right."

"From everything they tell me, this was a very minor event. I believe you should be released in another week."

"That would be great."

"Knowing you, I'm sure you can't wait to get back to work, but I want you to take it easy for a while. In fact, I'd like to see you take a brief vacation before you come back full time. Go someplace warm, drink pina coladas in the sunshine."

"Khaleem, I have to be honest with you. I won't be coming back."

There was a long pause.

"Come on, now," said Atalas finally. "You've had a rough time, first with your son and now this. I understand how you might feel at this point, but this isn't the time to be making snap decisions."

"It's not a snap decision. I've had the time to think, and I've considered this from every angle. I know you'll be disappointed, but I'm done. No one is sorrier than me to disappoint you, but I'm going to step down."

"Curt, look—"

"I'm almost seventy years old, Khaleem. I want to spend the time I have left with my family. I don't expect you to understand this. You're still a young man. But I've been in this game for thirty-five years, and it's time to get out."

"Step back a moment, if you can. Don't you think the attack on Curt Jr. has magnified the situation for you?"

"Yes and no. Don't misunderstand me, I'm not quitting immediately. I know you'll need some time to figure out a strategy going forward. You'll need to pick the right guy, and he'll have to be someone the Senate can confirm. I'd like to be out by the end of the year, possibly early next year, but I'll make sure you have a smooth transition."

"I understand completely how you feel. That's why we should have this conversation again in a couple of weeks."

"We can have it again anytime you want, but my mind is made up. I want to go back home. I want to spend some time with my grandchildren. I want to work on my golf game, when the weather permits."

Atalas grinned. "It won't help."

"Probably not. But I want you to know I'm serious."

"I know you're serious, because you're calling me Khaleem." The President stretched his legs. "And I appreciate what you're telling me. But please do me a favor and wait until you get out of here to finalize your decision."

"This is between you, me and my wife. And we'll talk again when I get out, and you can make the announcement when you feel comfortable. But you've got some tough days ahead, and you should have someone around who who's younger and in fighting trim."

"If you're talking about the detainees, I'm not worried. I can handle that situation."

"It's not just the detainees, although public opinion is turning on that issue, as you know. The midterms are coming up next year. The way it looks now, Democrats will get slaughtered. We'll end up with even bigger Republican majorities in both houses."

"I'm not convinced it'll go that way."

"The polling says it will. My guess is that you're not being overwhelmed by requests to campaign for the incumbents, are you?"

"Well," said the President, "no one's asking me to stump in Texas or southern California, no."

"Whether you do or not, you'll take the blame if it turns into a bloodbath."

"You know," mused Atalas, "you were my first pick. No one else even came close. Remember when it leaked to the press that I had asked you if you wanted to be on the ticket, or if you'd rather be Secretary of State if I won? Bethany Hampton went batshit."

"I'm glad I did it."

"You've done a hell of a job, and I think you still have some fighting days left."

"Thank you, Khaleem." Bassen smiled weakly. "But my time is over."

• • • • • • • • • • • • • • • • • • •

"Good morning, and welcome to Meet the Press. I'm Chuck Todd. My guest this morning is Representative Jeffrey Barrett, Republican of Texas. Congressman Barrett is chairman of the American Values Caucus, a group of 53 Congressmen devoted to advancing conservative causes. He is also the sponsor of House Resolution 42, known as the Repatriation Act—

or more popularly, as the Deportation Act. Congressman, welcome to Meet the Press."

"Thank you, Chuck. Good to be here."

"Why don't you begin by sketching out the intent of this legislation and give us some idea of how it originated."

"It's pretty simple stuff, Chuck. On one hand, we've got 100,000 illegal immigrants warehoused on the Mexican border. On the other, we've got a President who refuses to do anything about it. So a bunch of us were sitting around one day, reading the U.S. Constitution, and we realized we needed to act on this. Somebody's got to be the responsible adults here, and we think it's us."

"As I'm sure you know, President Atalas feels that the detainees are entitled to due process before they're deported. He believes there may be a number of legitimate asylum seekers in the group, people who would be in danger if they were returned to Mexico, and he wants to make sure those people are protected."

"We have a term for that where I come from, Chuck, but I can't say it on the air. As I see it, most of these folks didn't come here seeking asylum. Here's my thought process on that: they snuck across the border illegally, and they didn't head for the nearest immigration office to apply for asylum. If they hadn't been caught, they would have faded into the woodwork like the other 12 million illegals."

"Isn't it true that they were apprehended before they had a chance to do that?"

"Probably so, but here's what's also true: they are criminals who are in violation of the laws of the United States. And the 14th Amendment doesn't guarantee the right of due process to anyone other than an American citizen."

"I believe the 5th amendment is considerably more vague on that point."

"Maybe so. But I can tell you that I've been to those camps, Chuck, and the conditions are horrendous. You're talking about facilities that were built to house 8,000 or 10,000 people, and they're holding nearly 35,000 apiece. I wouldn't want to see my dog in a place like that. Now, I'm not familiar with the environment these folks came from, but I doubt that it was much worse than where they ended up."

"So you would have us believe that there's a humanitarian component to this on your end?"

"I wouldn't tell you what to believe. But this administration, don't forget, is supposed to be all about the rights of the downtrodden and the disenfranchised."

"You don't like the President much, do you?"

"Actually, Chuck, I have nothing against him on a personal level. Tell you the truth, I find him very charming. But we're not talking about personalities here. He was elected to enforce the Constitution, and quite honestly, he's failed to do that. He was elected to lead, and a lot of us can't see where he's even begun that task. Under those circumstances, someone has to take up the slack."

"Tell us a little bit about the American Values Caucus, for the benefit of those viewers who aren't familiar with it."

"Our group was formed with an eye toward having a true conservative voice in the House of Representatives. For many of us, you know, the Republican Party is the home team, and it's the only team we've got. But the way we see it, the recent Republican standard-bearers for President haven't been true conservatives. They've been more like Democrat Lite. So what we do is provide a voice for the causes we believe in: fiscal responsibility, personal responsibility, limited government, sanctity of life, and the rights of states to govern themselves. Because if we don't do it, it looks to us like nobody else will."

"How many Congressmen caucus with you?"

"There are 53 of us at the present time."

"Some commentators have noted that a majority of your caucus voted against the Restoration of Democracy Act, the bill that overturned the provisions of the Supreme Court decision in *Democracy Unchained*. Do you think their votes were influenced by large campaign contributions they might have received?"

"We urge everyone to vote their conscience, Chuck. But if we're gonna be honest, I think we have to admit that there were excesses on both sides following that decision."

"Congressman Barrett, where do we go from here? Your bill demanded immediate action by the executive branch, and it also excluded any legal delays. And, of course, you're aware that President Atalas has directed the Solicitor General to file a lawsuit in U.S. District Court challenging the legality of your bill. Are we heading for a confrontation, sir?"

"We see no problem with the President having his day in court, provided it doesn't drag on for months while the number of detainees increases, and while their living conditions continue to deteriorate. So if we can get a quick resolution to this from the judiciary, all well and good. But I do need to remind you that until we hear otherwise, the Repatriation Act is black-letter law."

"The reason I asked you that question, Congressman Barrett, is that there have been rumors swirling around this city for the past week or two about impeachment. Would you care to address that?"

"As I said at the beginning, Chuck, this is a pretty simple situation. This piece of legislation passed both the House and the Senate. It's now the law of the land, and we expect the President to enforce that law. I believe I also said that he's entitled to his day in court, and he is—provided that he's not just stalling us. I happen to think the judicial branch will see this our way. But we're not going to sit around and watch another 100,000 immigrants get stacked up on the border."

"So what's the answer to my question? Are some of your fellow members talking impeachment?"

"As a last resort, yes, we're prepared to go that route. If Khaleem Atalas won't enforce the laws of this country, there will be serious consequences."

Chapter 36

J orge Mendoza walked into the Starbucks in Lorton, Virginia, and glanced around the room. He walked over to the corner table, where a slim man in a dark blue suit fiddled with his cell phone.

"Is this seat taken?"

"I was saving it for César Chávez." Kevin Lapham looked up at him. "But you're welcome to keep it warm until he gets here."

"A fucking comedian," said Mendoza, pulling up a chair across from him. "Who would have thought?"

"How'd you know it was me?"

"I saw the limo parked outside, so I figured you were here. And I recognized you from a picture I saw in some Neo-Nazi magazine."

"Okay, we're even. Thanks for coming."

"No problem. I always drive twenty miles out to the boondocks to get myself a cappuccino. The journey clears my head."

"I figured that neither of us needed to be seen in public with each other. My instinct was it wouldn't play well with our respective constituencies."

"I suspect you're right. So tell me, Mr. Lapham, what have I done to deserve this audience? Have the Haft brothers decided to donate a billion dollars to Criollos Unidos?"

"We have some areas of mutual interest. I think we might be able to come to an accommodation."

"I'm listening."

"You've been quite outspoken recently in your criticism of Khaleem Atalas."

"I think he's a great man. If he wasn't holding a hundred thousand of my people in concentration camps along the Mexican border, I'd nominate him for the Nobel Peace Prize."

"As you can imagine, my employers share your disgust for the President. Although their specific reasons are different, of course."

"To be honest, he double-crossed us. And I do not like to be double-crossed."

"I think you're a man of principle, even though I may not agree with many of your convictions. And as I said, we're not fans of Atalas either. The only difference is that we haven't been surprised at the way things turned out."

"Before we join hands and start singing kumbaya, why don't you tell me why you dragged me down here?"

"I could have sworn you came of your own free will."

"I have to admit, I was curious."

"As I said, we find ourselves on the same side of this problem, but for different reasons. I was thinking there might be some way we could work together."

"What did you have in mind?"

"You are a respected national figure within your community—a community that carries considerable political weight, as you're fond of pointing out. Listening to you lately, I have the distinct impression that you would like to see Atalas out of the picture."

"I wouldn't be heartbroken at this point, no."

"Neither would we, obviously. So let's speculate a bit here. You know there are some elements in the House, particularly within the American Values Caucus, who are lobbying behind the scenes for impeachment."

"I've heard the rumors."

"Imagine what the repercussions might be if a prominent figure such as yourself aligned with them. It would have enormous impact. It would go way beyond a former ally and supporter calling for the President's removal—many people would see it as the canary dying in the coal mine."

"Hmm." Mendoza chuckled. "This is rich."

"What's so funny?"

"The concept of someone like me working with the American Values Caucus to oust the President. I agree that it would have a large impact, but you have to admit the thought is amusing."

"Perhaps, but unlikely coalitions happen all the time in politics."

"You know, I'm not sure if we'd be better off with Curt Bassen. He's more likeable on a personal level, but all these politicians are weasels."

"Don't worry about Bassen. If you read the newspapers, you're aware he isn't doing well."

"I know the man. The only way he leaves the White House is in a box."

"I'm not so sure that I agree with you. But even if he does take over, which I doubt, he would be free to be his own man. Whoever moves into the big chair is likely to feel empowered—although, if you remember the 22nd amendment, he wouldn't be eligible to run more than once, since he'd take over with more than two years left in the term."

"You guys think of all the angles, don't you?"

"Yes." Lapham stirred his coffee. "That's what we do."

"So tell me, Mr. Lapham: what's in it for us? Campaigns like these aren't cheap. It would involve a great deal of outreach, many pieces of direct mail, lots of polling."

"We'd be pleased to make a donation. Not a billion dollars, certainly, but I'm sure we could work out a reasonable figure. It goes without saying that any amount we might give would be anonymous."

"And beyond that, what's in it for me?"

"We'd also be willing to make a contribution to your future financial security."

"There'd be hell to pay if this got out."

"In your case, we're talking about depositing the funds in an offshore account that would be untraceable. We've done this before, and we're not amateurs."

"Well, well. Perhaps it was worth driving out to the boondocks after all."

"Give it some thought, Mr. Mendoza." He scribbled something on a piece of paper and handed it over. "Give me a call when you're ready to discuss the parameters of the situation. This is my secure line."

"You've given me a great deal to think about." He rose and extended his hand. "Maybe we can work together after all. Stranger things have happened."

"True," said Lapham. "Remember, the enemy of my enemy is my friend."

• • • • • • • • • • • • • • • • • • •

Vice President Bassen Released From Hospital
Will Work Part-Time Until Fully Recovered
By Kenneth Jablonski, National Editor
October 13: Special to The Washington Post

Vice President Curtis Bassen was released from Walter Reed Army Medical Center yesterday, after a ten-day stay caused by what doctors described as a mild heart attack.

"I'm feeling terrific," said a smiling Bassen as he was wheeled to his limousine by a team of nurses. "Ready to get back to work, but I might take some time to run a marathon first."

Bassen was admitted to Walter Reed on October 2 after complaining of chest pains. He was kept in intensive care for several days while doctors performed an exhaustive battery of tests. They eventually determined that the Vice President had suffered a mild heart attack.

Bassen, 69, has had heart problems for most of his adult life. His cardiac issues first surfaced nearly 25 years ago when he was in the Senate. However, his condition was brought under control by diet and medication, and he has had no recurring difficulties until recently.

Some observers have speculated that Bassen's condition was brought on by the stress of recent events. Shortly after Labor Day, his oldest son was attacked by a gunman as he left the Federal Courthouse in Dayton, where he works as a prosecutor. Curtis Jr. received a gunshot wound to the leg and recovered easily, but insiders say the attack took its toll on the Vice President.

"The Vice President suffered a minor cardiac event," said Dr. David Connelly, Bassen's personal physician. "However, we took it very seriously, as we would with all heart problems. His overall health is excellent, and we have no doubt he will make a rapid and complete recovery, although he's been advised to maintain a light work schedule for the next month or so."

Keeping the Vice President to that light schedule may turn out to be a task in itself. He is known to be a tireless worker who regularly puts in 70 to 80 hours in a typical week, according to aides. Members of his senior staff, some of whom are half his age, reportedly have difficulty keeping up with him.

Later in the day the Vice President made a visit to the White House, an appearance that was largely symbolic and ceremonial. He was greeted on the portico by President Khaleem Atalas, and the two men conferred privately for close to an hour.

"I'm delighted to see the Vice President up and about," said Atalas later, as the two men posed for a photo session. "I'm also pleased to welcome him back to work. I told him to take some time to relax with his family on a brief vacation, and I expect that he'll be returning to his old self very shortly."

From a political perspective, the Vice President's health issues come at a difficult time for the administration. President Atalas has been plagued by controversy for the past six months over the refugee crisis on the Mexican border. In the wake of the Repatriation Act recently passed by Congress, the President has filed suit in federal court to nullify the legislation. Many pollsters are reporting a sharp drop in the President's approval numbers, and it is generally believed that the Democrats will incur even further losses in next year's midterm elections if the immigrant crisis is not resolved quickly.

Chapter 37

D.C. District Court Rules Against
Atalas On Repatriation Act
President Vows Swift Appeal
By Kenneth Jablonski, National Editor
October 20: Special to The Washington Post

In an apparent effort to curb the powers of the executive branch, the U.S. District Court for the District of Columbia has ruled against the Atalas administration in the matter of the Repatriation Act.

The case, formally titled Atalas vs. Congress of the United States, was filed three weeks ago in response to legislation that mandated the deportation of refugees currently housed on the Mexican border. President Atalas has maintained that the detainees, who are immigrants arrested while crossing the border illegally, are entitled to due process under the Constitution. The lawsuit petitioned the court to nullify the Repatriation Act and grant the President executive authority to deal with the refugee crisis.

"This court is disturbed and alarmed at the excesses of executive power assumed by the administration in this case," said Clyde Davis, Chief Judge of the D.C. District Court. "We would remind them that the three branches of government are explicitly recognized as equals under the Constitution, and that no one branch has pre-emptive authority over the other two. The request by the President to nullify the Repatriation Act flies in the face of several centuries of precedent, all of which recognizes the responsibility of Congress to draft and pass legislation in the national interest."

Davis was appointed during the administration of President William Hampton and presides over a court known to lean toward the liberal end of the spectrum. The conventional wisdom among Washington insiders is that Davis would support the administration's claims for authority in this matter.

"The court takes note of the administration's argument that the detainees are entitled to due process," he wrote. "We recognize that while the Fourteenth Amendment guarantees this right to all U.S. citizens, the Fifth amendment implies that persons other than citizens qualify for protection. The court also asserts that the immigrants currently being held on the border came to this country in violation of our immigration laws. They are not being detained while waiting for their day in court, but rather because no one in authority has seemed to know what to do with them. In passing House Resolution 42, both houses of Congress acted decisively to resolve this situation and enforce the law. The President must now follow their lead.

"We further note that despite the administration's repeated claims that the immigrants are entitled to due process, very little progress has been made toward that goal. From our point of view, the Atalas administration is actually in violation of the Sixth Amendment, which guarantees the right to a fair and speedy trial. Under these circumstances and given the fact that no one disputes the violation of the law by the detained immigrants, we find that the Repatriation Act should be upheld and enforced without delay."

Current estimates on the number of immigrants detained at the three makeshift camps along the Mexican border range from 108,000 to 116,000. Living conditions have improved slightly *due to the construction of temporary housing by the U.S. Army Corps of Engineers, and the camps are patrolled by troops of the National Guard. However, tensions are still high—particularly at the Brownsville camp, home to an inmate group named "La Lucha," or The Struggle.*

During yesterday afternoon's press briefing, White House Press Secretary Josh Rulander was asked about the court's ruling and the President's reaction.

"He's disappointed, obviously," said Rulander, "and he believes the ruling to be incorrect. The President plans a swift appeal to the federal appeals court. He rejects the view that this issue is a matter of political expediency, and instead feels that we have a moral obligation to safeguard the rights of these immigrants. He is convinced that the legal process will ultimately agree with him, and he believes that future generations will view his position as compassionate and correct."

Around the city, there were some observers who did not share the administration's optimistic view of the situation.

"As I have maintained from the beginning, the refugee crisis is a disgrace," said Jorge Mendoza, head of Criollos Unidos, the nation's largest organization dedicated to safeguarding the rights of Hispanics. "Over 100,000 people are being cooped up like animals while the authorities argue over the right course of action. I call upon President Atalas to fulfill his oath of office and be the President of all the people, not just Caucasians. I also call upon the 55 million Hispanics and Latinos in this country, many of whom are citizens and have the right to vote, to determine in their hearts whether this man is truly fit to hold the highest office of the land."

• • • • • • • • • • • • • • • • • • • •

"So much for having a liberal-leaning court," said Khaleem Atalas with disgust, tossing *The Washington Post* on his desk in the Oval Office.

"I really expected better from Davis," said Curt Bassen. "But you know, it's been nearly twenty years since he was nominated. Sometimes these guys evolve on the bench."

"Tell me about it. Hopefully he's not expecting a promotion anytime soon."

"So where do we go from here?"

"The D.C. Federal Appeals Court. Dick Donovan is filing the papers now."

"What can we expect?"

"Hard to say—it all depends on the three judges we draw on the panel. It's a crapshoot. Let's keep our fingers crossed, because we'd be much better off settling this before it goes to the Supremes."

"If the D.C. appellate court sustains the ruling, you think the Supremes will hear the case?"

"It looks iffy, to tell you the truth. Gottbaum says he talked to Paul Gilliam, and Gilliam seems to have pretty much the same opinion as Davis. We don't have to wonder where the four conservative Justices would stand on this, but Gilliam would be the swing vote. And he's evidently shaky."

"That's not good."

"Gottbaum thinks they'll probably want to duck the issue altogether. Ever since the *Democracy Unchained* case, Gilliam is nervous about getting the Court involved in politics."

"So let's assume Davis's ruling gets upheld. What are you going to do?"

"Well, I'm not going to deport 100,000 immigrants before I know how many are qualified for asylum—I can tell you that much. But even if we lose, I won't have to deal with the situation until sometime around mid-November. At that point, if I have to, I'll drop the bomb."

"You're still considering the nuclear option?"

"If I have to, yes. Then a week or two after that, we can announce your retirement, if you're still serious."

Bassen grinned. "This almost sounds exciting enough to get me to reconsider. But to be honest, I just don't think I can stay on, regardless of how bad I feel about letting you down."

"Curt, you don't have anything to apologize for. You fought the good fight, and I'm grateful for the past five years." He smiled. "That doesn't mean I won't keep trying to talk you out of it, though."

"I appreciate it."

"What are you hearing from the political shop? How bad is it?"

"Pretty bad." Bassen shook his head. "Public sentiment is running strongly against you on the immigration issue. The Republicans smell blood in the water."

"Foolish me, wanting to give these folks their day in court. I guess we've arrived at the point in history where it's guilty until proven innocent."

"Jorge Mendoza is making some very ominous noises. If you didn't see his *60 Minutes* interview, I'll make sure you get a clip of it. It sounds like he's been approached by the American Values Caucus in the House, and they're trying to get him to support impeachment."

"That's not a reasonable scenario. Jorge knows we're the only game in town."

"Maybe, maybe not. When everything hits the fan, it's hard to predict what someone else knows."

"Can we talk to him? Appeal to his more practical nature?"

"I can try, but my understanding is that he's pretty pissed off."

"You know," mused the President, "at times like this, I think about something Lyndon Johnson once said."

"What's that?"

"Supposedly he looked at an aide one day and said, 'If I were to get up right now and walk on water across the Potomac River, the headlines in the afternoon papers would read: President Can't Swim.'"

Chapter 38

Richard Donovan had argued dozens of cases before the D.C. Circuit Court—or the U.S. Court of Appeals for the District of Columbia Circuit, as it was formally known. He had served on a Bar Association committee with Jefferson Osborne, the Chief Justice, who sat directly across from him today. He had also played golf with Lester Shapiro, one of the two Associate Justices on the three-judge panel hearing the appeal of *Khaleem Atalas vs. The Congress of the United States.*

But he had never encountered the type of behavior he was seeing this morning, either in or out of a courtroom. Osborne was scowling at him, as though Donovan had offered him a platter of week-old sushi. Shapiro drummed his fingers impatiently on the oak panel of the bench. Leslie McIntosh, the third judge, stared absently around the room, as if waiting for a bus that just wouldn't arrive.

"Your Honor, if I may add—"

"You may not," interrupted Osborne. "I think we've heard more than enough information to render a decision, and that decision is both clear and unanimous. But first, for the record, I want to express my disappointment with the government's conduct in this case. When I read the moving papers beforehand, I found it hard to believe the basis for the administration's objection to the legislation. I assumed there had to be more to their position than the mere fact that they disagreed with the provisions of the law, or that they simply didn't like it. I naïvely assumed that some rational argument about the constitutionality of the law would emerge, and I certainly never thought that their entire case would be based on the fact that they had a vague moral qualm about the legislation. Had I known what was to come, I never would have agreed to hear this case.

"I find the President's position here to be objectionable. As both a lawyer and a constitutional scholar, he should have known better than to waste our time and the taxpayer's resources with a case like this. There has been no convincing proof offered that the law in question violates the Constitution—in fact, there has been no evidence offered of any sort. While the President is correct that everyone in this country is entitled to due process, whether they are a citizen or not, he has made no apparent effort to guarantee the immigrants that right. As we sit here today, there are human beings who have been languishing in substandard conditions for most of this year, while the administration has done nothing to expedite hearings for them. As far as we can tell, the legitimate asylum seekers have not been distinguished from the hardened criminals. Under any sane and rational system of government, these individuals should have been turned back at the border if they failed to present a valid claim for asylum. This court has no idea why they have been imprisoned without the protections to which the President feels they are entitled, nor why the administration has not been more diligent in seeking a solution. On top of that, there is no reason to assume that a solution is even being contemplated, if the administration were to prevail here."

"Your Honor, if I may?"

"Go ahead."

"The administration's position here is very far from frivolous. We suspect that outside interference was a major factor in the involvement of the vigilantes on the border, and that this situation would never have occurred without them."

"If you're referring to the Angels of Democracy, no evidence has been offered, by you or anyone else. that they have done anything illegal."

"Even so—"

"Let me give you a hypothetical," said Osborne. "Say I die a wealthy man. This is an unlikely outcome, but let's assume it for a moment. I will my fortune to the local Boy Scout troop, with the proviso that they assist law enforcement as monitors at pedestrian intersections, where motorists are ignoring traffic signals. One year later, there are far fewer traffic infractions, and many citizens with multiple tickets. Those citizens are outraged, but the Boy Scouts are hardly to blame. They are not making the law, but rather helping to enforce it. The actions that were illegal prior to the enhanced enforcement are just as illegal in the present.

"The immigrants on the border are in violation of the law, and the administration has done nothing to help them. I strongly suspect that your assumption about outside interference is correct, but it's strange that no fingers are being pointed at the culprits. Given that the government has the full assets of the intelligence community at their disposal, it's reasonable to expect that you'd have some proof."

"We contend," said Donovan, "that there is a moral obligation to keep the immigrants on the border—in better conditions, certainly—until the government can determine who is entitled to asylum. Sending everyone back at once would likely result in a death sentence for some."

"Nonetheless, the law is the law, and the immigrants are in violation of it. The Repatriation Act is nothing more than a demand that the administration live up to its oath and its responsibilities. This court rejects the plaintiff's application, and we hold unanimously that the lower court ruling will stand."

"Your Honor—"

"And for the record, Mr. Donovan, we recognize that you are in a difficult position. Whether or not you agree with your client in this case, you have defended them with admirable zeal. You are, of course, free to appeal to the Supreme Court, but I cannot imagine that they would entertain hearing this case."

• • • • • • • • • • • • • • • • • • •

The buzzer sounded on Richard Haft's desk console.

"Yes?"

"Kevin Lapham on the secure line for you, sir."

"Thank you." He picked up the red phone. "Morning, Kevin. How are things in the belly of the beast?"

"I have an update for you."

"I'm all ears."

"We're locked and loaded. Everything is in place and going according to plan. We're just waiting for Bassen to resign."

"Good job. As soon as he quits, you can turn Jorge Mendoza loose."

"Will do."

"But not before. Is that understood?"

"Yes, sir."

"Timing is everything—this is a very delicate operation. We don't want any more screwups on the order of the Mexican restaurant. If anything goes wrong, there'll be hell to pay."

"Understood, sir. You can count on me."

"I'm not worried about you. I just don't want any of your colleagues to start feeling their oats and get carried away."

"Don't worry, everything is under control. There's no reason why anyone or anything should deviate from the plan." Lapham paused. "I should tell you that we have Eddie Lupin's medical records, just in case you ever need to release them."

"Absolutely not—under no circumstances. Is that clear?"

"Yes, sir."

"There's no need to subject him to that."

"I just wanted you to know that you had this ace in the hole."

"It's totally unnecessary," said Haft. "I've known Eddie for more than twenty years. Even if he wasn't sick, he wouldn't want to be president. Where are the records?"

"I have them in a vault."

"I'm going to hold you personally responsible for ensuring that they don't get out."

"Yes, sir. I've got this."

"Very good. Remember this: If everything does go according to plan, you're going to be a wealthy man."

• • • • • • • • • • • • • • • • • • • •

"I can't shake the feeling that I let you down, sir."

It was the day after the D.C. Circuit decision, and Richard Donovan sat in the Oval Office with Khaleem Atalas and Joel Gottbaum.

"Nonsense," said the President. "You did your best with a very weak case. Truth be known, we were just taking a shot."

"Even so—"

"Osborne was right." Atalas shook his head. "At the end of the day, all I have is an ethical objection to the Repatriation

Act. It's not as vague as he contends, but he's correct that it's moral rather than legal. I don't happen to believe that we should sentence the asylum seekers to death because the legal system has dragged its feet on the hearings."

"Is there any way we can accelerate them?"

"We've been trying all year," said Gottbaum. "The dockets are overloaded, and judges are overwhelmed with real criminals."

"What about retired judges, law professors, that sort of thing?"

"It wouldn't work," said Atalas. "Not on a wholesale basis, anyway. We'd be opening ourselves up to challenges and appeals from right-wing groups, and the whole thing would become even more of a nightmare than it is now." He looked at Donovan. "What's your sense of where we go from here? Is it even worth petitioning the Supremes on this?"

"It's bleak, sir. Osborne basically told me not to bother. I did reach out to Gilliam's office, and the reaction from Bindleman was lukewarm. It's a four-four split, as you know, and the Chief is extremely gun-shy about sticking his nose in politics ever since the *Democracy Unchained* case. Even if we got the four liberal Justices to agree to hear it, I don't think we could prevail."

"I understand. Still, I'd like you to go forward with the appeal."

"Are you sure about that, sir?"

"We have nothing to lose." Atalas shook his head. "Actually, that's not true. If we don't appeal to the Supremes, we give the appearance of not fully believing in our position, which is definitely not the case. So let's play this out, and let everybody declare themselves—both us and them."

"I'll get to work on it, sir. But it's going to take a while until we can get a resolution."

"That's fine." He rose and offered the Solicitor General his hand. "I appreciate all your efforts on this, Dick."

When Donovan left the room, the President leaned back in his chair, closed his eyes and pressed the fingers of his left hand to his temple.

"Well, Mr. Fixit?" He spoke without opening his eyes. "Any ideas?"

"You have to deport the immigrants."

"I won't do it."

"You have to," said Gottbaum. "The House Republicans will eat you alive. Send them back, and you can be full of moral outrage for the rest of your term. Maybe it even leads to meaningful immigration reform down the road."

"I'm not going do it, Joel."

"Somebody set you up. You were snookered. Now you're marching right into the center of the trap."

"What if they were Black, instead of Latino?"

"They're not Black. To be honest, it doesn't even matter. It's time to dial back your empathy and look at the big picture. When you sleep on it, you'll realize you have to send them back."

Chapter 39

On a cool, crisp day in early November, Khaleem Atalas and Curt Bassen approached the microphone in the Rose Garden.

"Good morning, everybody," said the President. "We both have statements for you today. I'm going to let Curt go first, after which I'll have something to add. In keeping with the seriousness of this occasion, we will not be taking any questions. Curt?"

"Thank you, Mr. President." Bassen squinted into the sun. He seemed to be looking at a distant point on the horizon, rather than at the assembled group of reporters and staffers. "Ladies and gentlemen. For nearly five years, I've been blessed with the honor to serve in this administration and give something back to my country. Of the many advantages I've had in life, one of the most significant has been the opportunity to work side by side with one of the greatest Presidents in modern history. It has been my good fortune to get to know him and to be able to call him a friend as well as a colleague, and I'm extremely proud of everything we've accomplished together.

"I've been faced with some challenges in recent months. I've had some family issues, which have been difficult but still surmountable—as many of you know, I've faced tragedies in my family before. However, my recent heart attack has made me acutely aware of my own mortality. Simply put, I'm not as young as I used to be, and I don't have the stamina I wish I had. I could certainly slow down a bit and continue to execute the responsibilities of my office at a more reasonable pace, as my doctors have advised me to do, but that would create an acute moral dilemma for me. I would not be performing at a peak level, which is what this office—and this country—is entitled to.

"Therefore, I have decided to step down as Vice President so that the work of the republic may be continued by someone younger and healthier than myself. I make this decision with both sorrow and regret, yet I am convinced that it is the right thing to do. I will work closely with the President and offer any assistance I can render in helping him select a replacement, and I will be available to provide advice and counsel to the man or woman who succeeds me.

"I could not possibly begin to thank everyone who participated in my extraordinary journey. I'm deeply indebted to my family, friends and colleagues, to the staffers who have worked so long and hard on my behalf, to the President and to the people of this great land. To anyone who is disappointed by my decision today, I say this: The republic will endure without me, just as it prospered before I came along. I look forward to watching its progress from my rocking chair."

He turned away from the microphone, and the two men embraced. After the back slapping, Atalas approached the podium with a sober expression.

"Thank you, Curt. As you can imagine, I'm more disappointed than anyone here today. Having Curt Bassen by my side has been one of the blessings of my presidency. I can't begin to express my gratitude for his help and his service to our nation. At the same time, I respect his decision and want the healthiest outcome for him." He flashed his trademark grin. "You better keep a phone near that rocking chair, because I'll be calling you frequently.

"In the weeks to come, I'll form an exploratory committee to assist me with the difficult task of replacing Curt Bassen. I'll quickly walk you through this process, since many of you weren't around the last time it happened, in 1973. According to the Twenty-fifth amendment to the Constitution, it's my responsibility to appoint a successor to fill the job of Vice President. That person will need to be approved by a majority vote of both the House and the Senate. As I have so many times in the past, I'm going to seek Curt's input on this decision and rely on his judgement to help me select the most qualified person to help carry on the work of this administration. There is no possible way that I could ever replace Curt Bassen, but I'm confident that we can find someone who will assist me in taking our mission the rest of the way. When history judges this administration, I'm confident it will rate Curt Bassen as an outstanding public servant, and an even greater man.

"Thank you."

As the two men turned away and walked under the portico toward the White House, the press shouted questions at their backs.

"Mr. President, will you deport the immigrants on the southern border?"

"What's the status of your appeal of the Repatriation Act to the Supreme Court?"

"Mr. President, Jorge Mendoza recently said that if the immigrants were White, their civil rights would have been protected. How do you feel about that?"

"This is just the damnedest thing I've ever seen," said Bull Caldwell, as he reached for another slice of pizza.

"That's the third time you've said that," said Chet Wallko. "Care to enlighten us as to the cause of your amazement?"

"I'm no fan of Khaleem Atalas, but he's not a stupid man. I have no idea of why he's doin' this to himself. For God's sake, the man taught Constitutional law—he knows damn well he can't reverse the Repatriation Act. Looks to me like he's spoilin' for a fight. It's like he wants to get himself impeached."

"I don't see the House voting impeachment," said Bob Insfield. "They know very well it doesn't go anywhere. He'll never get convicted in the Senate."

"Damn, you're naïve," said Caldwell. "It doesn't have to go anywhere. They got these cowboys over there in the House who are eatin' their Wheaties, guys like Barrett. And then you've got a whole bunch of spineless members who are catchin' hell from the folks back home. The redder the district, the more they want the President's ass on a platter. Gottbaum should know that."

"You just gave your own answer," said Carlton Bridges, the Senate's lone Independent. "It doesn't have to go anywhere. The guys from the redneck districts will make a statement, their constituents will be pacified, and they can get on with the daily process of doing nothing."

"And what about this whole business with Curt Bassen?" Caldwell looked like a toddler confronted with a complex puzzle he couldn't unravel. "That deal is stranger than strange. If it were me, God forbid, I'd lock Curt in the basement for the rest of the term and hire a body double to take his place."

Wallko laughed. "They've probably done that already."

"Don't joke, bubba," said Caldwell. "You may end up playing a bigger role in this than you want to."

"There's nothing to fear." Wallko stretched and looked at his watch. "He'll just appoint Marcus Kaplan as Vice President, and everybody will live happily ever after."

"Why the hell didn't he wait a few months to announce Bassen's retirement?"

"Probably because he doesn't want Curt dying on him," said Insfield. "He has enough problems as it is. Anyway, let's take Bull's hypothetical and kick it around. Say the House votes impeachment and dumps it into our laps. What happens then? You need a two-thirds majority to convict, which means you've got to get 18 Democrats to defect and vote against Atalas."

"It'll never happen," said Charles Moscone of Pennsylvania.

"The vote on the Repatriation Act was 58-42," said Wallko. "That means you had nine defections. Another nine is always possible."

"Chet's right," said Insfield. "You've got about 110,000 immigrants in these camps right now. Say it's a few months from now, and you're pushing 200,000. The inmates are rioting, they're dying like flies from a cholera epidemic, and the entire world is aghast. Do you stand by Atalas?"

There was silence as the group looked at Moscone.

"There you go," said Insfield after twenty seconds had passed. "He's from your state, and you can't even say you'd vote for him. What does that tell you?"

"It won't come to that," said Moscone.

Insfield gave him a broad smile. "Everybody loves a dreamer."

Chapter 40

*S**upreme Court Refuses to Hear Appeal of
Repatriation Act**
Lower Court Ruling Stands; President is Defiant
November 10: Special to The Washington Post
By Kenneth Jablonski, National Editor

*In a stunning rebuke to the limits of executive power, the
U.S. Supreme Court today declined to hear an appeal in the case of*
Atlas v. The Congress of the United States.

*Their refusal means that the lower court ruling will stand,
and the Repatriation Act is the law of the land. President Atlas
is legally obligated to begin deportations of the approximately
115,000 immigrants currently being detained in tent cities on the
U.S.-Mexican border.*

*In a terse statement, Chief Justice Paul Gilliam noted that
"The legislation is binding. According to the separation of powers
outlined in the Constitution, the administration has no standing
in this case. It is surprising to a majority of this court that the
appeals were even heard in the first place, and we will not pursue
this matter further."*

*It was widely expected that the Court would agree to review
the case and give a final ruling to settle the issue. Legal experts*

observe that four Justices are normally sufficient to hear an appeal, leading to speculation that the Court suspended their normal procedure and made their decision based on a majority vote.

No immediate reaction was forthcoming from the White House. At his daily briefing, Press Secretary Josh Rulander said: "The President is disappointed with the Court's lack of action, and he believes strongly that the Repatriation Act violates the constitutional rights of the immigrants currently detained on the border. He is consulting with his advisers on the best way forward."

Supporters of the Repatriation Act, on the other hand, were quick to make their feelings known.

"The legal charade is over," said Rep. Jeffrey Barrett (R-Texas), sponsor of the legislation and head of the American Values Caucus in the House. "It's now time for the President to stop stalling and obey the law, which is what he was elected to do."

"For the past six months, this country has witnessed a violation of civil rights on an unprecedented scale," said Jorge Mendoza, leader of Criollos Unidos, the nation's largest Hispanic advocacy group. "Khaleem Atalas has allowed more than 100,000 Latino immigrants to live in subhuman conditions, while voicing empty promises about due process. The legal system has now forced him to treat these immigrants as human beings."

The Supreme Court's refusal to hear the appeal brings to an end a month of legal wrangling between the President and the Congress, which passed the Repatriation Act on October 7. According to the provisions of the law, the President is obligated to begin the deportations "without any delay," and failure to do so would require the Congress to "take all necessary steps to safeguard the nation's security." Many observers have interpreted that last sentence as an implied threat about impeachment.

For his part, the President has consistently contended that the immigrants are entitled to protection under the Constitution, and he has refused to begin the deportations until they have received legal *hearings. It's not known how many of the detained immigrants have applied for asylum, but the core of the administration's position is that the lives of the asylum seekers could easily be in jeopardy under the scenario of a mass deportation.*

The three tent cities were originally built to accommodate no more than 10,000 people, and the population in each of them has swelled to nearly 40,000. According to reports published in the Post, conditions in the camps are unpredictable and dangerous. Riots are frequent, and health conditions are unsanitary. As of today, the death toll in the camps stands at 287. Officials at Doctors Without Borders, which is currently organizing an immunization campaign among the population, have expressed surprise that a full-scale epidemic hasn't yet occurred.

The crisis on the U.S.–Mexico border began earlier this year, when a group called the Angels of Democracy assisted the U.S. Border Patrol in detaining immigrants who had crossed illegally. Despite the insistence of President Atlas that the immigrants deserve due process, fewer than 2,000 have received hearings on their requests for asylum.

• • • • • • • • • • • • • • • • • • •

"Thanks for my tour of the White House kitchen," said Chet Wallko as he settled into a chair across from Khaleem Atalas in the Oval Office. "You know, I worked my way through college and washed my share of dishes. I could always lend a hand, if you're having trouble finding help."

The President grinned. "I thought that respecting your privacy was the best way to go."

"Plus, if I came in the front entrance, people would think I was being considered for Vice President. And we both know that's not going to happen."

"Actually, you were near the top of my short list. But I wouldn't offer, because I know you'd never accept it."

"It's worth a chuckle to contemplate."

"It's not as far-fetched as you might think. Remember Lincoln and his team of rivals."

"Sounds good in theory, but we both know the value of presenting a united front. You and Curt might have disagreed in private, but he always toed the line when the cameras were rolling."

"I'm going to miss him. He's a good man."

"One of the best." Wallko's eyes glanced around the room, and they came to rest on the bust of Martin Luther King Jr. on a shelf behind the President. "I think it's more likely that you brought me here to get a reading on your support in the Senate."

"Among other things, yes."

"Why not ask Marcus Kaplan?"

"Because I want the truth. You and I may disagree on many issues, but I value your honesty."

"Well, I'm glad somebody does." Wallko hesitated. "It's hard for me to say, because I haven't had a lot of 'what if' conversations. I can tell you, though, that the few I've had haven't come out in your favor. The public is outraged about the situation on the border, and their elected representatives are feeling the heat."

"So I understand."

"Remember that you had nine defections on the Repatriation Act vote. If push comes to shove and the House votes impeachment, that puts you nine votes away from going home early."

"Just out of curiosity, what would you do?"

"I assume you're asking about the immigrants. I would have sent them back a long time ago. They broke the law."

"To you, it's that open and shut?"

"To me and many others. Look, sir, you say you value my honesty. I say you walked into a trap here."

The President smiled. "That's what Gottbaum tells me."

"The DNC had intelligence before all this started on the Angels of Democracy. They were also aware of the camps being constructed on the border."

"That's true, but no one put it all together at the time. Hindsight is always perfect."

"But here's the thing: If you're sounding me out on your support in the Senate, that presupposes that you're not planning to send the immigrants back."

"I haven't made a final decision."

"Frankly, I don't see what there is to decide. They're here illegally, the conditions are horrible, and you're concerned about their constitutional rights. It's a lose-lose situation."

"That's exactly the difficulty. If I keep them here, we're all in violation of the law. If I send them back, I'm condemning them to the misery of the life they tried to flee. Plus, I'm probably sentencing the asylum seekers to death." The president leaned back in his chair and rubbed his temple. "You know, I keep thinking about my father, who came here from Indonesia. He escaped poverty, and he dodged the possibility that he could be killed in some meaningless tribal warfare. Everyone deserves a chance."

"Sounds like my father's father, who came here from Poland. He came here legally, as I bet your father did." Wallko paused. "With all due respect, sir, that's the crux of it—you're entitled to your opinion, like any other citizen, but you can't arbitrarily decide which laws you're going to follow. You say you'll be sentencing the asylum seekers to death if you send them back. The way things are going, they'll die in the camps if they stay here. It's a miracle there hasn't been some sort of epidemic."

"I'm aware of that. We're working on improving the conditions."

"Improving the conditions?" Wallko could barely contain himself. "The number of detainees is increasing every day. You can't stop the Angels of Democracy, because they're not doing anything illegal. With all due respect, sir, you're missing an opportunity here. This is your chance to talk about significant immigration reform—or at least it was, before this thing spiraled out of control."

"I'm afraid you're right. It's now to the point where I have to make a decision."

"If I were you, I'd send the immigrants back yesterday."

"Good thing you're not me." Atalas rose and offered his hand. "Thanks for coming. I appreciate your input."

"I don't think I've been very helpful," said Wallko as they shook hands. "All I can tell you, sir, is don't let this go to the Senate."

Chapter 41

Under normal circumstances, the event would have been televised by Univision, Telemundo and possibly C-SPAN.

However, these were very far from normal circumstances. When Jorge Mendoza came to the podium to address the annual conference of Criollos Unidos, the ballroom of the Washington Hilton was filled with camera crews from every network and cable outlet in the country. Mendoza received a standing ovation that continued for more than five minutes.

"My fellow warriors," he said when the crowd finally quieted down. "It is my pleasure to be here with you today as we gather in the midst of our common and ongoing struggle. I thank you for coming, and I know that God will guide your steps when you leave this hall.

"This has been a difficult year. When President Atalas first took office, many of us harbored the dream that we could begin a dialogue about twelve million of our brothers and sisters who came to this country in search of a better life. Almost all of them were poor when they arrived here. Many were desperate. Without exception, they loved this country and the opportunities it provided.

"These brothers and sisters took the jobs no one else wanted. They worked in the kitchens of restaurants, cleaned houses, and mopped the floors of office buildings. They endured discrimination. They were hired for low wages and dismissed without cause, with their employers knowing that they had no way to complain. They survived, they endured, and they built a future for their families.

"Today, these twelve million brothers and sisters are still in the shadows. Their hard work has not been rewarded, and they have not been given a path to citizenship. They are condemned to live in fear, knowing that they may be rounded up at any moment and sent back to the life they desperately wanted to escape.

"A few of them—a very fortunate few—were able to become citizens of this great country. They believed in the democratic ideal, with both a small and a capital D. They knew that the United States was a paradise compared to the land they had fled, and they hoped that someday the privilege of citizenship would be available to all.

"The lucky few also believed in the principles of the Democratic Party. They were taught that the Democrats were on the side of the worker and the common man, the disadvantaged and the downtrodden. This was the legacy of Franklin D. Roosevelt, Harry Truman and John F. Kennedy. They knew that if they gave their support to the Democrats, that their interests would be represented. They believed that someday, they would be granted the dignity of citizenship.

"When Khaleem Atalas ran for President, he promised comprehensive immigration reform. He spoke with compassion for the twelve million, and he pledged to us that they would not be forgotten. As I stand here today, five years have passed. Do we have immigration reform?"

"No!" roared the crowd.

"Have our twelve million brothers and sisters come out of the shadows?"

"No!"

"I ask you: Are we better off today that we were five years ago?"

"No!"

"Certainly not. Most certainly not. This man is no Franklin D. Roosevelt. He is no John F. Kennedy. It is painfully obvious that he is a bag of wind, a collection of empty promises. For all our loyalty to the Democratic Party, let us not forget that the last significant immigration reform came during the administration of Ronald Reagan, who extended the possibility of amnesty to millions of our people. His efforts weren't perfect, but at least he tried. And Ronald Reagan, let us not forget, was a Republican.

"I am forced to recognize the painful truth that the Democratic Party has abandoned us. They no longer seem to care about our hopes and dreams, about whether we are treated fairly. All they seem to care about is themselves.

"To make matters worse, there are currently more than 100,000 of our people being held in concentration camps along the U.S.-Mexico border. I call them concentration camps because the conditions, in some respects, are no better than what people endured as prisoners under the Nazis. They are filthy, they are overcrowded, they are violent and dangerous places. The prisoners held there are being caged like animals.

"Khaleem Atalas has the power to do something about this situation. If he cared to, he could use this terrible state of affairs to bring about true immigration reform. But he doesn't do that. In fact, he doesn't do anything—despite the fact that sending the immigrants back to Mexico at this point would almost be the compassionate thing to do, compared to keeping them enslaved in subhuman conditions.

"I have been fortunate in life, but my most fortunate realization was this: You cannot be disenfranchised unless you consent to it. There is no way that you can occupy an inferior position in society unless you have the misguided belief that you're not entitled to a better outcome.

"So I call upon you today to treat the Democratic Party as they have treated us. I call upon you to remember the mistreatment, the broken promises, the political expediency that took power for themselves while denying it to others. I call upon you to remember it during next year's midterm elections, during the next Presidential election, and during every political campaign to come. If we disavow the Democrats and align ourselves with politicians who represent our interests, we stand a chance for equality and justice. It is obvious that we will never get those things from the Democratic Party of Khaleem Atalas.

"Let the Democrats know that they can no longer take us for granted. Let them realize that there is no safe Hispanic voting bloc, that there are no safe inner-city Congressional seats. Above all, let them know that life is not a one-way street.

"As I stand here today, I know all too well that millions of our people are suffering. But I also know that we can and will triumph. With the determination to succeed, and with God on our side, we can achieve the basic dream of all mankind: to be treated with dignity and respect.

"God bless you, my brothers and sisters."

• • • • • • • • • • • • • • • • • • •

"Good Lord," said Linda Buckmeister, as she watched the Criollos Unidos speech in Chet Wallko's Senate office. "What on earth happened to him?"

"Damned if I know," said Wallko. "He's got a bug up his ass, though, no question about it. Maybe somebody got to him."

"You think so? He never seemed like the type."

"Who knows?" Wallko shrugged. "I've always said that it's the true believers you have to worry about. When they get pissed off, they can jump ship in a flash."

"It looks like they all jumped ship. The crowd is eating it up."

"One thing's for sure: I wouldn't want to be sitting in the offices of the Democratic Congressional Campaign Committee right about now. Even worse, I wouldn't want to be Joel Gottbaum."

"Well, you certainly won't be their pet charity going forward."

"I never was. But it looks like nobody's going to be their pet charity, at this rate." The buzzer sounded on his desk console. "Yes?"

"Senator Insfield is on the phone for you, sir."

"Put him through." He punched several buttons simultaneously. "Hey, Bob, you're on speakerphone. It's just me and Linda."

"What the hell's going on here, Chet?"

"Your guess is as good as mine."

"Whatever it is, this is just the beginning. He'll be wall to wall on the talk shows for weeks. I'll tell you what, it's a good time to be a moderate."

"Yeah." Wallko laughed. "Call Bull Caldwell and let him know it's safe to go back to Morton's."

"Don't joke around, my friend. You'd better hope that Eddie Lupin feels healthy."

"If Atalas has any sense he'll appoint a Vice President now, before things escalate any further. The Senate would confirm Kaplan in a heartbeat."

"What makes you think he has any sense? From everything I see, the man thinks he's been sent direct from God to straighten out the mere mortals."

"When push comes to shove, he'll do the right thing."

"You'd better hope so. Otherwise you could inherit this mess."

Chapter 42

On November 17, one week after the Supreme Court declined to hear the administration's appeal of the Repatriation Act, Khaleem Atalas asked for television time to address the nation. Shortly after 9:00 p.m., the cameras focused on the President as he sat behind his desk in the Oval Office. He looked tired and somber.

"Good evening, my fellow Americans. I come into your living rooms tonight to speak to you about a matter of urgent national importance.

"For the past six months, as most of you know, there has been a backlog of immigrants detained on the border between Mexico and the United States. This situation came about due to legal and enhanced surveillance activity on the part of American citizens assisting the U.S. Border Patrol. The number of detainees has been steadily growing.

"As of tonight, there are nearly 120,000 immigrants housed in three makeshift camps designed to hold no more than 10,000 people each. In addition to being desperately overcrowded, conditions in these camps are both violent and dangerous. We have deployed as many security personnel and health-care professionals to these sites as we could muster, but the situation is growing more unmanageable by the day.

"From the beginning of this crisis, I have consistently maintained that the detainees are entitled to their day in court. Most legal precedents support this belief. Our Constitution provides for due process for all, whether the individuals in question are U.S. citizens or not.

"Unfortunately, our legal system is currently too overwhelmed and understaffed to give these detainees the speedy hearings they deserve. Many of them have applied for asylum. They came to this country as a safe haven, knowing full well that their lives and the lives of their families would be endangered if they stayed at home. For some of them, I have no doubt that sending them back to their home country would amount to a death sentence.

"For months, my administration has struggled with the best way to handle this issue. I regard the situation as not just a legal challenge, but also a moral imperative of the first order. I have repeatedly said that I regard immigration as the great moral challenge of our time, and I believe that future generations will judge us based on how we respond to this situation.

"After intensive consultations with the Departments of Justice and Homeland Security, I have settled on the following course of action:

"First, the Justice Department has reviewed the criminal records of the detainees. To the extent that we can verify their identities, we've determined that slightly fewer than 10,000, or between six and seven percent, have felony convictions in their home countries. The number of immigrants convicted of violent felonies is roughly 8,000. I am ordering that those detainees be deported without delay, for the sake of everyone's safety.

"For the rest of the detainees, I am issuing an executive order granting them amnesty for any crimes they may have committed during their illegal entry into the United States. My administration will work diligently with the Department of Homeland Security to settle these folks in communities around the country. Initially, they will be placed in sponsored homes and given assistance finding employment, so that they may begin to pay taxes, support themselves and their families, and begin the long journey toward citizenship. I will issue this order tomorrow morning.

"I'm well aware that this is a decision that will spark controversy in some quarters. To those who disagree, I say this: The integrity of any society can be judged by the way it treats the less fortunate and disenfranchised among them. This is a moment when we are called upon to do the correct and moral thing. I will not shrink from that responsibility, and I hope that many of my fellow citizens will embrace it. Given a combination of a few unlucky breaks and the whims of the universe, any one of us could find ourselves in the place of these detainees. And if we were, we could only pray for the compassion of humanity.

"God bless you, and God bless the United States of America."

• • • • • • • • • • • • • • • • • • •

The response to the President's amnesty declaration was immediate, volcanic and explosive. Even CNN and MSNBC were cautious; while praising the executive order as a courageous form of civil disobedience, both liberal-leaning outlets gave substantial airtime to experts who claimed the order was illegal. On November 21, the deans of the country's top 50 law schools issued a statement condemning the action. The gist of their argument was simple: By allowing the Justice Department to selectively enforce existing immigration law, the President's order called the legitimacy of the entire legal system into question. Snap polling conducted immediately after his speech showed the public evenly divided, with those who supported the measure swayed by the morality argument. One week later, approval of the measure had dipped to 31 percent. The drumbeat of outrage continued in the media, and the streets of the capital were filled with both demonstrations and counterdemonstrations.

On November 25, the day before Thanksgiving, Rep. Charles Barrett (R-Texas) filed the following Article of Impeachment in the House:

Resolved. That Khaleem Mohammed Atalas, President of the United States, is impeached for high crimes and misdemeanors, and that the following article of impeachment be exhibited to the United States Senate:

Article of impeachment exhibited by the House of Representatives of the United States of America in the name of itself and of the people of the United States of America, against Khaleem Mohammed Atalas, President of the United States of America, in maintenance and support of its impeachment against him for high crimes and misdemeanors.

Article I

On the occasion of his two inaugurations, Khaleem Mohammed Atalas swore to "preserve, protect and defend the Constitution of the United States."

Implied in this oath was fidelity to the laws enacted by the duly elected representatives of the people, the stated powers of which derive from the U.S. Constitution. Throughout this year, Khaleem Mohammed Atalas has failed to protect the natural borders of the United States of America, and he has aided and abetted those who would violate those borders. He has disregarded common standards of detainee treatment, in particular: imprisoned individuals without notifying them whether or not they have committed a crime; continued to hold them prisoner without explanation of the charges against them; denied them competent legal representation; housed them in circumstances proven to be inhumane; and withheld from them the right to a speedy trial.

On October 7, the Congress of the United States passed legislation commonly known as the Repatriation Act, which provided for the deportation of those individuals currently detained without charges or trial on the southern border of the United States. Khaleem Mohammed Atalas has refused to follow this law, and he has falsely and repeatedly asserted executive authority against the expressed will of the people. He has continually asserted the right of the detainees to a fair and speedy trial, while making no effort to provide one for them.

In doing this, Khaleem Mohammed Atalas has undermined the integrity of his office, has brought disrepute on the Presidency, has betrayed his trust as President, and has acted in a manner subversive of the rule of law and justice, to the manifest injury of the people of the United States.

Wherefore, Khaleem Mohammed Atalas, by such conduct, warrants impeachment and trial, and removal from office and disqualification to hold and enjoy any office of honor, trust or profit under the United States.

• • • • • • • • • • • • • • • • • • •

"How are you holding up?" asked Chet Wallko.

"Just great," said Joel Gottbaum. "The press is going through my garbage and tailing my every move. That's why I'm calling you on the phone and not there in person."

"Well, it does look like you're not going to be inducted into the Political Consultants Hall of Fame at this rate. How can I help?"

"Give me a reading on the situation. My perspective is what you might call warped."

"There's good news and bad news. On the plus side, there's only the single article of impeachment."

"Thus far, you mean. It's labelled Article One, which means they can add to it any time they get the inspiration. What's the bad news?"

"Your guy is guilty as hell. I mean, he did refuse to enforce the law."

"I'm aware of that."

"Can't you reason with him?"

"He's on a kamikaze mission, Chet. He's steering the ship."

"What about the wife? Can't she bring him down to earth?"

"She's worse than he is. The two of them think they're replaying the '60s. In their minds, this is a campus demonstration and they're the leaders of the SDS."

"Charming. But if you want a reading on the situation, Joel, shouldn't you be asking Lupin?"

"Sorry, I didn't make myself clear. I don't need to talk to Lupin, because this thing is a slam dunk to pass in the House. I really wanted your sense of how things shake out in the Senate."

"Then I guess you're taking this seriously?"

"Damn right. Believe it or not, I think the only thing that really worries him about conviction is passing the office to the Speaker, who happens to be a conservative Republican."

"He also happens to be sick, so all bets are off."

"Not so sick that he might not do it just to spite the President. He could always serve for a while and then hand it off to one of his ideological cohorts."

"If he's so worried, why the hell didn't he appoint Marcus Kaplan as his VP? You know we would have confirmed him.

Then he could have passed the baton to another snowflake liberal and ridden off into the sunset."

"God only knows. I urged him to do it, but he never pulled the trigger. In the meantime, you haven't answered me—how do things shake out in the Senate?"

"The honest answer is I don't know. But I'll take some preliminary soundings and get back to you."

"I'd appreciate that. How about you, Mr. Moderate? Where do you stand?"

"It's complicated." Wallko hesitated. "You know, when I met with the President recently, I reminded him that that vote on the Repatriation Act was 58-42, which represented nine Democratic defections. The Senate would need a two-thirds majority to convict, which means they'd have to come up with another nine. You have to think that it's entirely possible."

"That doesn't tell me where you stand on this."

"I'm leaning strongly toward conviction, to be honest. He did ignore the law, and I find his arrogance to be personally offensive. On top of that, when I was home during the last recess, I found that a majority of my constituents seem to agree with me."

"Could you at least do me a personal favor and not try to sway people toward your point of view?"

"No problem. Remember that my situation is different from Lupin's. I'm not standing over these guys and brandishing a club, threatening their committee assignments."

"Well, that's something."

"Since we're speaking confidentially, how about answering one question?"

"Shoot."

"Can you explain why your guy appears to be intentionally walking off the side of a cliff?"

There was a long pause on the other end of the line. "His psychology is complicated," Gottbaum said finally. "There are times when I'd almost swear the prospect of becoming a martyr is appealing to him. No matter how he leaves office, of course, he'll be a hero to certain constituencies—he'll write books, give speeches and have a grand old time. This way, though, he gets the stature of Dr. King without being shot."

"I'm sorry, Joel. I know you've had a bad week. Just remember that you still have a future ahead of you."

"Sure," said Gottbaum. "When this is all over, I can manage the campaign of some schmuck running for Mayor of Cleveland."

Chapter 43

One by one, the members of the House of Representatives filed up to the podium to cast their vote. Since the early 1970s their decisions had been recorded electronically, but there was still an element of theater to the process. Khaleem Atalas and Joel Gottbaum sat in the Oval Office, watching the proceedings on C-SPAN.

"Ever read *A Tale of Two Cities*?" asked the President as the vote passed the halfway point.

"I think so, but I tried my best to forget Dickens—he was a terrible writer. Why would you ask?"

"Doesn't this remind you of the procession to the guillotine?" Atalas grinned. "I guess that would cast Lupin as Madame Defarge."

"You're pretty sanguine for a guy who's about to be sent back to Pennsylvania. What's that about?"

"I'm less worried about the outcome than you are."

"You should be worried. This is no joke."

"I just don't think the Senators will want to deport the immigrants, particularly the asylum seekers, and have blood on their hands."

"It doesn't seem to bother this group of patriots, does it?"

"The Republicans have a twenty-eight-seat majority in the House, so we know this is going to pass. Look, Joel: Only three Presidents have ever been impeached, and none of them were convicted by the Senate."

"That's because Nixon resigned. He would've been convicted in a heartbeat."

"You're comparing me to Nixon?"

"Of course not," said Gottbaum. "But we don't know what the head count is in the Senate, do we?"

"When I met with Wallko, he didn't sound like the world was coming to an end."

"Well, I talked to him last week, and he was waffling all over the place. I'd take this more seriously, if I were you."

"It looks like I have the public on my side."

"Initially, you did. But that was before they realized the immigrants might move in with a foster family next door to them. Now they're singing a different tune."

"Speaking of singing differently, what's up with Mendoza? You'd think he'd be happy that I put my ass on the line for 100,000 brown people."

"I don't know." Gottbaum shook his head. "It's very curious. In fact, it almost makes you think there's some mischief going on behind the scenes."

"Have you talked to him?"

"I've tried, but he's not taking my calls."

"Screw it," said the President. "We're going to get through this."

· · · · · · · · · · · · · · · · · · ·

House Votes Impeachment of President Atalas
Senate Trial Set for January

December 9
By Kenneth Jablonski, National Editor

By a vote of 309-136, the U.S. House of Representatives yesterday approved a single count of impeachment against President Khaleem Atalas. Although the measure had been widely expected to pass, 14 Democrats joined the Republican majority in voting to advance the measure to the Senate. The impeachment trial is expected to begin after the Christmas recess on January 8.

The measure was drafted by Rep. Charles Barrett (R–Texas), and introduced on November 8. It charged that President Atalas had violated his oath of office by refusing to enforce the Repatriation Act, which demands that the immigrants currently held on the U.S.-Mexico border be immediately deported.

In addition, the Article of Impeachment alleged that the President had "disregarded common standards of detainee treatment, in particular: imprisoned individuals without notifying them whether or not they have committed a crime; continued to hold them prisoner without explanation of the charges against them; denied them competent legal representation; housed them in circumstances proven to be inhumane; and withheld from them the right to a speedy trial."

Many political observers were surprised by the size of the majority voting to impeach the President. The Republicans currently control the House by a margin of 28 seats, but the 309–136 tally was unexpected.

"If I were Khaleem Atalas, I'd be very concerned with this outcome," said Keith Englehart, who served as an advisor to five Presidents of both parties. "Anytime you have 14 Democrats crossing party lines to vote against their leader, you have an indication of deep-seated problems. Remember that it will only take 18 Senators to cast their votes against Atalas to remove the President from office—slightly more than the number of cross-over votes he received in the House, although obviously the Senate is a different story."

Some of the Democrats in question were unavailable for comment, but those who agreed to speak on the record indicated that their decision had been influenced by pressure from constituents.

"Citizens are very disturbed by this situation," said Peter Buckley (D–MT), one of the defectors. "Back home in Montana, we don't have a problem with immigration, but people are very strong believers in individual rights. They see this as a case of false imprisonment and unfair treatment."

Others were blunt in their assessment.

"I represent a very diverse district," said Claire Villanova (D–CA). "We have a large population of Jewish people, African Americans and Japanese Americans, all of whom have suffered discriminatory treatment in the past. When they look at the situation in the detention camps, and particularly the administration's response to it, it makes them very uneasy."

Yesterday's action by the House represents only the third time in history that a U.S. President has been impeached. In 1868, Andrew Johnson dodged conviction during his Senate trial by a single vote. William Hampton was acquitted in 1998 by a party line vote, and Richard Nixon resigned before his impeachment trial could be brought to the Senate.

"This is an interesting case," said Seymour Goldfarb, Dean of the Columbia University School of Law. "The article of impeachment is very narrowly drawn, and Khaleem Atalas is guilty on its face—he did, in fact, refuse to enforce the Repatriation Act. So his predicament is less of a legal one and more of a political one. I think the outcome depends on whether or not the Democrats in the Senate are willing to turn on a President of their own party."

During the Senate trial, conviction will require a two-thirds majority, or 67 votes. The chamber currently consists of 51 Democrats and 49 Republicans, so 18 members of the President's party would need to vote against him in order to remove him from office. Political analysts seem to agree that a great deal depends on how the President conducts himself between now and January 8.

Chapter 44

Between November 10, when the Supreme Court refused to hear the administration's appeal of the Repatriation Act, and December 8, when the House of Representatives voted on the Article of Impeachment, Jorge Mendoza made thirty-one media appearances. He was on CNN fourteen times, and he became a sought-after guest on the Sunday morning talk shows.

To influence the largest possible proportion of the public, Mendoza abandoned the sound and fury of his Criollos Unidos speech. He played the role of a thoughtful but wounded former supporter of Khaleem Atalas, a man who represented the nation's largest cultural minority and who had reluctantly come to understand the President's disappointing performance on immigration.

"We know that you were once an enthusiastic cheerleader for the President," said the CNN host during his first appearance. "Could you sketch out for us the series of events that convinced you he wasn't sincere about immigration reform?"

"Sadly, yes." Mendoza was attired in a plaid shirt and red knit tie, a touch that made him seem like a retired Boy Scout troop leader. "Like many of my people, I harbored great hopes for Khaleem Atalas when he was first elected. I understand that the man faces full-scale political pressures, and sometimes a leader in his position must do what is expedient. But the situation on the U.S.-Mexico border has been tragic, and it has been marked by a pattern of inaction from the beginning. The immigrants were first placed in county jails, which were overcrowded to begin with. When conditions became intolerable, they were moved to the detention camps, where things went from bad to worse. Any reasonable and compassionate person would realize that it would be far better to send these immigrants back to their country, rather than keep them cooped up like animals in cages. For myself, and millions of others like me, it has been heartbreaking to watch. Those detainees could easily have been our sons, brothers, and fathers.

"Khaleem Atalas may be President, but he is only one man. We realize that he cannot solve the problems of the world on his own. But when you look at these camps, you regrettably have to ask yourself: Where is the compassion for one's fellow man? No one expected special treatment, but we certainly aspire to be part of the human family."

As the weeks passed, CNN seemed fascinated by Mendoza: he was the cheerleader who married the boy next door, and her fiancé turned out to be an ax murderer. Their interviews with him were often split-screen shots, with Mendoza's mournful face sharing the TV with images of rioting inmates and overcrowded, filthy bunk rooms.

He was front and center on November 18, the night after the President's address to the nation.

"I wonder, Mr. Mendoza," asked the anchor, "how you feel about the President's decision to resettle the majority of the detainees in sponsored homes and integrate them into society?"

"I applaud him for doing the right thing, but I fear it will turn out to be too late. As you know, Criollos Unidos conducts lobbying efforts on Capitol Hill, and we maintain a dialogue with many members of Congress. I can tell you there has been significant support for impeachment in the House for quite a while, and this latest action will inflame the members who already lean in that direction. I only wish the President had taken this course of action from the beginning—it could have worked, and it might have led to significant immigration reform. Now I fear the consequences will be more drastic for him."

And on the Sunday preceding the impeachment vote, he was the featured guest on *Meet the Press*.

"Above all, Mr. Mendoza," said David Gregory, "we're curious to get your prediction of what will happen in the House of Representatives this week, and what that will mean for the country."

"This is a very sad episode in our history, David. Khaleem Atalas is our legitimately elected leader, a man who took office carrying the hopes and dreams of many disenfranchised citizens with him. Somehow, he has lost his way. He was meek when he should have been bold, cautious when the moment called for decisiveness. I'm very glad I'm not in the position of the House members who will be called upon to cast this difficult vote, but I remain hopeful."

"So you're relatively confident the President will survive this?"

"No, no. I'm speaking now as the child of immigrants, and as someone who believes in America. I am confident the House will come to the right conclusion, and that our great democracy will endure."

• • • • • • • • • • • • • • • • • • •

"Good afternoon, Mr. Marshall," said Kevin Lapham. "Sorry it took me so long to get back to you."

"No worries—I know you're a busy man. Sounds like we have a bad connection, though."

"I'm calling from the plane, so I'm on a satellite phone. If we hit a rough spot, I'll call you back."

"That's a plan."

"I imagine you're calling to get a sense about the future. Now that the project is close to completion, you probably want to know where we go from here."

"How did you know that?"

"Instinct. So I'll give you both the short-term and long-range view of things. Between now and the time Khaleem Atalas leaves office, it's business as usual. You keep your men on point, you continue to detain immigrants crossing the border illegally. Nothing changes until we tell you to cease and desist. Is that clear?"

"Absolutely."

"When the project is successfully completed, as I'm sure it will be, you'll be paid according to the terms of the contract. I imagine you'll probably get a substantial bonus as well."

"I certainly wasn't expecting that."

"That's the way Sheldon and Richard operate—if you produce and get results, you're rewarded for your efforts. You've done a great job for us, and everyone is appreciative. Either way, the financial future of you and your family should be secure."

"I don't know what to say."

"What questions do you have?"

"I'm not sure if you've seen the conditions in the camps, sir, but they're pretty brutal."

"In many cases, Mr. Marshall, it's no worse than what the immigrants had to endure back home."

"Even so—"

"I'm sure your empathy is sincere, but it's a little late. What else?"

"The trend of events is a little overwhelming, to be honest. I never expected that the President would be impeached."

"Well, I wouldn't shed any crocodile tears over the future of Khaleem Atalas. He'll be pardoned, and he'll give speeches at a hundred grand apiece. The liberal think tanks will drool over him. He'll be a hero. If things get slow, he can always go on TV and tell people he was ousted because of an invisible racist conspiracy."

"Even so—"

"Let me put it another way, Mr. Marshall. When you gave that speech at the high school auditorium, the one that brought you to the attention of Sheldon and Richard, you were quite sincere about wanting meaningful immigration reform, weren't you?"

"Yes, sure."

"You know very well that was never going to happen while Khaleem Atalas was in office. For convenience sake, I'll use the old, tired analogy between the workings of government and the making of sausage. Both are unpleasant to watch, and squeamish people need to keep their distance. You, sir, got a job in the sausage factory. Now that you've seen it up close, you know it's just as messy as everyone always said it was."

"So you saw all of this from the beginning?"

"It's certainly what we hoped for, yes."

"What happens to all the agents we've hired?"

"When the project concludes, we'd like you to review their performance records and isolate the ones who've been most effective. We'll probably keep the best of them on the payroll. Otherwise, remember that they were hired on a one-year contract with a sunset provision. You can give preference to the original members who were with you from the start."

"It sounds like there will be more projects in the pipeline."

"Of course. Sheldon and Richard are always thinking. Whether you choose to participate in the future is entirely up to you. But given the way you've performed here, I'm sure they'll conclude you're worthy of an ongoing investment."

"I guess my father was right. He used to tell me that life isn't fair."

"We operate on the merit system. We believe that's fair, and I'm sure you probably agree. Khaleem Atalas, of course, thinks that everyone is equal. And potentially, they are—but once you see what they do with that potential, I don't believe you can turn back the clock."

"I'm sure you're right."

"Welcome to the sausage factory, Mr. Marshall."

Chapter 45

Although it should have gone down as the historic Christmas vacation that toppled a President, many in Washington remembered it as the holiday recess when everyone had to work. For the first time since taking office, Khaleem Atalas decided to forego his annual Caribbean retreat and remain in the nation's capital. Many House members followed his example: some would be directly involved in the upcoming trial, while others simply wanted to keep their fingers in the air. On the Senate side, nearly ninety of the one hundred legislators stayed in the city—the only exceptions were Senators from Northeastern or Mid-Atlantic states who were less than a two-hour plane ride away, and they restricted their absence to a day on either side of Christmas.

The staffs of Senators on the Judiciary Committee slept in their offices, working nonstop to prepare for the trial. There was little precedent to go on: Andrew Johnson had been impeached nearly 150 years before and Nixon's trial had never materialized, so William Hampton was the only available role model. As December progressed, it became apparent that the atmosphere was very different than it had been in 1999. Back then the Senate had been composed of fifty-five Republicans and forty-five Democrats, and no one in the President's party voted for his removal from office. This time, the outcome of the impending trial was haunted by the vote on the Repatriation Act, when nine Democrats had defected. Putting aside that the Atlas administration had been dismissive and high-handed with Congress from the beginning, many Senators were uncomfortable with the fact that the President had flouted the law and was now asking them to do so.

As usual, the Nevada Gaming Commission prohibited Las Vegas sports books from accepting wagers on the outcome, but betting was brisk in Europe. Most of the action taken by London bookies ran overwhelmingly against Atlas, and betting $1 on conviction in Dublin netted a mere 60 cents. The touts were taking no chances.

Handicapping the situation from the White House proved to be more difficult. The office of the Chief Justice, who would be conducting the Senate trial, maintained radio silence for the month of December. As the New Year approached, Gottbaum found it increasingly difficult to contact Senators by phone, and he was reduced to analyzing the situation through daily snap polls. Atlas began the month with an approval rating of 44 percent, with 52 percent of the public stating that the President should be retained in office. These numbers held steady during the Christmas shopping season, when most of the electorate was too preoccupied to focus on the upcoming trial, but they slipped steadily as the month progressed. By December 26, approval was down to 38 percent and 54 percent felt the President should be convicted. At that point it was fair to say that the case was being tried in the press, and most of the media had lost sympathy for Atlas.

"Damn," said Bull Caldwell on December 22, on a phone call with Senator Bob Insfield. "Either I'm a greased duck, or this is the most inscrutable thing I've ever seen. Nobody knows where the bodies are buried here."

"I have to assume a lot of us are waiting for Lupin," said Insfield, "and he's not talking. If anybody could get a reading on what his plans are, it would make the decision much easier."

"Bet your sweet patootie on that, Bob. How are you leanin'?"

"I'm inclined toward conviction—but again, I don't want to hand the White House over to Lupin."

"Things could be worse."

"Of course, they could." Insfield chuckled. "You could be his Vice President."

"Don't worry 'bout a thing, bubba. They're not lettin' me near that party."

Representative Edward Lupin (R-Minn.), the Speaker of the House, was indeed the most important player in this drama. According to the Presidential Succession Act of 1947, the Speaker was third in line behind the Vice President in case of the President's death, incapacity or removal from office. Directly behind him was Chet Wallko, President Pro Tempore of the Senate. Lupin was undergoing treatment for prostate cancer, and it was unknown whether he would be willing or able to take office in case of a conviction. Despite being followed by dozens of reporters during every waking moment, the Speaker offered no clues. He emerged from his Capitol Hill townhouse each morning, waved cheerfully to the camera crews staking out his house, and went about his business with the imperturbability of a Buddha.

• • • • • • • • • • • • • • • • • • •

"Buenas noches," said Chet Wallko as he walked through the White House kitchen.

"Buenas, señor!" The dishwasher grinned. "Cómo está?"

"Muy bien, gracias."

"I wasn't aware that you spoke Spanish," said Bob Insfield.

"Three years in high school. That's about all I remember."

They followed the military guard through the bowels of the building toward the West Wing. When they got to the Oval Office, the guard opened the door and stood at attention. Khaleem Atalas was waiting for them.

"Evening, guys." He gestured toward the sitting area. "Let's be comfortable. Thanks for coming."

"Whatever we can do, sir," said Insfield. The two Senators sat down on the sofa facing the President. "I imagine you want our best sense of the situation."

"Exactly."

"We're not whips," said Wallko. "We can't claim to have the head count."

"Well, you know more than I do."

The two men glanced at each other.

"It's not good, sir," said Wallko. "I'd say you're very close to having eighteen Democratic votes for conviction. I can't tell you for sure, but my sense is that it's right on the edge."

The President grinned. "So you're the lynching party?"

"You could say we're the bearers of bad news."

"What about you, Bob? Do you agree with Chet?"

"As he said, we're not whips. But I think he's on target."

"These eighteen Democrats," said Atalas. "They don't mind removing one of their own from office and risking a Republican takeover? What about you guys? Are you in that group?"

"I'm afraid so," said Insfield.

"And this doesn't bother you, even in principle?"

"What bothers me in principle," said Wallko, "is how this whole thing was handled. I'm no Boy Scout, and I don't even play one on TV. But I am an attorney, and I can't look people in the eye and tell them that I support disregarding the law."

"I see." The President stared out the window, and the two Senators waited. "What about Selma? What about the protests over the war in Vietnam? They were violating the law, and yet most people today would say they were morally right."

"Maybe they were," said Wallko. "But some people were arrested back then, and others were killed. That's the chance you take."

"So your educated guess is I'm not going to make it?"

"We can't say for sure," said Insfield. "The question is whether you want to chance it."

"The real question," said Wallko, "is whether you want to put yourself and the country through this. Say you pull an Andrew Johnson and squeak by with a margin of a vote or two. What do you think the next three years will be like? Is it really worth it?"

"On top of that," said Insfield, "what's it really going to accomplish? The Repatriation Act is law, sir. The immigrants are going back. You have to ask yourself if you want to burn at the stake for them?"

"They wouldn't let me play Joan of Arc in high school." The President's grin showed all his teeth. "Must've been that biracial thing."

Insfield forced a smile. "With all due respect, sir, this is pretty serious."

"Of course, it is." Atalas leaned forward earnestly. "I'm trying to safeguard the asylum seekers. Justice tells me there could be as many as 12,000 of them."

"Then why don't you send the rest of them back, and just keep the asylum seekers here until their stories can be verified?" asked Insfield.

"We're way beyond that now, Bob," said Wallko.

The President nodded. "So it appears. I guess this is a classic case of no good deed going unpunished. Mendoza obviously wants my head on a spike." He looked at Wallko. "What's the bottom line here, Chet?"

"I think it's time to go, sir. For your sake and everyone else's."

Atalas walked to the window and looked out at the South Lawn. The two Senators waited in silence.

"I'm not going until I hear what Lupin is going to do," he said finally.

"I'll sound him out," said Wallko. "I can talk to him."

"If he thinks he's going to stage a palace coup, I'm going to ride this out. Make sure he understands that."

Chapter 46

Wallko made the call the following evening.

"I've been waiting for you," said the Speaker. "In fact, I'm surprised I haven't heard from you thus far."

"I'm not much on small talk, as you know. But it's crunch time, Eddie—what are you going to do?"

"I'm deeply conflicted. I never wanted the job, or I would have run for it."

"That goes for the two of us. Who the hell needs that aggravation?"

"To be honest, I don't think I'm up for it. I'll be in treatment for the next year or so, and I'm likely to be fatigued. The White House isn't a place where you want to be fatigued."

"What's your prognosis?"

"It's hard to get anything concrete. When I ask, I get the standard line: with the proper care, the chances are good I could live another ten years. But that assumes a normal stress level, of course."

"Better than I would have thought."

"Absolutely, and better than I had expected. But on the other side of all this, there are the political factors."

"True."

"No matter what happens, we've got an unelected President on our hands, which circumvents the public's right to choose their leader. And don't tell me that you won't run for election after you serve out the rest of Atalas's term—by then, you'll be so in love with the situation that you'll never want to leave. No one is without ego."

"That's if I even make it three years. Some responsible citizen will probably shoot me."

"Hopefully not, but consider this: If you take office now, you have the option of running for a full term."

"God forbid."

"You never know. What's certain on my end, though, is that I'll be ousted as Speaker."

"I doubt that. You were just reelected."

"They'll call another election and toss me out, and deservedly so. I can barely do the job now, to be honest— I'm only still there out of sympathy. But if I hand the White House over to you, the Tea Party guys will be out for blood."

"All right," said Wallko. "How about this: I'll promise you that I won't run. But you have to issue a statement now, for everyone's sake. There's no point in prolonging this."

"I'm sure you'll change your mind when the time comes," he said after a long pause. "But I'll do it. I'd have to do it eventually, so there's no reason to stall."

"If I were you, I'd go back to Minnesota and play with my grandchildren."

"Not me. I'm going to stay in the House." He chuckled. "I'm not a quitter, Chet. I'm no Khaleem Atalas."

• • • • • • • • • • • • • • • • • • •

Citing Health Concerns, Speaker Lupin Removes Himself From Line of Succession

By Kenneth Jablonksi, National Editor

January 2

Rep. Edward Lupin (R–Minn.), the Speaker of the House, announced yesterday that he would not serve as President if called upon to do so after the Senate impeachment trial of Khaleem Atalas.

In a terse and carefully worded statement, Lupin put an end to speculation as to what might occur in the wake of that trial should the President be convicted. Here is the text of his announcement:

"My fellow Americans: As you know, the U.S. Senate is getting ready to begin the impeachment trial of President Atalas. Many of you are concerned about the outcome of that trial, and some are wondering what could happen if the Senate votes to remove the President from office.

"Since there is currently no Vice President, the Speaker of the House is directly in line to assume the duties of the office if the President is removed. For most of the past year, I have been undergoing treatment for prostate cancer. While my outlook is encouraging, the treatments often leave me weak and tired. I feel that I would not be able to devote my full energies to the office of the Presidency, should it come to me in the course of events. Therefore, I am removing myself from the line of succession.

"Partisanship obviously played no role in my deliberations, since my decision means that Chester Wallko would become President in the wake of a conviction. I've known Senator Wallko for many years, and have always admired his intelligence, vision, and patriotism. At a time like this, there are no Democrats or Republicans. There are only Americans. This is a time for the citizens of this great country to unite, as I know they will.

"I wish you a happy, healthy and prosperous New Year."

While not unexpected, Speaker Lupin's announcement was yet another twist in a political year full of surprises. Officials in both parties are still trying to make sense of the President's decision to grant amnesty to the immigrants detained on the U.S.-Mexico border, even as the public attempts to absorb the swift and dizzying chain of events that have sprung from that decision.

Senator Wallko could not be reached for comment, and his office issued an equally terse reaction:

"Edward Lupin is a true patriot. We admire his selfless actions and wish him a speedy recovery."

Chapter 47

O n January 4, President Atalas asked for television time to address the nation. When the cameras zoomed in on him in the Oval Office, he looked somber and haggard. "My fellow Americans, I come before you tonight to talk to you about a matter of great national importance.

"I'm sure most of you are aware of the chain of events that have led up to this moment, so I won't go into them in detail now. For the past year, the news has been dominated by the refugee crisis. My response to that calamity is what has brought us to this point. I'm sure you're also aware that the Senate is scheduled to begin their impeachment trial four days from now. Before I tell you about my decision concerning that trial, I want to share some of the emotions and reasoning that went into making that decision.

"My entire life has been devoted to defending the underdog, because I was an underdog myself: the biracial son of an immigrant couple who came to this country in search of a better life. My background has motivated everything I've done in my career, because I felt a special responsibility to protect people who were unable to defend themselves against the tyranny of the state. I felt an obligation to defend their rights, so I've worked as a community organizer, pro bono attorney and public servant. Throughout all of those experiences, I've always been on the side of those who were less fortunate, who didn't have some of the opportunities that this great country granted to some of us.

"The refugees currently detained on the U.S.-Mexico border are not criminals, regardless of what the law may state. They are human beings who came to this country to avoid poverty and violence, and to provide greater opportunity for their children. The Congress has passed legislation requiring me to deport them, and I have refused to do so. After being unable to seek redress in the courts, that same Congress has accused me of high crimes and misdemeanors and demanded my removal from office.

"If we have come to a point in this country where defending the rights of the less fortunate has become a high crime and misdemeanor, then I cannot continue to serve that system. Throughout my lifetime, I have seen noble and selfless acts of civil disobedience. I witnessed the struggle of Martin Luther King Jr. for civil rights, and I grieved over his death. I joined in the protests against an unjust and unnecessary war in Southeast Asia. Time and time again, I have realized that in moments of moral crisis, it is imperative that individuals do what is right.

"In this situation, the right thing to do is very simple. We have a moral obligation to accept the immigrants detained on the border and integrate them into our society, as generations of immigrants before them have been assimilated. However, the Congress and the judicial system refuse to do that. I believe they are wrong, and I firmly believe that history will view me as correct.

"Therefore, I have refused to accept the mandate to send the immigrants back, and I will not be judged for taking a position I view as morally justified. I will step down from the Presidency at noon on Thursday. Senator Chester Wallko is next in the line of succession, according to the Constitution, and he will be sworn in at that day and time in this office.

"To my many supporters, I urge you to harbor no bitterness at this turn of events and give Senator Wallko the prayers he will need to succeed. To those who disagree with me, I offer my forgiveness.

"Thank you for your time this evening. God bless you, and God bless the United States of America."

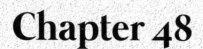

Chapter 48

Shortly after 8:00 a.m., President Chet Wallko relaxed on a sofa in the Oval Office. He hated the Resolute Desk. *It makes me look like a pompous ass, rather than the coach potato I really am*, he thought. And thus, he had used it exactly three times during his first month. Linda Buckmeister, his Chief of Staff, sat on the sofa opposite him.

"So what excitement do I have to look forward to this morning?"

"You have the CIA briefing at nine. Homeland Security will come by around ten to discuss the situation on the border. At eleven, Vice President Insfield is going to report on the Youth Opportunity Initiative. After that, you're free as a bee until 2:00 p.m., when the Prime Minister of Japan is scheduled to visit."

"Great. Maybe I can sneak out for a shot and a beer."

"Good luck."

"What's happening with the detainees? How are we coming along with the deportations?"

"I'm not updated on the precise details."

"Give me the overview."

"Justice separated out the legitimate asylum seekers—the total was right around 12,000, as Atalas had said. We've put their feet to the fire, so they're moving forward with the hearings. Subtracting them from the total, along with the 8,000 felons who are already gone, that left around 90,000. About one-third have been deported. We should be done by the spring."

"I hope so."

"Do you want to appropriate money to clean up the camps afterward?"

"Surely you jest. That's not government land, last time I looked. Let the Hafts clean them up. It's their mess."

"That's about it." Buckmeister glanced at her legal pad. "We keep getting requests from the Preservation Committee about when you'll want to redecorate the Oval Office and the residence."

"We've been through this. The office looks fine to me, and the residence is considerably better than a Holiday Inn Express. So the answer is probably never."

"What do you want to do about the money set aside for the project?"

"How much money are we talking about?"

"One hundred thousand from the general fund. Plus you have offers from donors that bring the total to about a half million."

"I say we use the money to buy breakfast for inner city school kids with single mothers who can't afford to feed them. That makes more sense to me than a new set of drapes."

"Spoken like Khaleem Atalas."

"Maybe. But he never gave them so much as a pancake, as far as I know. He did spring for new drapes, if I recall—one of his many protests against the tyranny of the state."

"Speaking of donors, I've been approached by three different groups. They want to set up exploratory committees and PACS for your election."

"God almighty." He shook his head. "I've been here slightly over a month, and I haven't even located all the bathrooms yet."

"They're well intentioned. At some point, you'll have to think about the future. And I'm sure your wife will want to redecorate sooner or later."

"Think so?" The President glanced up the picture of the pig , which occupied a place of honor near the entrance. "Tell them I have all the décor I need."

• • • • • • • • • • • • • • • • • • • •

On the top floor of Haft Industries' executive offices, the atmosphere was celebratory but controlled. A light snow was falling, much as it had been fourteen months before when the plan to fund the Angels of Democracy had been conceived. Sheldon Haft sat behind his desk, underneath the Thomas Hart Benton mural, surrounded by his brother and Kevin Lapham. The TV on the opposite wall was silently tuned to CNN, which was covering President Wallko's press conference.

"Brilliant," said Sheldon, his eyes trained on Wallko. "I have to admit I was skeptical at first, Dickie, but you saw the whole thing from the beginning."

"Kudos, sir," said Lapham.

"I assume you've got the tally, Kevin?" asked Sheldon. "Going forward, we'll want to look out for the people who were helpful."

"It's all in the little black book, sir."

"Excellent. As I mentioned, we'll stagger your bonus in stages, to reduce your potential tax liability." He smiled. "Not that you're going to pay taxes on it, since it's all going offshore."

"You've been more than generous, sir. I appreciate it."

"The real question," said Richard, "is how we're going to keep Wallko on the reservation. Don't lose sight of the fact that he's a Democrat."

"I wouldn't fret over it," said Sheldon. "You can't get to him, but the odds are we probably won't need to. He's a Libertarian at heart." He gestured toward the TV. "Let's turn it up, Kevin."

As the volume increased, a reporter from *The New York Times* rose to ask the President a question.

"Sir, we're six weeks in, and roughly thirty percent of the detainees have been sent back. What would you say to the critics who feel you're not moving fast enough on the deportations?"

"I'd tell them to go on down to the border and lend a hand." Wallko grinned. "We can always use volunteers, and there's no law against pundits doing an honest day's work. We've got government planes that can get them from D.C. to Brownsville in three hours or so."

"That's our guy," said Sheldon. "Nothing to worry about."

"Even so," said Lapham, "I'm compiling a list of second-string appointees who may cause problems and will need to be replaced—undersecretaries, career diplomats, what have you."

"Well, that's prudent," said Sheldon, "and that's certainly what we pay you for. But I want to proceed slowly on that front. Keep me posted, but make sure you check in before you take any action."

"Will do, sir."

Sheldon turned to his brother. "So, Dickie. What's next?"

• • • • • • • • • • • • • • • • • • •

Discuss this Book

1. Many of us make our voting decisions based on whether or not a candidate's views on key issues agree with our own. Issues are important, but issues also come and go. Thinking about Chet Wallko, would it be better to find someone who we can admire for their underlying values and assume the issues will fall into place? Is it possible to find such a politician in the current climate?

2. In the book, the Supreme Court decision on Democracy Unchained is obviously based on Citizens United. Should money be regarded as the equivalent of political speech? Is it fair that people with more resources be given a greater voice than others? How does this affect the doctrine of "One person, One vote?"

3. The events of 2020 sparked a national debate on the role of the police, Army, and National Guard in keeping order. The scenario of a group like the Angels of Democracy now seems more plausible than ever. How do you feel about the legality of a "peacekeeping" force created by someone with an agenda?

4. How else might this saga have ended? What outcome were you expecting? Are there other courses of action that President Atalas might have taken? And what does the outcome say about Atalas as a politician and as a human being?